ABOUT THE AUTHOR

Dogside Story

Patricia Grace is the author of five novels, four short story collections and several children's books.

Awards for her work include the New Zealand Fiction Award (*Potiki* 1987), the Children's Picture Book of the Year (*The Kuia and the Spider* 1982) and the Hubert Church Prose Award for best first book (*Waiariki* 1976). She was awarded the Liberaturpreis from Frankfurt, Germany (1994) for *Potiki*, which has been translated into several languages. *Dogside Story* was longlisted for the Booker Prize and winner of the Kiriyama Pacific Rim Book Prize in 2001.

Patricia Grace was born in Wellington in 1937. She lives in Plimmerton on the ancestral land of Ngati Toa, Ngati Raukawa and Te Ati Awa, in close proximity to her home marae at Hongoeka Bay.

Published in North America by
University of Hawai'i Press
2840 Kolowalu Street
Honolulu, Hawai'i 96822

First published in New Zealand by
Penguin Books (NZ) Ltd
Cnr Rosedale and Airborne Roads
Albany, Auckland 1310
NEW ZEALAND

Printed in Australia

Library of Congress Cataloguing-in-Publication Data

The record for the book is on file.

ISBN 0-8248-2584-5

DOGSIDE STORY

Patricia Grace

Talanoa: Contemporary Pacific Literature
UNIVERSITY OF HAWAI'I PRESS
HONOLULU

ACKNOWLEDGEMENTS

My thanks to the Arts Board of Creative New Zealand for assistance while writing *Dogside Story*.

Thanks also to the staff of Te Puna Matauranga o Aotearoa and of the Tolaga Bay Community Library.

Special thanks to Ray Binet, Don Milward, Ludmilla Smith, Charlene Williams and Kaya Grace.

For Joyce and Te Aomania

ONE

THIS FIRST part of the story is about two sisters, Ngarua and Maraenohonoho, who quarrelled over a canoe.

The sisters lived on the coast of the north side of a tidal river that came down from far back in the ranges and mouthed out into a wide bay. Far beyond the bay was where the morning sun tipped up out of the sea and flipped back across the sky like a slow, many-coloured fish, travelling the high arc until it dropped and splashed down again beyond the mountains. This northern curve of the bay was bordered by rock and steep white cliffs. In the clearings, here and there between the inlet and the cliffs, people had built their ancestral house, their sleeping houses and cooking shelters, and had made their gardens.

On the other side of the inlet, bordering the south end of the bay, were low cliffs of yellow rock centred by a blowhole which at low tide stood dry, enabling a way through to a sheltered cove which was a favoured fishing place. At this time no one lived on the south side.

The canoe that the sisters quarrelled over was small and old and suitable only to take a single paddler from one side of the inlet to the other. Once across, the paddler would have to take the canoe to high ground and turn it upside down to get the water out of it and allow it to dry.

There were other canoes and other ways of crossing the inlet. On most days at low tide there were places where the inlet could be easily forded on foot, and even at half tide it was possible to cross on horseback. In good weather it wasn't too far to swim. Also there wasn't much necessity for crossing the inlet unless it was to hunt pigs on the scrub-covered hills beyond the rocks or to go overland to the cove or perhaps make a journey south, but for such crossings bigger craft with room for goods or equipment were needed.

But the canoe had belonged to Ngarua and Maraenohonoho's brother who had been fifteen years old when the elder of his two sisters was born. He'd looked after them ever since they learned to walk, been patient with their games, listened to their complaints, allowed them to sleep one each side of him at night, and had always tried to show even-handedness when they competed for his attention and affection.

By the time the two women were in their thirties both their parents had died and it was their brother who was their champion when elders wanted to marry them off to two old men seeking wives. He'd stood firm in refusal on his sisters' behalf and had sent them north to relatives, out of the way until the fuss died down.

While they were away the sisters, who up until then had shown little interest in marriage, found prospective husbands without help from anyone, and eventually returned to their brother's place to seek family approval.

So not long after their return they were married—though it was said that what love they had for their new husbands never ever matched the love they held for their brother. Even after some years of marriage, and with children who could have distracted them from it, they still became jealous if they felt their brother had shown favour to one of them above the other.

When their brother died they were distraught. They had to be pulled off the casket when the pallbearers were ready to head the procession to the urupa, then once there, had to be dragged away from the graveside when they attempted to throw themselves into the hole and onto the box along with their brother's gun and his clothing.

After the burial, and after the burning of his death shelter and his palliasse, there was only one thing remaining that was personal to their brother. That was the canoe that he'd made when he was a boy. He had sat them in it and pushed them about in shallow water when they were babies. They had waited in it while he fished. Now both claimed the canoe, and though it was of no real use to either of them they pretended that it was and made up excuses for needing to cross the inlet in that canoe, that and no other.

They began removing the canoe from its usual place by the water and hiding it from each other. Ngarua would hide it, and Maraenohonoho wouldn't rest until she'd found it, waiting until Ngarua had her back turned so she could hide it somewhere else.

The sisters would go to extremes in order to distract each other while they searched for the canoe. Once Ngarua led Maraenoho-noho's children into heavy bush and left them there, and while her sister and the people were searching for the children she dragged the canoe to a new hiding place. On another occasion Maraenoho-noho reported seeing someone fall from the cliff tops onto the rocks below. She set out along the shore with the searchers but turned back in order to get the canoe and hide it in the trees.

The people soon became tired of all this. There had to be an end to it and they were awaiting an opportunity to break up the canoe, perhaps set fire to it, or hole it and push it out to sea, but in the end they never got the chance.

The sisters guessed what was in the people's minds and realised the canoe would never be safe in any hiding place now. It had to be where they could see it and they had to watch each other and everyone else as well, after all the canoe was not just a canoe, never had been just a canoe to them. It was the memory of their brother. It *was* their brother. It was all that he'd meant to them in the past, and it was all that he meant to them now. It was his heart, his love for them, and each wanted that heart and that love for herself. Neither of the sisters held any love for each other and one would have died rather than let the other have this, their brother's heart, their brother's love.

One night the sisters were sitting on the banks of the inlet, separate from each other but both keeping the canoe in sight, waiting for the other to be distracted in some way. There was a horn-shaped moon giving ragged light to the water through the branches and foliage of trees that lined the inlet, and it was when a cloud passed over the moon that Ngarua and Maraenohonoho both saw an opportunity and raced to snatch the canoe with the intention of taking it across the water and remaining with it on the other side. Ngarua, who was smaller and quicker than Maraenoho-noho, reached the canoe first, pushed it down and into the water, stepped in and pitched away from the shore.

Seeing that Ngarua had beaten her to it, Maraenohonoho took up a heavy piece of driftwood, rushed out and launched the branch through the water, cursing as best she knew how. The wood struck the already frail canoe and made a large hole in it.

Ngarua continued to paddle as the canoe began to sink, then as it went from beneath her she swam, finally walking out on the other side of the inlet from where she never returned.

The canoe was never retrieved from the water.

The next morning Ngarua's husband rolled blankets and clothing into a bundle and tied it on to the back of his horse along with a billycan and his gun. At low tide he tied their youngest child to his back, then leading his horse bearing the three older children, crossed the inlet to join his wife, followed by several dogs who thought there was a pig hunt on.

During the next few days Ngarua and her husband were joined by others who found themselves in sympathy with Ngarua, or who may have had their own dissatisfactions with life on that northern side, or who maybe followed because their dog had gone. Over the years, disagreement or whim caused further defections from the north side, and gradually the populations of Northside and Southside evened out.

Though the division had come about because of jealousy and quarrelling, people on the north side held no severe animosity against those who had crossed over. However, they did hold disdain. They, the Northsiders, were the stayers, the originals, those resident in the place where their ancestors' bones were buried. They had established gardens on the fertile areas of flat land at the base of the hills and were the caretakers of lands, sacred sites and of the ancestral meeting house—all of which made them superior, at least in their own eyes.

Neither did the Southsiders have outstanding bad feeling for those they'd left behind. They were all family after all and they'd lived together well enough for many generations. But the inlet-crossers now saw themselves as the ones who'd stood no nonsense, those who'd acted on principle, and this is what they believed gave them the edge. Adventurers they were. Movers, changers, seekers.

As quickly as they could, after making their houses and setting up fireplaces, the Southsiders made gardens of their own, increasing them in size each year until they were more extensive than those on the north side. In response to the situation of ancestral remains they established a new burial ground. This was at the time of the death of an old woman who had crossed the inlet not far behind Ngarua's husband and children. They couldn't pretend that this was quite the same however, after all there were many chiefly people and many loved people buried in the old place, including the brother. There was nothing they could do about that.

But once they were established, Ngarua spoke about a new

meeting house as a way of stamping authority on the new settlement, and people began to plan. The new wharenui was larger and more strongly built than the old one of Northside, and according to those who had made it, more finely decorated.

Modernity and size didn't impress the Northsiders, or if they were impressed they didn't admit to it, after all theirs would always be the first house, the senior house, which gave it greater importance. Anyway, they thought the small amount of carving on the exterior of the Southside house to be unstylish and rough, and weren't surprised that there were no interior carvings if that was the best their cross-over relatives could do. The rafters—that important place of ancestral backbone and ribs, the place where stories hang and where talk is recorded—they considered to be meanly decorated and wondered why they'd bothered at all.

The new meeting house must have struck a note on a hollow bone somewhere, however. Not long after it opened Maraenohonoho announced that they, of Northside, would build a church. It was the first but not the last of many churches that were eventually built on Northside.

Before the sisters died they saw roads go through the area, saw bridges, shops and banks built. Coaches and eventually motor vehicles arrived, and so did farmers. They witnessed the softening of the land.

Northside and Southside children now went to school together, their parents and grandparents met in the stores, the clubs, the pubs and the churches. They came together for tangihanga and when there was a Northside wedding or other event the relatives from Southside always attended, and vice versa.

But there was competitiveness about what one side or the other could provide for such occasions, whether it was fish or pork or produce. One side was always looking for reason to feel high-souled about the other.

According to the Northside story, the reason that it was Ngarua and not Maraenohonoho who reached the canoe first on its final night on water was that Maraenohonoho was preoccupied with God when she was taken advantage of by Ngarua. Maraenohonoho, they said—to whom legend had given exceptional beauty, grace, dignity and goodness—was deep in prayer, so her distractions were for high and holy reasons and were therefore understandable. Maraenohonoho began to be seen as the saviour of her people who was second only to the Great Saviour. She was the one who had chosen to remain with her lands, her people, their bones, their ancestral house. The other side of the inlet was another country.

To subsequent Northside generations this all translated into them seeing themselves as cultured, devout, principled, steadfast people who deserved and enjoyed the love of God. They cared for their churches, their families, their houses, and later their vehicles and their lawns. They kept order. They dressed their children properly, cleaned their hair and made sure they attended school. They paid attention to teeth.

They had opinions about their relations on Southside based on what they knew of Ngarua and on what they saw with their own eyes. These Southsiders were rough and ungodly, loudmouthed and without morals. Their houses were falling down, their clothes were shabby, they drove round in clapped-out cars and were always accompanied by their mongrel dogs. They were alkies and no-hopers, useless hua who sent their kids to school barefoot and let them run wild. They were dog thieves too.

But the Southsiders knew their ancestor Ngarua had just been too smart for Maraenohonoho, who they said was a foolish, lazy woman who had not been engrossed in prayer at all but had gone to sleep at a vital moment. Ngarua, of great patience, intelligence and beauty, had skilfully judged the moment to get up and lead them all off into adventure. That was why they, the Southsiders of today, in their own opinion, were so outgoing, so fun-seeking and resourceful. They were generous, intelligent and unafraid, and their kids didn't need shoes and flash clothes in order to outdo their crybaby, stay-at-home cousins at school. They saw the Northsiders as people who had no idea of how to enjoy life. They were sore losers who lived beyond their means, and even though they were bike-riding, bible-bashing teetotallers, they were known to be light fingered as well.

The number of churches on Northside led to it becoming known as Godside, while the number of dogs on Southside led to it becoming known as Dogside.

From now on the story becomes one-sided. It favours Dogside.

TWO

THAT KID.

Stretched out flat with water now almost reaching the foot with the good shoe on it that had been given to him by Arch, and with his head resting on a stone that was rough and becoming uncomfortable, and even with his eyes closed while he waited for Jase and Bones to come and get him, Rua knew it was Kid up on the beach creeping down. It was Kid his dog had gone up to meet.

Eyes on him he could feel. Two black spiders were her eyes.

In her mouth were words, waiting.

If he'd been two-legged he'd have waited, let her come close, then he would've flipped up, yelled, dropped his tongue, scared the wingnuts out of her and chased her home. But he was stuck. Even the crutches were too far away for him to grab and jump up. She knew that.

Or he could do a quick roll, grab one of the crutches, aim, fire—tada dada da, tada dada da—which wouldn't scare her, stop her coming square and flat-faced with her black spiders and her words.

He'd have to shift in a minute before the water got to his shoe, which was a pretty flash sort of shoe, flasher than what was necessary to get him into the pub dressed in Tidy Dress—in clean jeans with one leg pinned up, black tee shirt, black jacket which at the moment was folded there on the crutches. His head was resting on a bloody sore rock to keep the sand out of his hair, keep his hair tied back for the tidy-dress pub. The cousins were late picking him up. The tide was just about getting in old Arch's shoe but if he moved Kid would know he wasn't asleep.

Pain, her.

She knew he wasn't asleep anyway.

She knew he knew she knew.

No, Arch, who had a thing about shoes, who was a real shoehead, wouldn't like it if he saw the tide getting up around this one now that he'd parted with it. 'On'y you, Son. On'y you, Rua. On'y one I'd give my shoes to, in honour of the misfortune that has come to you. Come wit' me.'

Archie had taken him, along with Jase and Bones, into his new bedroom and shown him a row of pairs, heels hard up against the whole length of a wall, like lined up ready to march or dance forward.

He'd seen all these shoes while he was growing up, not all set out like that, but usually just one pair at a time. Seen them stepping out, going for the bus during Arch's working years—lifting, lifting, so as not to get marked from the holey, dusty road. Or he'd seen them dancing at weddings, or rocking and jumping heel to toe at a guitar party or planted each side of a guitar when Arch decided to upend the instrument and play it as if it were a double bass.

Later, after Arch's retirement and after the older uncles and aunties had died, the shoes had appeared more and more often at hui at the marae. There, planted at the paepae. There, slow step, quick step, back and forth, turn, at the ends of tidy ankles, while Arch dished out his welcomes and his words to the visitors, on on on. Black, light brown, dark brown, white, blue, mix, high and low, buckled, laced, fringed, shining—quick, slow, back and forth, turn.

A black lace-up was what he'd chosen, the one with water getting into it now. If he moved Kid would see. 'Take 'em both,' Arch had said. 'You don't have to disrespect the other leg just because half of him's not there, just because we put him down on top of your cousin. Take your old leg a shoe too.'

'Or you could give it,' Bones had said. 'Give it. Find somebody with only a right, a right with a foot on it, aa aa.'

'No good to that old fella in the hospital with you that time Cuz, with two . . . two off. Gone. Right and left, e heh,' Jase had said.

'Don't mean the old fella couldn't have shoes,' then Arch had started up, gone on on on, with them waiting to take unwanted shoes and get out. History of this pair, that pair, on on on for half the morning. 'I had shoes when I was a kid, two shoes, but both the same side, both left. Woulda been good for you Rua, Son. So on'y wore them at night, in the dark when there were visitors in the house. Run up and down outside the house making a noise so visitors know I got shoes. Singing out loud so they know who it is who got shoes, then hide them under the steps 'til nex'time . . . And take slip-ons too, Son. Easy to get off when you go inside.'

So he'd got out of there last with the black lace-ups and brown slip-ons thinking he'd never wear them, not even the left ones. But now he was wearing one. All right for a night out. Two bands down the pub. Money in his pocket for the cover charge and a few rounds.

Kid wouldn't be roaming about if The Sisters were home. She'd be home doing dishes instead, cleaning out, making their cups of tea, running to the shops for their smokes and lollies. The Sisters were probably down the pub all done up, sitting on laps, looping themselves round dart throwers come for the tournament. Someone should do something about Kid. Someone should take her away from those two. He could hear water beginning to spill out through the blowhole.

Tomorrow he'd have to be up and about, get himself through the hole to the cove before the tide came in, otherwise he'd have to go up the tracks and down the ridges, taking him ages and making him too late for the crays.

Someone should.

Kid was close up looking down on him waiting for his eyes or his foot to move. She had hold of his dog. Any minute she'd give up waiting and come out with her words.

Arch or Wai. One of them should do something. He'd heard Aunty Wai going off at The Sisters for how they treated Kid so why didn't she do something? Jase and Bones were bloody late. They could've all been down the pub half off their faces by now.

Shouting match. Sisters had told Wai to mind her own business. 'You had your chance, you had your chance, you all did,' that smart Babs had said, chop chopping beans and nearly sending her fingers along with them. The day was fading on his skin, on his eyelids, on eyeballs under his eyelids, but at last he could hear the car arriving giving a toot toot.

So . . . Kid.

He rolled for his crutches and hopped up, shaking water off the black lace–up, swinging the jacket. Jase and Bones were grinning out the windows. They had . . . Remelda and someone.

'Go home. Go on,' he shouted at Kid as he lunged past. Blink, blink. Spiders knitting their legs.

'You,' Kid yelled after him. 'You Rua.'

THREE

HE REMEMBERED waking as the car wove its way along the home road towards the sun, which had its forehead just up out of the water, splashing it all over red and colouring the sky at its fringes. At the end of the straight where it was meant to make a turn, the car had kept on ahead, going up over the verge of dune grass and washed-up sticks until it buried its four wheels up to halfway in sand.

He remembered Jase slumping forward on to the steering wheel, the horn blasting, Jase sitting up then getting out and going, leaving Tina asleep clamped back against the front passenger seat with the belt adjusted for someone even skinnier than she was, her head dropped forward and gently swinging.

No Bones. No Remelda.

He'd got out of the car and lain down on the sand with sky bleeding across his eyeballs for a moment before he closed them again and slept.

With the tide already sinking, Archie Shoes had driven along in his station wagon with the trailer hitched up behind and come down onto the beach, shaking him by the black lace-up, 'Tide's on the way,' he'd said. 'You lot better get going.'

'My sticks,' he'd said to Arch, and his uncle had reached into the car and handed him the crutches.

'Faw, stinks in there,' he remembered Arch saying.

He'd propped himself against the car and dropped his head back letting his bloodied eyes fall shut again, not wanting to throw up while Arch was there.

'Be around with the boat later to pick up the crays,' Archie called as he left. 'Ha ha, you all need a drench, you lot.'

Now with Arch gone he removed the shoe and went down into the water, throwing the crutches back up on to the beach, launching them like spears and letting himself fall flat, hair floating, shirt shunting up under his armpits and the jean legs filling out like balloons—empty one ballooning more than the other one, as though it was the one with the leg in it. He turned the whole bundle of himself, lying face down for as long as he could before rolling again, spurting, rolling and going down.

Under water he clawed along from stone to stone, from clump to clump of weed, surfacing and diving, surfacing and diving until he reached the flat water beyond the shore waves where he lay face up—sun eyeing down, birds eyeing down, maybe waiting for his stomach to unbolt.

Stroking his way back to the shallow water he let the waves take him in. Tina, who had woken by then and was sitting on the shore, stood and came down swinging in his crutches. As he scrambled out she shot them to him. 'How'm I getting home?' she asked, but he had no answer to that, had his own problems as he reached into the car for his jacket wondering who was going to give him a hand. Saturday, and he and his two cousins were meant to be going to the cove to get crayfish for the wedding, now here he was on his own. Bones off with Remelda, Jase gone to fix himself up and asleep by now.

But it was too late to worry about who. He had to get through to the cove now before the water got up too much, had to take his stomach, his head, his pumice mouth, his sunshot eyes through to the cove and just hope someone would turn up to help, even if it was only to hold the bag.

Kutu? Didn't know where his dog had got to.

It was too late to go back to his own place for his gear so he looked along the row of houses to see who might be home to give him what he needed.

Nobody.

They were all down the end getting things ready for the wedding, expecting crayfish by mid-afternoon. So he made his way along to Wai's place to look for shorts, a shirt, backpack, jandal, something to wrap round his hands.

Just as he reached the house his dog came rushing over from next door making jagged movements and sharp noises, and he realised Kid must've taken him home with her after he left.

Out in the garage were overalls, old coats and rugby jerseys hanging on a row of nails. On a row lower down were snorkels, a pair of goggles, old backpacks, sacks, life-jackets, a string of cork floats, fishing reels. He took a rugby jersey, a backpack, a bundle of sacks. No shorts there, but he found a pair on the clothesline— yellow and black Adidas—a bit too good for diving around the cove, too flash for salt water, but they'd have to do. Old singlets to wrap round his hands. No jandal.

Sitting on the step he took off his jeans and underpants and put on the shorts, and as he was pulling off his shirt Tina came into the yard asking about a phone. 'Inside,' he said. 'Kitchen by the fridge.' He heard her ring through and ask about the kids and tell about the car. Someone was going off at her at the other end.

'I know, I know, someone come and get me,' she kept saying. 'Shut up, just come and get me.'

He hung his wet clothes on the line and gave them a quick hose down thinking they'd be dry by the time he came back, good enough to change back into later.

'Some der-brain,' he could hear Tina saying. 'Some dipstick, hardly said anything, just bought me drinks all night.'

Well the clothes would be good enough for the after-wedding party once they'd cleared the tables and everyone had casualled out a bit. Two nights in a row he was going to be inked up.

'And I lost one of my crystal earrings . . . Nothing, he done nothing, just didn't take me home . . . He's an egg . . . Somewhere, some beach, how would I know. Shut up, just come and get me.'

Hooking his arms through the straps of the backpack he went swinging along on the crutches with Kutu keeping ahead of him, down the driveway and off towards the blowhole. Half a wave to Tina who was heading back towards the car.

Down the end there was smoke rising from the hangi fire in the marae paddock, but he was pleased he didn't have that job today. He was a bit useless when it came to that type of work anyway, and the others didn't like him round the pit jumping about on sticks, reckoned he might fall in, reckoned he wouldn't taste good—or thought he could be all right salted down. How to get the crays on his own, have enough before the tide got too high?

As he passed by the marquee that they'd put up the day before he could hear Wai and the others in there discussing tables, how many rows, how many to each row. There were more trestles to come, Archie was getting them from across the river, Cass was saying. And ferns. Once the hangi was down Jackson and Joeboy were going up the back to get ferns to decorate the entrance. 'The sooner we get our new dining room the better,' he could hear Wai saying.

Kid.

She was sneaking up behind him, which meant The Sisters weren't home yet, The Aunties. It meant they'd scored, got lucky with dart throwers. It meant Kid had been left on her own all night with only Kutu for company. He decided to take her with him and get her to hold the bag.

Swinging along the rough track with his sticks, over the shingle and the washed-up wood and weed he knew he could easily outpace two-legged walkers and even dogs. Kid and Kutu were puffing and panting behind him.

They caught up to him though when he came to the narrow ledge leading to the blowhole where he had to slow down. He shifted sideways, put his back against the bank and edged round the jutting rocks and bushes before turning into the cold, salt air of the opening with its curved dark walls as smooth as skin, its floor of round, velvet-nubbed boulders with their attachments of silky orange tufts, coarse black strands, trails of beaded hair, limpets like little tattoos. In among the boulders were the fresh, shadowed pools.

After making his way over the stones and around the pools with Kid and Kutu splashing along behind him, he came into the bowl of sun, where the water was like rubbed pots. The amount of sand at its edge showed the tide to be a full bite down.

Gulls, rising from the grassy slopes, twanged like broken strings and herons lifted out of the trees, sweeping round high and slow over water the colour of their wings, legs trailing like rags. Pressing himself back against the rocky bank he felt the sharp edges digging into the back of his head and shoulders, felt colour leaching from his sunrise eyes, but none of that was enough to distract his stomach from unleashing.

He leaned and threw, down into the gap the missing leg had left, while Kid dropped, flopped herself on the track, laughing, 'Rua. You . . . Th th th, ahh ahh.'

Sailing over the mess he'd made and up onto the grass where he could've slept if there'd been time and where Kutu had found a shady place already, he removed the sacks from the backpack. Kid followed after him loose and boneless, laughing all round the cove.

'You got to get out by the near rocks,' he said when she plonked down beside him. 'You got to wait there in the water with the

backpack. I bring the crays one at a time and you got to hold on
. . . hold on, then we bring them back, put them in the wet sacks
and go back for more. Got it?'

'Got it.'

'Give us your hair-tie, uh.'

She took the band from her hair and passed it to him. He
hooked his own hair through it and rolled down the grassy slope,
over the stones and sand and into the water with Kid running after
him laughing and dragging the backpack down.

In the water they went together to the beginning of the channel
where the first crayfish rocks were, then he left her there, dipped
down, shooting along with herrings swarming one-legged ahead of
him. The tide was right, the water was clear and he knew he'd get
what he wanted as long as there was enough time, or maybe if Jase
or Bones showed up soon to help, not that he expected his cousins
to get down to the difficult stuff, but one of them could hold the
bag for him while the other took Kid to work the easy places. He
surfaced and stroked towards the far rocks. Forty big-sized crays for
the tables was what was needed, and a few for the cooks if he was
quick about it. A wedding without crayfish on Southside? Nah, too
shame. He needed big ones so no one'd say he was robbing the
nursery. It was up to him because he was the one now who knew
what to do and at the same time was fit enough to do it—though
he'd never had to do this on his own before.

Kid.

Last time they were here, just the two of them, he was fourteen.
Ten years ago. That's how old Kid was now, ten. Ani Wainoa was
flying away, shouting down, leaving the two of them there in water
making for the shore.

Coming to the place where the water was dark with submerged
rock he made his first dive, deep down to where the cavity in the
rock was large and open, and the crays were easy to see but not
easy to get to, snapping their tails and backing into the hole as he

came. He went after them grasping one of the large ones across the back with both hands and pulling it up against his chest on to the heavy fabric of the jersey, and turning, pushed his foot against the rock, shooting for the surface. Kid was paddling towards him and he went to put the cray into the pack.

Leaving her to zip the bag he returned to the rock to make his next dive, aware that the water was already deepening. After several quick dives he moved to the next rock, then the next, working round the holes until the water became too deep and the crays too far back for his breath to last.

But he was satisfied with what he'd been able to get from the deep places, knowing the next rocks would be easier. Kid helped him pull the full pack ashore where they put the crays into sacks which they tied and put into the shore water ready to be taken home. They swam out to the near rocks and here he didn't need to dive. He crouched, bobbed down and reached under the shelves pulling the crays out by their feelers, selecting the large ones to put into the pack that Kid held open for him.

When they'd finished he sat in the shore water with the bags, moving them higher as the tide rose. He was thinking of food and sleep, and of Kid who probably hadn't had breakfast, maybe hadn't had tea the night before. She was up behind him on the grass walking with his sticks, 'Tell me. Tell me Rua,' she said.

'Uncle Archie,' he said as he heard the boat rapping across the bay.

'Who cares?'

The motor cut down as the boat came round the island and through the rip, and soon afterwards they watched it coming towards them. Archie was bringing the boat in, at the same time swearing, ripping into him for coming there on his own, still half cut with only a kid helping. 'I woulda come if I knew,' he said. 'Someone else coulda got tables and stuff from Other Side if I knew, stupid bugger.'

He hauled the bags one by one alongside the boat where he steadied himself and edged them in over the side and, after sending his dog home, helped Kid into the boat and pushed it out, flipping himself in over the stern.

FOUR

WHEN THESE Southsiders, Inlet Crossers, Dogsiders built their first meeting house in the time of Ngarua, all the cooking for visitors was done out of doors. In bad weather, shelters and windbreaks of brush and harakeke were erected, and when the house was moved to its new site not long after the death of Ngarua, a lean-to was built where the cooking fires were under light shelter.

In recent times a more permanent structure was put up where cooking could be done and people could sit down to eat, and though it lacked many of the conveniences of more modern wharekai around the coast, it served well enough until it was destroyed by wind and flooding a year before Blind's dog died, Ani Wainoa left and Rua arrived wet in the wharenui with a bundle.

At first nobody noticed too much the loss of the wharekai. Seeing the broken up pieces of it floating out with the tide was not as absorbing as other dramatic events going on during that time.

The people had been talking for some time about the need for a new wharekai anyway, but with all else that was going on it was more than a year after the cyclone that they began planning a new one. What they had in mind was a concrete block structure on a concrete base, with a good iron roof, something that wasn't going to blow to pieces in high wind, or float off down the inlet to be swallowed up by waves—something more substantial than the tinny Skyline buildings being put up on neighbouring marae.

Getting money was the problem.

They began fundraising, travelling to the early morning flea market held in the city on Saturdays, to sell their cakes and produce and crafts, but accumulation of funds was slow. They did better with the raffles and batons-up, and the sausage sizzles outside Pak'n Save, and made good profits selling hot dogs and paua fritters at Pa Wars, but Pa Wars only happened once every two years. They came to realise that the funds they were trying to build grew so slowly that they couldn't even keep ahead of the rising costs of materials. Added to all this they'd been ripped off a couple of times by their own relations who'd lost count with raffle money or forgotten to charge for sausages—that was until Wai took charge.

In the meantime people didn't stop dying or getting married, and now here they all were in this last year of the millennium, with another wedding and still without a wharekai, still putting up marquees for their visitors and having to prepare food on rigged-up benches under plastic flaps and tarpaulins, not too much different from cross-over days.

On this morning of the wedding Babs, who was over the gas ring burning sugar for the steam puddings, pushing the spatula so the sugar wouldn't stick on the bottom of the pot, was thinking that if it hadn't been for this marriage she and Amiria would've been off to the tournament with number one and number two dart players. She'd been telling everyone all about their night out and how they were expecting Andy and Dave to come along and party-up later. She turned the gas down.

Her sister Amiria, flouring raisins and sultanas, was fed up with Babs and her big mouth. Babs was telling it all round, and now if the men didn't turn up how did that make them look? This lot, who were taking in everything her sister was saying and already rolling their eyes at each other, already silently busting themselves laughing, would be wisecracking as soon as their backs were turned. She drove her hands through the fruit and flour. Her sister was brainless.

But Andy and Dave weren't the only friends Babs and Amiria had invited to the wedding.

In her job as the local Post Shop supervisor Babs came into regular contact with most people of the district and was the first-call information link between Southside and their relatives on Northside, as well as with other residents of the town.

Post Shop was also the place where Kid went every day after school to sweep out, empty paper bins and slot junk mail into the post boxes, and where occasionally, on opening the back of the box there would be a face looking back at her, voices to be heard, or a hand coming through as her own hand reached in to deposit fliers, Warehouse and supermarket ads, shop-by-mail catalogues, coupon books and holiday programme leaflets from the Info Centre.

Post Shop, being situated in a corner of Mil and Milly's general store, meant that Babs also met with most casual visitors to the town—people calling in on their way round the coast, summer holiday makers, sales people. Of those who stayed, visits were seldom long, some staying for a night, a weekend or maybe a week at the camping grounds or the nearby motel.

There was one visitor however, who had taken a unit for two months at what had previously been called Bay Motel. Because of the approach of the new millennium the proprietors had renamed it Firstlight Motel in the hope of attracting those with an interest in being among the first in the world to see the first sunrise of the year two thousand.

Dawn Anne Brown of Warkworth, writing her twenty-fifth romance, though entrenched in old themes and storylines, had come to the district in search of new backdrops, new characters, a new outlook, different colour.

She quickly realised the place was a mine. There were horses galloping along sandy beaches, boats on water, far and near horizons, waves crashing up over the rocks and onto shores, moonlit banks, shadowed bridges. It was really only the people who needed making over.

Babs was a mine as well. To a lesser degree, so was her sister Amiria who worked across the road from Mil and Milly's, at Bay Fish. Dawn Anne couldn't believe her luck. Not only had she found a willing informant, but she'd also found her olive-complexioned, green-eyed heroine, only needing to strip off years and weight, re-outfit her and place her in a earlier time. She was going to call the new work 'Tides of Ecstasy'.

'Dawn Anne and I are like *that*,' Babs would say, crossing a middle finger over a first finger and holding her hand up to show her relatives how close she and her new friend had become. It was natural that she would want this author of twenty-four books, many of which Babs had read even before meeting the writer, to come to the wedding. People would see for themselves how 'like *that*' they were.

'So-o-o-o, there you are,' Babs said, as Kid lifted the flap and came in.

'Who said you could take off?' Amiria asked.

'She's been helping me,' Rua said coming in behind her.

'And she can get helping at home right now,' Amiria said swiping her hands. Dustings of flour clouded the space in front of her face for a moment then floated down, settling into the large basin that she'd been working her hands in. She scooped sugar from a bag and scattered it in handfuls.

'She's having a feed first,' Rua said.

It was the first two words of Rua's sentence that caught people by the ears—'She's having'. Not asking, just telling. This was pretty sharp coming out of Rua who they knew must be wild about something. Teria, who had peeled twenty-four onions and was crying and chopping them, stopped what she was doing, washed her hands in a bowl, damped down a cloth and began dabbing her eyes so she could see better what was going to happen here. Brig and Moana let up on the noise they were making counting out bowls for the salads, and Awhina cutting rewena, stopped being so vigorous about pulling and pushing the knife. Mereana paused in her tin buttering, rolled her sleeves and waited. Pita and Joyleen who had been asked to bring in a form for people to sit on came in carrying it between them. They put it down and sat.

'She can eat at home,' Amiria said biffing a fistful of salt in with the rest of the dry ingredients and shuffling a hand in the basin to make a well for the milk and burnt sugar as Babs came across with the pot.

'Then she can clean up the dog hair and kitten mess all over the place,' Babs said.

Everyone had heard all about this earlier from Babs too, how Kid had locked the kitten in a room and it had messed, how there was dog hair all over the settee and how Kid was now off somewhere hiding.

'She's having a feed first,' Rua said.

Wai, outside the tent arranging a space in the hangi baskets for the pudding tins, was saying to the two men attending the fire, 'Still no wharekai, no roof over our fires, no roof over our cooks.'

'Well, not raining at least,' one of the men said.

She could hear the exchange going on inside the tent and was glad young Rua was standing up to The Sisters. There was something she wanted to say to them too and she might as well say it in front of everybody as soon as she got a chance.

The men at the fires also heard what was going on, lifted their eyebrows at each other and let their ears hang open as Wai went to the opening and looked in.

The burnt sugar liquid and the milk with soda dissolved in it were all in the well now, and Amiria and Babs with ruby and amber rings removed and resting on the bench beside them, were pushing their lovely hands through the wet mixture. Both their mouths were open.

'Come on you two,' Wai, from the flap, said to Rua and Kid, 'Boil-up for the cooks out here on the fire.'

'She can eat at home. It's none of his business,' Amiria said.

Those listening noticed the word 'his' rather than 'your'— cheeky enough they thought, though Amiria had not been willing to directly challenge Wai who was a generation older than she was.

'She's not going anywhere 'til she's had a feed,' Wai said.

'None of his business.'

'It's everyone's business who eats,' Wai said. 'And another thing . . . You don't leave her home on her own when you go out, you hear. You send her over my place. Told you before.' Wai put a hand on the back of Kid's neck and turned her towards the fireplace.

So, it was all over. The talk started again, as did the chopping, cutting, counting and carrying. The Two with their hands sliding in the pudding said nothing more, knew they were on shaky ground even though they did believe Kid was big enough, old enough to stay home and look after a cat on her own, big enough, old enough to keep the place from getting messed up. She was sly. And it *was* nobody else's business. That young Te Rua Tapaerangi was getting too smart for his boots.

Or boot.

One leg and he thought he could get away with murder.

But it wasn't quite all over.

'Then she's going home to get a dress and coming back to the wedding,' Rua said. He left them with that and went out to where Wai was dishing bones and watercress on to two plates for them, and where the men were chopping wood, boosting the flames and hosing fresh water into two big pots.

'Like we're still back last century,' Wai was saying to the men. 'Outdoor kitchen. One drop of rain, up to our ankles in mud. No rain and we got dust over everything.'

Jackson and Joeboy came up from the hangi area, slinging a basket down between them and returning at a fast walk to the pit. Other men came after them taking baskets away. Babs and Amiria in their rosy aprons, their Starboks, their high-up hair came out with the foiled tins, their angry puddings, and stacked them in the last of the baskets, then the two men who had been looking after the fires took this remaining basket between them and followed the others to the pit, leaving the newly filled pots on the fire for the crays.

Down on the marae atea the groom and his family were being welcomed, and through the fringe of trees at the edge of the marae, those at the fire or coming to the flap of the tent could see one of the visitors on his feet, pacing, talking. He had everyone laughing.

'It's that blow bag from the other side who married my mate Neta,' Wai said. 'Hasn't showed his face round here since he was treasurer of the rugby club and absconded with the funds years ago. Praise the Lord through Sunday, him, rip off the people Monday. Been up and down the country into one rip-off scheme after another, one wife after another too, and never been to jail once. Now he's big chief, I heard, Piiki Chiefy, some wallah wallah in the Corrections Department, some sort of kaumatua. And now . . . now little Tia's marrying one of his nephews. God almighty that kid she's marrying better be better than the uncle.'

The hangi makers were returning from the pit slow legged, cooked looking, eyes bugging, taking turns at the hose flushing out their faces and washing their heads. They sat on the bank in the grass from where they could watch proceedings through the trees.

FIVE

HE SAT on a box by the fire keeping it stoked until the water was at full boil before lifting the first of the crayfish out of the sack by its feelers. Thought he should've put them in fresh water to drown first but there hadn't been time.

As soon as they arrived back Arch had gone home so that he could clean up and get back down to the marae before the visitors arrived, leaving him there with the boat and the crays. Jackson and Joeboy had come over from the hangi to unload the bags and carry them up on to the grassy patch by the fire for him. Now he could see Jase coming.

As he lifted it the cray opened itself out in air, reaching out its jointed legs, flicking its tail down segment by segment until it was fully stretched, fitted and fluted like a musical instrument. 'Mind out,' he said to Kid who was still picking away at her food and as he let the cray down into the pot, swinging himself away as it tucked its tail and pushed, splashing the boiling water. It tucked again and then stopped. 'Where's your aunties?' he asked.

'Home getting dressed.'

He began stacking the crays in, holding the lid of the pot up like a shield against the hot splashes. 'Go home and change too,' he said. 'Wait 'til you see them coming back then go and get a dress. Go and see the wedding.' When he finished he began spreading the embers with a stick, bringing the water in the first pot down to an even simmer as the crays began to lighten in colour. 'And,' he said, 'take Kutu along and tie him up at Aunty Wai's or he might go down and jump all over the bride.'

'You shoulda got me,' Jase said, emptying one of the bags out on to the grass.

'Too late. Tide already down,' he said.

'Who? Who went?'

'Me, her.'

'Just youse?'

'Just us.'

'But Maan . . . But Bro you were pissed as.'

He boosted the fire under the second pot while Jase began untangling the second lot of crays and letting them down into the water. 'What about the car?' he asked.

'Rocks under the wheels and Tina's sister give us a tow . . . What you think, Tina?'

'Aaa. Shitty when she woke up,' he said, 'Supposed to drop her off, you.'

'Nnn . . . Well . . . Didn't tell me where, did she? Somewhere down Ludfield all I know. Bones and Remelda gone, you out of it, her out of it. How was I to know?'

They left the first lot of crays cooking and went to sit with the workers on the bank who were resting and watching through the trees. The crowd down on the marae had gone quiet, the singers were arranging themselves and the kaikaranga was standing ready to call the bridal party.

'My volley ball shorts I'll have you know,' his cousin Eva whispered beside him. She was dressed in a black skirt and white top ready to be a waitress.

'Too bloody small, your shorts,' he said,

'Don't bust my shorts, you.'

'Chopped in the goolies when I sit everytime.'

The shorts were chafing him now that he'd steamed and drip-dried. Kid was down there, up in one of the trees with Georgie and Hinewai getting a good look at everything. No dress, just clean shorts and a tee shirt like the other kids. Kid with other kids, Kid with her cousins doing what other kids did, watching the bride come in.

Discarding one of the crutches he leaned himself against the bench and propped his left elbow into the other crutch because he wanted to do the job himself. Jase was too heavy, too rough, and the crays could end up smashed, legs missing or busted. Jase went round to the other side of the bench to turn the crays over, lay them out and hold the legs away. 'After this,' Jase said, 'ring her . . . Might.'

He pushed into the cray's head with the knife that had been sharpened so many times it was like a needle, bringing it down through the centre of the body, down through the length of tail, then after completing the cut pressing the two sides apart until the back shell cracked. White flesh, shitty heads still steaming. Picking up the knife again, he got his balance and pushed the point hard into the next one. 'You got no phone number,' he said as he drew down.

'Hnnn,' Jase spread the next cray. 'Sister going off her nut about her not coming home, sister babysitting for Tina.'

It was meant to be a night out at the local. They were meant to get home and have a sleep then get themselves off to the cove this morning. Instead they'd ended up in the city at an all-night party getting stewed with friends of Remelda's.

'Out of it, her. Up and down Ludfield,' Jase said. 'Asking . . . but she's out of it.'

'Aaa . . . You kept filling her glass all night.'

'How do I know?'

'Mmm.'

It was true. His cousin was clueless when it came to all that. 'You got the wobbles on the way home. Wobble wobble, next thing wheels up in sand, you asleep. Remember that much, me.'

'Hnnn, well anyway what about you? What about that one, that one . . .?'

True, what about him? What about that one, Donna. Him being one-legged hadn't put her off, didn't put any of them off, he didn't know why.

'What we doing with these here? Trays? Basins?' Jase asked.

'None left. We got to empty the water out the big pots and stack our crays back in. They send someone when they want them down there on the tables.'

'You know, that one . . . Donna . . . I reckon you coulda got lucky anytime.'

If he wanted.

Looking in under the flap of the marquee, he felt satisfied about the way the crays had been set in the middle of each table on the platters with lettuce, tomatoes, parsley. There was condensed milk and vinegar dressing in glass bowls by each one.

Everyone was seated now, and at one end of the main table the minister was tapping a glass with a spoon and beginning grace while Eva and the others in their black and white clothes went from table to table, reaching across to remove the gladwrap from the salads, creamed paua and fish, and the tinfoil covers from the bowls of hangi. He stank of crays and the shorts were choking him but he was free to go now, get back to Wai's to shower and change, or better still he could go back to his own place for a sleep then stoke up his bath. When he came back they'd give him a barman job, stick him behind the keg.

He made his way along the track over the hill and through the manuka to the deeper green of karaka, ponga, nikau, rangiora, akeake and the black bush floor. The black earth of the track, criss-crossed with tree roots, was packed solid even though it didn't get used much. Only his one-legged self and his four-legged mate came through here now that there were easier places, easier ways to the eel spots and the watercress. Kutu was keeping within sniffing distance of the hangi bone he'd wrapped and put in the backpack.

They had come this way twice a week when he was little, Mum, Moananui and himself, to bring Nanny Blind's bread and fish, and each time they came he'd heard his mother trying to persuade Nanny Blind to come home with them because her house was too damp in winter, too old, too cold, too far in the trees, no electric. 'Leave me, leave me,' Nanny Blind would say.

'And Ani Wainoa. You and Ani Wainoa come and live with me.'

'Leave me, leave me and my girl.'

'Or Wai's place, or Archie's, whatever you want. They all want you to come and live with one of us now that your sister's gone.'

'Leave me and my girl. Leave me and my Toss.'

Before going home they'd go up the creek for watercress and on their way back along the track his mother would call through the trees to Ani Wainoa on her way home from school with books she stole. 'You tell Nanny Blind you want to come and live with us now,' his mother would say. 'Tell Nanny you want to come home to Mummy now, Ani Wainoa.' And Ani Wainoa would slit her eyes, look sideways out of them and bite her big teeth over her bottom lip as though she was thinking hard, as though she was giving the idea all her consideration. She always was bullshit that Ani Wainoa. 'Now that Nanny Ru's dead and there's only Nanny Blind we want you to come,' his mother would say. 'You tell her, you tell her Sweetie you want her to come, tell her you want to come home to live with Mummy now.'

Ani Wainoa would nod in a serious way and then smile, her neck lengthening, her big teeth parting and her dark cheeks forming up into tight balls. Her eyes would tilt and her eyebrows would lift like birds. 'I'll go to Nanny Blind,' she'd say. 'I'll explain everything to her.'

They'd watch her in her white clothes, her black hair flying, running and making her own track through rotting leaves, fern and overhangs, in those days before he started school. The white clothes that she always wore—shorts and tops, cut-off baseball pants, curtains and cloths, skirts, singlet and dungarees—she had sorted from bags of stuff people had given her. Red, yellow, green, blue, brown all discarded, thrown in the trees. It had all seemed part of her cruelty.

On the way home his mother would gasp and huff and laugh and talk to him while she carried Moananui on her back. He'd be ahead listening to this and that his mother was telling him in her wheezy voice, following Moimoi and carrying the wet bag.

Then he'd had to go to school. His mother and Moananui still went two days every week to Nanny Blind's. For how many years? He knew that there *were* years. There had to be years. Moananui had turned five and followed him to school, their father had continued to go to work in the early mornings in the yellow Humber, continued to play in the band on Friday nights and to get drunk on Saturdays.

But it hadn't seemed like any years at all from when he was five until he was nine and their loud-talking, powdery, dancing, laughing, sweaty, baggy mother with her round face and hard hands, and with fat bulging round her eyes right up to her mostly pulled-out eyebrows which she had redrawn in arches with a bit of pencil, had become someone changed and opposite.

He dropped the bone in the grass, hung the pack on a nail and pushed open the door of his falling-down place with its wavy floor, its smell of baked boards, old ashes, fish and smoky blankets. Letting go of the crutches he rolled onto the bed.

It would be his father getting out of bed, moving about in the dark, that would wake him. He'd wake hot, never remembering how he'd got there into the big bed. On the other side of him, his mother, with Moananui on a pillow by her face, would snore a bit, shift a little, but keep on sleeping. In a while there'd be a thin line of light coming from under the bathroom door, and even with the door shut he would hear the scratch scratch sound of his father shaving. He'd fall asleep again and not remember his father leaving for work, or know that his mother had fed Moananui or got up to change her. He wouldn't know anything more until he woke again at daylight alone in the big bed.

Sometimes he'd make a cave, pulling the pillows down under the covers to make the walls. He'd make a little opening then hide in there and wait.

'Where's that Te Rua Tapaerangi? Where's that boogey boy gone?' his mother would say when she came in. Out he'd come, roaring. She'd laugh and laugh and put Moananui in bed with him while she had her bath. Or on cold mornings she'd sometimes say, 'You got me a warm place? Come on give me a warm.' Bringing Moananui she'd get back into bed with him, sweaty, giggling, her milk running and smelly and her straight, black hair coming out of its band.

In a while she'd say, 'Come on Boy, up time,' and the covers would seem to float away as she lifted them and rolled herself to sit on the edge of the bed, feeling for her jandals and jabbing her feet into them and slap, slapping on the boards as she went to run the water. 'Put Bubby back in her bed, good boy,' she'd call.

So he'd get up and lift Moananui into her cot and wait until his mother came out in a dancing dress, powdery, brushing out her hair. The dancing dress was a pink cotton wrap-around with palm trees going sideways that she'd pull tight under her tufty armpits, streaky from damp powder, crossing the cloth and rolling it above her milky bowls. When he was dressed he'd be allowed to go out and let Moimoi off the chain and go and find Taku and Shania.

SIX

WHEN HE woke there was a candle burning and Kid was sitting in Nanny Blind's chair. Kutu was stretched out on the floor in front of her, just the way that Toss used to lie waiting, wide as a table, dusty and tangled, stinking and slow, to take Nanny Blind to the lavatory, the wood pile, the creek, out to the bushes where she spread her washing. Toss's eyes would move your way but you were nothing to do with him. He was hers, only for her. That time he came with the baby Toss was dead.

'Tell me,' Kid said.

'You better get off home,' he said, but could see it was too late, too dark for her to go home. Why should she anyway?

'No.'

'Huh, you don't say that to your aunties ay, "no"?'

He went out into the trees where he had his bath set up on bricks and emptied a bucket of water into it. In the dark he scraped together dry twigs and leaves, gathering them into the paper that the bone had been wrapped in, and lit a fire under the bath. When the flames had spread through he put in a few larger pieces of wood and went down the creek bank for more water which he could get one bucket at a time, sliding on his bum.

'Aaay, that's your bath?' Kid called and started to laugh.

Back in the house he lit the lamp and sorted out some clothes to wear, gears good enough for a barman at a wedding, good enough to dance at a wedding. When he went out again Kid was feeding sticks into the fire. 'That's enough or you boil my bum you, Kid.'

He woke next morning face down on the beach with the water high and the sun right over him. Kutu was sniffing round the shore rocks and his crutches had gone awol. Propping himself on his elbows he could see people moving about and vehicles backing round and driving away. There was smoke and the smell of leftovers cooking— hangi fry-up—and John Rowles was doodling out over the speakers as the clean-up was going on, *only had time, only time*. His leg was bloody sore, wrecked from dancing—come on you, come on you, come on you—all night. 'I'm minding the bar, me,' he'd kept saying.

'Come on, come on, plenty other barmen.'

'Pick on them, get one a them to dance.'

'Got two legs them, ha ha handicapped.'

He rolled on his back and closed his eyes, making up his mind he wasn't going anywhere until his sticks turned up. Kutu's wet legs went past, toenails clicking on the stones.

Hard case party and he reckoned there'd still be half a keg left back there for the workers and thought Archie, Wai and them might be already cracking it. The water was running full in the blowhole.

No years at all for someone to change size, shape and colour, and to feel and sound different, to taste different, to have a different smell. No years before that bed, that same early morning bed, had in it this small, white, hairless woman whose arms, that she held out to him each afternoon when he came home from school, had been just hanging flaps of skin, whose hands picking at his face and scratching in his hair were like the twists of newspaper she used to get a flame from the stove element to light her cigarette with. The powder smell had gone and there was a smell and taste of ditches, a little voice that said good boy, you been to school, you come home to Mummy.

Kid.

'Give my sticks you.'

'Tell me.'

'Give them.'

'Tell me.'

'There's nothing.'

She was off, swinging down the road on his sticks, his dog following, tail going, jumping round like a picnic. 'Tell Jase I want him,' he called.

'No.'

Now coming towards him was that out-of-luck wife of Piiki Chiefy, still in the dress she'd worn to the wedding. Looking for her old man or what? Looking for that blow-bag from Other Side or what? She wouldn't find him because he'd gone off with the writer, everyone knew that. Anyone going out of a marquee in the middle of a party couldn't not be seen. Anyone not coming back couldn't not be noticed. Blow Bag leaving first and that Dawn Anne leaving a few minutes later wouldn't fool anyone, especially since the two of them had already spent half the night gabbing in each other's faces.

Baggy eyes, baggy face, been crying or had a hangover? Or still pissed? Mmm, still had a skinful he reckoned and needed a sleep, walking to keep herself awake. Guessed she'd been up all night with Arch and the other stayers. Cigarette in one hand, lighter in the other. He shut his eyes. 'He's such an arsehole,' she said.

There was only one thing wrong with having one leg instead of two, only one real thing, nothing else was any big deal. While it was true he couldn't play rugby any more he didn't really care about that. Though he sometimes thought he wouldn't mind driving a car and probably could if he got himself an automatic. What use was a car when you lived in the bush?

Also it was true that no one wanted him wobbling round the hangi pit, but he could still stand back and give them all a bit of jaw if he wanted to, and it was true too he had trouble getting up ladders, which wouldn't be too good if he wanted to get his old job back.

That's if.

But no big deal all that because he could still play 'My Dog's Got Fleas' on the uke, still take his turn on the guitar, do his stick dance, smoke some stuff, get wasted now and again.

Women? It wasn't a missing leg problem.

And if he ever wanted to win a gold medal he could train up for a swim at the paralympics, haa.

The main thing was he could still get himself through the blowhole, get himself into water. That was the big thing, the biggest thing, and meant his life wasn't all that much different from before.

So if there was anything wrong with his life now it was nothing to do with his missing leg. It was all right. He liked it if only people knew. Being one-legged made him think better, gave him a physical life.

'Even if he'd come back at daylight, or early,' she said, 'so we could pack up and go, then people could talk about him as much as they liked, or feel sorry for me as much as they liked after we'd gone. But it's bloody embarrassing being stuck here and everyone looking through their eyelashes at you and trying to be polite.'

There was only one pain-in-the-arse thing about having one leg instead of two, only one thing, and that was that people he didn't know—strangers—all thought they could tell him their aches and pains and problems. They thought being one-legged made him worse off than they were, so believed they could hammer him on and on about how they'd been done over by shopkeepers, politicians and gangs, about how they'd been beat up by their children, how their lungs and livers had packed up and their houses had been burgled. Then there were their toothaches and emphysema, their dead daughters, their stillborn babies, their Aids, their shot livers, their cancer of the brain.

He got it from taxi drivers, hairdressers, nurses, physios and other people's hospital visitors; from people any size any colour any age; in waiting rooms, at bus stations, in post shops and banks.

Now from people on beaches.

Your problems were greater than theirs, they thought, therefore you'd understand about their bad secrets, their sick bodies, their domestics, their stuffed-up lives.

'Can't stand it,' she said.

Sore head or husband, he thought of asking. Take a seat, he thought of saying.

As though she'd heard this last thought and taken the invitation seriously, she stepped down on to the stones in her wedding heels, hooked her muscly arms behind her and smoothed the flowy stuff of the dress down over her big backside, holding it there behind her knees while she seated herself. The cigarette jigged in her mouth as she got it going, smoke easing up round her big face. She was breathing it in again through her nose he noticed, smoking it twice.

'Bloody embarrassing being stuck here without a car and everyone having a laugh. You want a smoke?'

'Nah. No thanks.'

'She'll end up paying the bill, that Dawn Anne. No out-on-the-beach-under-a-starry-sky for him. He'll take her off to the flashest place around, everything laid on, wine, room service, the lot. Before she knows it she's paid up, thanking him.'

Now Kid was back, hanging around, blinking, spidering. He should hop up, hop off, get out of it. Should go up and get some beers into him and never mind being polite and being stuck there listening.

'She'll be so impressed with his Micky underwear, his leather toilet gear, his silky pjs, she'll think it's worth it.'

Or he could strip off and roll into the tide, wander about under water until the coast was clear.

'No marae sleeping for him I thought when I saw him packing his bag before we left yesterday. I reckon he didn't even put a towel in. Big dreamer . . . I saw you at the wedding Darling Girl, up a tree.'

'Give them Kid,' he said.

'Tell me,' Kid said.

Smart, getting at him in front of a stranger, but there was nothing he could tell her, or nothing he would tell different from what she already knew.

'You know already,' he said.

'Tell.'

'There's nothing.'

She turned and was off again bloody Kid, running up to meet other running kids, shooting them with his crutches—poom, poom, poom.

'It's really something watching him in front of some motel mirror in his Miki Kiore shorts, with his hairless chest, his hard arms and his not too flabby middle, lathering up and scraping his loose doggy face down clean, looking at himself looking at himself. That voice in the shower. Then it's the aftershave slap, the roll-on underarm bit before he gets into his perfect clothes. She'll think it's worth it.'

She stopped talking while she lit another cigarette. The kids were running down to the water past where he sat, kicking up sand, stripping off and throwing themselves in. Kid doing what other kids did. Kid playing with cousins. She'd hidden his sticks somewhere, knowing not to take them into the water, knowing he could easily get her there.

'He buys you flowers, you get the bill. But still they are the best flowers, wrapped in real stiff, classy paper with heaps of proper ribbon. You think you're married to this perfect man. Look at him and your heart goes funny. He talks to you, your stomach goes funny and you forget you're one of many, you forget you're paying for his car, his home gym, his bets, his debts and everything.'

She was a talker this one, and still more than half cut, spilling it all.

'And why me? I mean . . . the younger woman and all that, but that usually means *attractive* younger woman don't it, like skinny, like stylish. That's what he goes for . . . but still he came after *me*. Ended up married.'

'Do you want to look behind those logs for my sticks?' he asked.

'Monkey isn't she, doing that?' She held the shimmering skirt bunched in one hand, the cigarette in the other as she walked back and forth looking behind the driftwood piles. 'Sweet monkey though. Little trick. Gorgeous really . . . He went off with my bag in the boot of the car of course. That's why I'm still in this stupid outfit, these stupid shoes. Went off with my money is why I can't call a taxi . . . We would've seen her I suppose, that monkey one, if she put them anywhere down here.'

'Back there in the bushes.'

'I'll go.'

'Nah. Just pass me that bit of wood by you, and another one the same.'

'What happened to your leg?'

He said what he usually said, 'A shark got it.' Said it loud and it shut her up.

She didn't believe him, knew she knew he was giving her the message to mind her own business. Well the other thing was, that after they'd told you about their diseases, their depressions and their stuffed relationships—after they'd come to an end of talking about themselves, they'd always want to know. Payback time. Only they didn't usually ask straight out like this one here, gawping at his gone leg as though it was some fascinating baby.

The sticks she gave him were about the right length, anyway good enough to get him up as far as the bushes. He started off ahead of her showing her half a clean pair of heels, which was something he wouldn't mind saying to someone, haa.

But she was getting along at a good rate and overtook him in the end, banging about in the bushes, slapping about in the grass, the dress catching on branches and her just ripping the cloth away. Now there was Eddie calling him over the mike, 'Where are you? Come in Te Rua. There's a few cold beers up this way.'

'She's a trick all right that little . . . Who?'

'Kiri. Pain in the bum.'

'Here, there, look. One in the grass one in a tree.' Big-teeth smile. 'Who's her mum and dad?'

'Aunties. The Sisters.'

'Ah, Amiria and Babs. Saw them shooting off in a mini while I was out lighting up under the trees.'

'Aiming for dartists.'

Her head dropped back, smoke shooting from the small whistle-hole she'd made with her lips, then she leaned forward into a big, deep laugh, like a gush of tide and a back wash.

'Lolly Sisters,' he said. 'Candyfloss . . .'

A gush and clatter like a wave busting over stones, before she fell down in a big heap in the grass in her snagged clothes, her laughter bobbing her about as though she was on water.

'And . . . and Peppermint Stick.'

'You . . . You're a crack-up, you.'

Eddie was on the mike again calling him.

'You want to go up and get blind?' he asked her. Blinder, he could've said.

SEVEN

ON THE first school morning after burying their mother, Aunty Wai had come in to help them with their breakfasts and their school lunches. Their father had already gone to work.

When it was time to go he'd gone into the bedroom to say goodbye and had seen the bed not only flat but empty. It had been made up with the cover pulled tight and tidy and the pillows gone. The curtains had been taken down and the windows were all open. Cold air was coming in and he'd felt as though he was being strangled, as though there were fingers round his throat stopping him from screaming.

He'd gone off out the door, running for the cove. When he arrived at the blowhole the water was breaking through and he'd removed his shoes and socks and shorts, pushing in against the water which was sucking him into the hole and licking at him as he moved through holding his schoolbag above the splash. Through the other side he'd walked the ledge out onto the grassy slope where he'd taken off the rest of his clothes and gone into the water.

It was the beginning of winter and the water was rising, beginning to break dark and heavy over the rocks and up onto the sand. The cold of it had loosened him, unlocked his throat and his chest as he pushed in against the first wave and the next until it all became easier—making his way out, swimming and diving until he was beyond the breakers.

By then he was feeling warmer but had kept underwater as much as he could, out of the wind that was roughing the surface. A fish among rocks and weed he was, a fish among other fish— gurnard, moki, sand sharks, octopus; barracuda slinking by; jellyfish with their coloured bits of ribbon; flounder which were just shapes, like hand-prints in the sand.

Kicking his way round he'd begun exploring the near cray holes, the shellfish beds and the weed, then realising the cold was getting to him had stroked hard for the far rocks near the cove entrance. Out there he'd climbed one of the rocks and dived, getting into the waves that had taken him headlong, shoreward, and he'd felt all right, knew he'd be all right.

Using his shirt for a towel he'd dried off, rubbing and rubbing, getting warmth into himself before putting on his socks and shoes, pants and jacket, thinking that if he had matches he could've lit a fire. Thought of going back over the hill to Nanny Blind's for some, but didn't want to go there or anywhere else, or to see or talk to anyone.

By mid-afternoon the wind had died away and he'd eaten his school lunch sitting on a ledge in the cold sun. Afterwards he'd nosed about the shore rocks and shore pools for a while then decided to get into the water again. It was calmer by then and though still cold he'd climbed down and lay on the water, closed his eyes and let himself wash this way and that in the ripples. Seaweed he was.

'That's how dead people lay down in coffins.'

Above him on the bank, Ani Wainoa with a sword, was wearing softball breeches and a white singlet. He didn't want her to be there because he'd found a place to come to—which wasn't a new place.

They all came there nearly every day in the summer holidays, sometimes camped there. Came in weekends throughout the year to get their fish and mussels and crays whenever the weather and tides were right—but it was new being on his own there, or anywhere on his own for that matter. On that day he'd wanted to be by himself and had found the right place for it.

By the time he dried off and put his clothes on again, Ani Wainoa had found another sword and tossed it down to him. So he'd gone up on to the ledge to face her. They'd touched sword tips and begun a careful tipping and tapping back and forth along the ship's side which was the bank of the cove. As he warmed up he'd allowed Ani Wainoa to come at him, backing him down onto the grassy deck where there was room to move about—defend, attack, whack whack whack whack—all the time watching for the change that he knew would come, the change that had caught him out at other times during games played along the creek, along the ledges, or in and out among the trees at Nanny Blind's.

When it came, the two-handed swipe that should've knocked his sword from him, he was ready for it. He'd sidestepped, ducking under the swing, unbalancing her for a moment and moving her backwards down the sloping deck until she managed to turn and run to a place above him, coming at him again. But a one-handed hack and Ani Wainoa's sword broke in the middle. He'd pointed his sword into her chest and she'd raised her head and looked to the sky, letting her arms fall and allowing the remaining piece of stick to drop to the ground. Not that she'd fallen down dead as she should've. She always had been a cheat that Ani Wainoa.

Instead she'd waited, suddenly grabbing the end of his sword that he had pointed into her heart shoving it so hard that his end of it had shot back through his loosened grip and scraped his face, making a rip by his ear and causing him to fall.

Ani Wainoa, now with his stick, held the pointed end of it to his eye, not quite touching.

'Nex'time, loser walks the plank,' she'd said.

'You for sure,' he'd answered.

It was getting dark by then and the water was high in the blowhole, so he'd had to go the long way home, first of all running with Ani Wainoa up through the trees and down to Nanny Blind's.

He left her there and she'd called after him about nex'time as he ran along the long track to the beach, then home.

When he arrived he saw that his father and Uncle Archie who were already home from work, had dismantled the bed and were taking the pieces out to put on a trailer.

'What happened?' his father asked, seeing the blood on his face.

'A stick.'

'Taku and Shania been looking for you. Said you didn't go to school.'

'Down the cove swimming.'

'Hold the door back for us Son, then after that go over Aunty's for tea.'

Nex'time was two weeks later. It was on Nanny Blind's bread day when Wai made bread that Ani Wainoa collected on her way home from school. But Ani Wainoa hadn't been at school that day, so when he arrived home Wai had given him the bread to take.

He ran with it along the shore in the wind that was rocking the sea and whisking up sand. It was cold. Ahead of him Kutu was floating up canopies of seagulls.

Away from the beach and out of the wind, the tracks led him in under the dark trees with their black skins, their shadowy arms, their talking leaves. Kutu was ahead sniffing and pissing and it was silent behind him.

On his own he'd been able to run the wide stretches and the narrow edges in a way that he'd never been able to before—no waiting, walking slow, turning back, no gritty breathing, no one for him to be slow for. He was able to walk the side paths made by

Ani Wainoa, and to stop and disturb the eels, watch them slide in the dark places of the creek; able to run up the rise and down the other side without stopping, resting, waiting or stepping carefully on the narrow path down.

At the house he'd found Ani Wainoa sitting among the books she stole, waiting, dressed in white breeches and blouse, with a black sash round her waist, a strip of curtain lace tying back her hair. For him, in a tidy pile, she had blue track pants, a long-sleeved blouse, a coloured sash and headscarf.

Down in the cove where the wind was blowing cold they'd found their own swords and begun tapping, tapping, moving back and forth watching each other, testing each step, circling the low and high parts of the grassy decks, then moving along the ridges and back, feeling their footsteps, bracing against the wind, back and forth until they could scarcely hold up their swords. He'd used his to help him down to a lower path while Ani Wainoa ran back to the slope and sat waiting in the long winter grass where he could only just see her.

Waiting until he felt the strength coming back into his arms he'd gone after her, but when he was just a little more than a sword's length away she'd rolled a hunk of wood at his feet so that he fell. She'd placed a foot on his back, the tip of her sword touching the back of his neck. 'The Plank,' she'd said, as he lay there wondering how he could get the better of her.

The Plank was a piece of tree trunk growing horizontally from the bank overhanging the water and he'd jumped from there many times, as they all had. But that was in summer.

Now it was July with a wind like needles and a raw sea. He'd rolled from under the pointed sword and run down the slope and up onto the ledge. Removing the track pants, he'd walked quickly out to the tip of the side-on tree and dropped into shocking water that had shot up his bum, up his nose and rattled the bones of his head.

Down there he'd waited, waited, waited, then grabbed for the surface popping his face and going for shore where Ani Wainoa screwed her eyes into him, furious that he'd done it, wishing that she'd been the one to walk and jump—doing it exactly the way he had—straight off, dropping into icy water.

So, ana, Ani Wainoa!

His dog was barking up and down the shore.

'I'll do it, I'll do it,' Ani Wainoa said, but he'd left her there while he set off for Nanny Blind's, knowing she wouldn't jump without him there to see. 'Well nex'time then, nex'time,' she'd called, coming after him as he ran with his teeth clamped to stop them cracking together and to stop his head from aching.

Nex'time.

But it might not ever be as cold again, and by nex'time Ani Wainoa would probably have something worse thought up that they liked better, for them to do.

On his way home, Pop Henry at the gate in his balaclava and coat waiting for Marley to bring his paper, had called out to him, 'You seen a ghose, you Rua?'

EIGHT

IT WAS all set up under the plum trees—beers on a table along with a last few slugs of hard stuff, ice coolers and a couple of nearly finished chateau cardboards. Not enough to get blind unless you were nearly blind already, as she was. Eddie and Jase were rolling up extension chords and Jackson and Joeboy were tying forms and tables down on Archie's trailer.

'Crack you a can,' Dion, the best man, said to him.

'And here, throw this in you,' Wai said to Maina pouring whisky on to a lump of melting ice. 'Forget about him, the bugger. Hnnnn, we know him from way back . . . Trade him in's my advice.'

'Get me a trade, I'll take it.'

The mother and grandfather of the bride, who'd left the party early the night before, had cooked up the left-overs and were bringing it on trays from under the canopy, making a space on the table for it and calling the kids to come. Kid wasn't among them he noticed as they all came running, and Wai seeing him looking for her said she'd gone off home. 'Her and your dog. Seen the mini coming just before you two come up out of the bushes, and off she went.'

'Pain in the bum, her,' he said.

'Little thing, little Kiri. Cheeky,' Maina said.

Archie who hadn't been to bed yet and whose wife Cass had come to get him, was dashing at his ukelele, bundled over it and singing, '*When I die chus bury me please . . .*' likely to fall forward if his feet stopped rocking toe to heel.

'Do it yourself, bury yourself easy, you don't watch out,' Cass said.

'*Underneath a manuka tree . . .*'

'Archie'll tell you, ay Arch?' Wai said.

'*Mingimingi at my head and feet . . .*'

'Con man and a rip-off artist from way back. Married Neta. Left her when he ran off with the rugby funds, right Arch?'

'*Chus like I gone to sleep.*'

'I know, I know. Clever the way he puts himself across,' Maina said. 'Nice the lies he tells, the way he tells them. Thank god I already had my kids to my first husband . . . who was a little rat Aussie drug pusher who took himself off home to Sydney and ended up in the clink.'

'You know how to pick 'em,' Wai said.

'And a pack of losers in between,' Maina said.

'*Freitrain, freitrain, goin' so fast . . .*'

'Across the lunch table at this hui where I was note-taker for the AGM and he was offering me watercress in a bowl along with waanderful advice, is where I met him,' Maina said. 'Nex'thing I know I'm riding off into the sunset in this unpaid-for flash car, and married to him.'

'Off up country with the footy funds and a new woman by the time the shit hit the fan,' Wai said. 'Neta on her own with the kids. Good, good. Lucky for her.'

'Don't know why me,' Maina said.

The fry-up was swimming about in his stomach and he didn't want to drink any more, thought he'd wait around for the tide and get off to the cove again. Good day, good tide. He reckoned everyone would be heading for the cove later, even Archie who'd been up singing and dancing all night. Wobbly now, but he'd have a couple of hours' sleep and come over ready for some action, no headache, nothing. How did he . . .? Maybe a matter of practice.

'Ditch him why don't you?' Wai was saying to Maina as she poured. 'Here, get this into you while you think about it.'

'I got six hundred dollars off my dad when we first met you know. Lied to my father . . . lied that I needed the money. Bloody hell, dad sold his old car. That was the . . . that was . . . I mean . . . '

'We-e-ll. Well, your dad won't be the first one sold a car because of him and his deals. We heard about Laundromat, Dial-a-Hangi, Car Yards, treks through the ponga forest . . . all shonky. The people end up with no deal, no money, ay Arch?'

'That was, that was . . . the worst thing . . . the old man's car . . . '

'Ahh, you think he just making a sandwich and he takes off wit' the bread?' Arch said, singing and strumming it. 'That's it, ha, ha, everytime.'

The boys had returned with the trailer and Dion and Jase went to help them stack the last load of tables. When they'd gone Jase came and sat by him, holding out his hand with a phone number written on it. 'Give it me last night, Remelda,' he said.

'Where are they? Bones, Remelda?'

'Off somewhere . . . What you reckon? What you think Cuz?'

'Ring it.'

'You reckon, you reckon?'

'Yeh ring it.'

'You. You ring it. You like her nnn?'

'My fingers drunk,' Archie said handing the uke to Pare, grandmother of the bride, 'Taking my fingers home, me.'

'*To the place I belong,*' sang Pare plucking the strings, '*West Virginia . . .* '

'That's my man Arch,' Cass said.

'Won't bother you know, to lie,' Maina said. 'I mean, I mean . . . I should go off . . . have an affair myself . . .'

'True . . . You should, you should . . .'

'Except . . . couldn't be bloody bothered.'

'Come home wit' me, me and my drunk fingers, Girl,' Arch said.

'I would, would too . . .'

'Could rent him out,' Cass said.

'Won't even lie. Expect me . . . expect me to find my own way home then he won't even lie. Too full of himself to lie . . . like . . . like any other decent . . . adult . . . adulter.'

'Mind you, he'll be useless,' Cass said. 'Won't you my Arch?'

'Want her money back,' Wai said.

'. . . erer, adulterer. A liar any other time . . . but when it comes to that he don't.'

Now Pare had handed the uke to him. He passed it to Jase who picked a few strings and put it down. 'Why not Cuz. You ring . . . her, Tina . . . I come with you.'

'Or I could make out I was, huhuh . . . Like, hide out a few days and make out I was, if . . . if I could think of . . . huh.' She was lighting up and handing her nearly empty cigarette packet round. 'Be a laugh. Whoosh, gone . . . if I could think . . . think where.'

Everyone was making a move to go, collecting the empties into a rubbish bag and carrying them to a trailer, talking about how they'd been lucky with the weather—no cooking in the rain—which started Wai off again wondering when and how they were going to get their new wharekai.

Before he knew he'd opened his mouth he heard words coming out of it. 'I know where,' he said to Maina.

'The boys have got one more trip, taking the rubbish bags to the tip,' Cass said to her. 'Then I'll have the car. Take you home, if you want.'

'It's OK, who bloody cares. Too shickered anyway. Have a sleep down on the sand. It's what people do round here, sleep on beaches. Nice. Just lay down on the sand and wait down there, me. He'll turn up later, won't even be embarrassed . . . thinks he's such a big shot. Me, I'm the one embarrassed and . . . And I'll just get in the bloody car like usual, go home pay all the bills like usual, get him out of his failed . . . failed . . . enter . . . prises like usual . . . pack up and leave with him when it all goes wrong like usual. I should just . . . '

'When Tamarua and Renie got married was the last time we had a proper roof,' Wai was saying. 'Broken down but better than no roof at all . . . But tell you what. The army boys are leaving us the marquee 'til Monday week. Can't come for it 'til Monday after next. So what say we use it to have a fundraiser for our wharekai next weekend? What you say? Be us lot doing all the work again?'

'I know where . . . a place,' he said to Maina.

He could see his dog returning.

NINE

IT WAS six months later, at the beginning of the summer after his mother died, that his father had gone out one Saturday morning and returned in the late afternoon with Renie and Tommy John. His father was jittery and pale and looked as though he'd been drinking for a week and he took him and Moananui over to Wai's place where all the people were sitting about waiting.

After his father had taken Renie and the baby round the lawn to greet everyone, he sat down on Wai's step while Aunty Wai took Renie to sit with the aunties on a fold-out chair covered in giant flowers. He remembered how quiet it was, and that no one had growled at Taku and Shania or made them get down out of Aunty Wai's coral tree. So he'd gone to join his two same-age cousins in the tree, waiting to see what would happen.

It was a long wait, with people talking in low voices, eyeing up this Renie that his father had brought home and wiggling their eyebrows at Tommy John.

After a time Pop Henry had begun making noises, blowing his nose, clearing his throat and getting up ready to speak—which he did on on on, stamping his feet and waving his arms about, jabbing his finger in the direction of the urupa.

He hadn't realised at first that Pop was having a go at his father—for playing around while his wife, their niece, was sick all that time, and for coming there now, today, bringing a woman who looked like a schoolgirl with a baby already more than a year old.

On on on, giving his father a tongue bashing that had lasted until the sun began to drop behind the hills.

Over there on the slopes their own niece was hardly under, hardly cold was what Pop was going on about.

All this while his father had sat without moving, leaning on his knees looking as though he was enduring a hangover that he'd decided was nobody's business but his own, waiting for it to be over.

People had sat about, becoming shadows, scraping their hands up over their legs and arms, swiping in front of their faces and snorting down their noses at the mobs of sandflies that were attacking them.

Then it was done. Pop Henry stopped and sat down on one of Wai's chairs of big flowers without even singing his song—that's how wild he was. People stopped waving at sandflies, kids stopped lugging the baby and he and his cousins had taken the opportunity to get down out of the tree.

What next?

He remembered that all eyes had been on his father to see what he would do, but his father did nothing. Eyes looked about to see if anyone else was getting up to say anything but it seemed not.

All over.

Lights went on in the house and when he went inside with his cousins, his aunties were in the kitchen slicing a cold leg, buttering bread, boiling water and laughing, ha ha, Tamarua sitting there like a kehua.

'Pop dishing it out to him, laying it on. Wild as anything.'

'Tamarua not a word to say.'

'Scared he make matters worse.'

64

'Ha, good way to spend a Saturday, you think?'

'True.'

'Well . . . Who can blame him anyway?'

'A man is just a man.'

'That's a fact.'

'Of course that Renie . . .'

It seemed they'd all seen her in her little dresses, her short hair, all arms and legs dancing in her diamond shoes, even if today she did just look ordinary in her long skirt and white top, like an ordinary mother of a little kid. The baby was fat and nice, all had agreed about that, and agreed too that it was something to ring up and tell the other relations about. Juicy it was.

As they were discussing all of this Nan Tini had come in bringing her old cousin, Nanny Blind, and the aunties had begun pushing furniture out of the way and getting an armchair ready. Tini had led Blind and her dog there, sat the old woman down in the chair and begun pushing her arms into a cardigan and buttoning it as though Blind couldn't dress herself.

They'd all started bossing, 'Look now, look at your legs.'

'You can't stay there living in the trees with those.'

'True, you can't . . . She can't.'

The legs were big and fat he'd noticed, her feet pumped like balloons, and they'd all begun promising Nanny Blind that if she came out front to live with Arch or Wai, or any of them, they could rub her legs with Deep Heat or a slice off their aloe vera plant. They could soak her feet in boiled kawakawa or Vicks and warm water and rub in their creams, take her to town and get her an outfit for the wedding, get her some shoes, give her hair a trim. She could be near doctors. Also, they'd said, it would be closer to school for Ani Wainoa and better for her, because . . . because . . . because they didn't want Ani Wainoa growing up in the trees, weird.

Blind listened, and now and again he'd seen her lift her eyelids just far enough to show spooky half rounds of useless pale centres, rimmed by dark outer half rings, then whites that were bluish as though smoke had leaked into them. But Blind hadn't been interested in his aunties' rubs and cures, or in leaving her falling-down house and coming to live with anyone, or in outfits and hairdos, or in being near doctors and closer to schools. What she'd wanted that evening was descriptions.

'T'is new woman of Tamarua?' she'd asked.

'Ah, Renie?'

'Renie. Well, one of these skinny-as-a-stick ones with boy's hair, all neck and arms and legs.'

'Ah it's a fact.'

'Dressed in a yard of ribbon like Audrey Hepburn in old movies.'

'True. Black version of Audrey.'

'Long neck like Audrey.'

'True, and black eyes.'

'Skinny. Half a head taller than him.'

'And . . . tis it his, tis it his?' Blind had wanted to know.

'Ah Tommy John. It is, you can see it.'

'True you can see. Those fat photos of Rua and Moananui when they were babies, just like that, fat and nice.'

'Her dad works on the trawlers,' someone had said. 'One of those town Hakopas, and the mother from up Wellington.'

'Ah well, Hakopa,' Blind had said. 'Got a dance band all t'ose Hakopa, after the war when we go to socials and dancing, and I dance around seeing with half of one eye. Ronny, Chock, Tutu and their cousin Takumoana with only one hand after the war, so he have to be the singer. Hmmm, could be dead all t'ose.'

On Blind's dog were big fat fleas.

When they went out again their Uncle Arch was pouring double slugs of whisky into two glasses for Pop and his father telling anyone else who wanted one to get themselves a glass. Renie was sitting by his father with a drink in her hand. Yes she had a long neck and kept swallowing even though she hadn't started drinking—sitting really still, flicking her black eyes. Everyone was laughing and slapping the bloody sandflies, shouting and having his father on, 'Ha ha Brother, all right, when's the wedding?'

TEN

DURING THE wedding ceremony when his father and Renie were married at the end of that summer, he'd watched Ani Wainoa— who was wearing a dress, a back-to-front waistcoat and an admiral's hat, but for once nothing in white—edging away from Nanny Blind and making her way towards where he'd found a standing space along the back wall of the wharenui. She'd squeezed in beside him, made a hole in the side of her mouth and said, 'The treasure of the boiling deep lies there, and the monster of the treacherous crossing is asleep.'

He'd tipped his head in the direction of the door, letting her know to follow him, and together they'd slid out on to the veranda and looked across the marae to the water—which on that day was the shiny blue of bridesmaids' dresses. They'd made their way round to the back of the meeting house from where they could see the blowhole, high, dry and open for them. Off they'd gone running.

When they arrived at the cove they'd made their way up and along the track to the plank from where they could look out towards the last rock standing at the cove entrance, then past there to the wide band of water where, on that day, they could see that the taniwha was asleep. Beyond there was the island and Cave Rock where the treasure lay.

It was the right day and they were alone.

There had been other good days during the summer, but on those occasions there'd always been others there too. They'd had to wait all summer to be by themselves, because they knew that what they had planned, what Ani Wainoa had planned for them, wasn't allowed.

The log that they had practised with was above the high tide mark where they'd left it. It was long enough for both of them to sit on and had enough branching pieces on it to prevent it rolling in the water. They'd taken off their outer clothing and slid the log down into the water going one each side and kicking for the far rocks.

From there they'd looked out over the forbidden band of water, which on most days was whipped and orderless, with waves that were tipsy, dislocated and skew-back because the taniwha was awake and raving. On this day, being a day of taniwha sleeping, the stretch of water was just bridesmaids' dresses, with a frilly place out in the middle of the stream, tucked and pinned from breathing and snores.

It wasn't allowed, but they had positioned the log, angling it towards the island and the nearest side of Cave Rock, pushing off through the first band of water, ironed and satiny. When they came close to the strip of rucks and pinnings they'd prepared themselves, breathing in, propelling forward, cutting water with their fast, paddling feet and their one-armed stroking.

And they'd almost made it, could almost have touched the outcrops of Cave Rock with outstretched hands, but the log had begun to turn and they'd realised there was nothing their kicking or one-armed stroking could do. All they'd been able to do was cling to the log as it began rotating in the currents at the same time washing them sideways, out from the island where it spilled them into the calm water of the open sea.

Climbing onto the log and laying flat along it, they'd leaned first to one side then the other to keep it balanced, knowing there was no way back and nothing they could do but allow the current to take them towards the shore of the next bay.

Once there they'd rested, waiting until the sun began to go down before starting off around the cliff edges, climbing the jagged rocks and lower cliff faces to avoid what was now high tide water beating its way through the channels.

It was night by the time they reached the cove and the familiar paths. On the grassy slope they'd waited for cuts and scratches to stop bleeding before putting their wedding clothes back on and setting out on the home tracks carrying their shoes.

The tables had been cleared by the time they arrived, and the last of the dishes were being stacked in the wash-up area. Before coming out into the open they'd waited until there was only Uncle Morehu looking after the fires, knowing he wouldn't ask any questions and would just give them kai.

A year later when his father and Renie decided to move and take the family where there was work, he'd decided not to go with them. He couldn't think at the time why he didn't want to leave, only saying to himself that there was treasure lying at the bottom of the boiling deep. It hadn't seemed to be the real reason, but even though he'd felt sorry for his father who had kept saying, 'Your mum would want me to keep you kids together,' he'd kept with his decision to stay there with Aunty Wai.

After his father and Renie and the children left, life had gone on much as before even though it had people missing from it.

ELEVEN

HE SENT Kutu on ahead. Maina followed, coughing and staggering, slapping her snagged skirt down with the shoes that she'd taken off and now held either side of her. At the creek, where he could swing through to the other side so easily without getting wet, she made no attempt to cross on the stepping stones but waded straight through and up the sloping bank, breathing so hard he thought she might pass out.

From there the track narrowed even more, going up and over the rise. He slowed down when he reached the top, sat and waited, looking out over the cove to the island and beyond to a flat horizon.

In the other direction he could see over the bushes to the clearing and the tipsy chimney of the falling-down house that Nanny Blind had given him—after Toss died, after Ani Wainoa left, after Blind had gone to live at last with Archie Shoes.

'His feet,' Maina said, flopping down beside him, 'you know . . . these perfect . . . feet. Sings to his feet, soaping, rinsing off, drying every bit, every baby toenail. A whole newspaper on the floor . . . sits there with clippers . . . files, making . . . making art . . . of feet.'

Private life of Piiki Chiefy. She was a crack-up all right.

'It's a wreck,' he said. 'Falling down,' excusing the house and thinking now that this wasn't a good idea, wondering why he'd opened his mouth to say I know a place, wondering why he'd gone down to the beach and said it again, I know a place. He pushed the door and she went in, not hearing what he was saying, not understanding what he was talking about but just dropping her shoes, falling onto his lopsided bed asleep.

Collecting his tent, sleeping bag and fishing gear into his backpack he prepared to go and join whoever would be spending the afternoon at the cove, intending to stay the next few nights there.

When he arrived back at the old house the next morning with fish, her clothes were draped over a bush and she was sitting on the creek bank by the wash pool wearing a tee shirt of his and one of his beach towels.

'Embarrassing,' she said, 'in this morning-after light. Sounds good when you're drunk as a skunk, maudlin over your glass.'

He unhooked his frying-pan from where it hung on the tree, set it up on the stones and lit dry grass and sticks under it. He filled his water pot and put it to one side of the fire.

'Anyway just waiting for my things to dry and I'll get moving.'

That was a relief. There'd been no rain and the tank was just about empty. There were no supplies apart from a half loaf of old bread, a bit of flour, a few cans and a handful of teabags. He went inside for the tin of fat.

'I mean I always end up going back to him anyway,' he could hear her saying, 'so why hang around just to try and prove a point. Prove what point? Or . . . or pretending?'

He went out, scraping away layers of fat from the tin until he came to the clean stuff which he scooped into the pan. It slid and melted and began spitting.

'Woke up in the bloody dark and didn't know where I was. And didn't care, just went back to sleep.'

When the first fish was in the pan he went to the tank for a pot of water which he put on the side of the fire before returning to the house for plates, cups, salt and teabags.

'Woke up again it was daylight and still couldn't remember much really. All I knew was I had no smokes, no clean clothes, no nothing. Found me a piece of soap and had a nice cold wash in the creek, in the hollow. Washed my things and it was just really, really . . .'

She was a talker this one. He slid his knife under the fish and turned it. The cooked side had browned, the skin had crisped and the whitened flesh was beaded with juice.

'And I was just sitting here, wanting a smoke, realising it was Monday and thinking I should ring in to work . . . ah, on a bush phone or what? But you know, I think I was so dead asleep last night that my watch stopped. Ten past two it says, so I don't even know, no idea . . . what it is . . . don't care really.'

With his knife under the fish, he eased it onto a plate and handed it to her, then put the second fish in the pan and boosted the fire.

Not long after sunrise he'd thrown his line out and spent about an hour before catching the two fish, then he'd scaled and cleaned them, washed up, taken his time coming back. Probably getting on for eight o'clock. Anyway it was all his own doing, getting her to come here. Why had he? He turned his fish and shuffled the pan, and when the fish was ready removed the pan from the fire and shifted the water to the middle.

'This is um, it's aah . . . unbelievable. I mean . . . My god . . . it's . . .' She was lifting the flesh away from the bones with her big fingers, which were full and round except at the tips where they looked as though they'd been sharpened—an expert when it came to cleaning up fish, he could see.

'He goes to Wellington today, which is something I didn't remember until my head cleared, another of his jaunts. Got a suite in a posh hotel down there that they reserve for him. Must just about own the place by now, or the Runanga must, since they're the ones paying. That goes for the taxi company too—and Air Enzed. Once a month, all laid on.'

When the water boiled he filled the cups and put a teabag in each. 'There's condense milk if you want.'

'I'll get it.'

'On the shelf with the other tins.'

'I haven't had it since I was a kid,' she said when she returned with the can. 'Tea and condense milk, Weetbix and condense milk, condense milk on bread if we could get away with it.' He bunged two holes in the can and she let the milk slug out into her cup while he whisked it with his knife. 'Well, as for all that—flash hotels, flash women, someone else's money—he can stick it. This . . . this is my idea of the good life.'

She lay on her side facing the fire, resting on one elbow, shaping her mouth to sip the tea, 'But I suppose . . . after this I'll get going.' Then she asked, 'Who knows I'm here?'

'No one asked.'

It was true, no one at the cove the previous afternoon had mentioned seeing him leave the beach with her and set out on the tracks, no one had asked about her or if anyone had come to pick her up.

'It's just that . . . well it's embarrassing. My big mouth gets me in trouble sometimes when I've had a few. It just won't shut up. I remember yesterday . . . life history, then before we went up to get your sticks, still half plonked asking about your leg.'

So she wanted to bring that up again, only more carefully this time, still wanted to know.

Nose trouble.

Well the subject of his leg was fine, safe. He could talk about it anytime because it was nothing, and she was a stranger anyway, a piece of landscape lying there on her side changing the shape of the creek bank. She was someone he hardly knew, who would stand up soon and push off—maybe after he'd given her the piece of information she wanted, which it would take only one breath and one sentence to give. Lost in a car accident.

Nothing secret about that. One sentence, or he could tell it all if he wanted to.

On other matters there were things he'd never told and never would. Kid was the one asking him but she wouldn't get it out of him, the secret for life, the one to die with.

Did this one here know he wasn't fooled, that he didn't have to tell if he didn't want to, that if he did decide to speak it wasn't because she was there getting it out of him.

Lost it in a car accident. Time to go. Ka kite ano.

And if he put it that way, decided to say it like that, he'd be telling her that was all the information she was getting. She was waiting, her dark eyes dulled like Marmite. Wiped. She'd pulled right back after putting out bait, that's how badly she wanted . . . to know?

Or, to have conversation? A reason to stay a while?

Anyway there was no way for her to get home now, because even if she did walk back along the tracks and then the three k's into the township in her wrong shoes there wouldn't be a bus at this time of day.

'After a year at the High School where I didn't do much good,' he said, 'I was packed off to boarding school with money sent from Aussie by my father. Homesick the whole time and always in trouble for standing up for myself. I missed home, missed my cousins, especially Taku and Shania because we'd always been together.'

He'd started too far back but it was because he wanted her to know about Taku and Shania before he came to the leg bit. Or was it because he wanted to have conversation, an excuse for her to stay a while?

'My cousin Dion was at the school too, the one that was best man the other day. He was two years ahead, two years older, and that helped a bit but I never really got over my homesickness. I stuck it out for two years then they let me come home, but I had to promise to complete everything at the local High so I could go to university. It's what my father and the rest of the whanau had in mind for me.

'So I did the first bit, got through the exams, but there was no way I wanted to go to university—nothing there to interest me. Not academic like Dion, wanted to be a builder.

'Anyway it wasn't a good time for builders and the nearest type of training I could get was to go on a Home Maintenance course which I thought would be a way in, maybe with an apprenticeship to follow or a job doing building labour. What we learned was to replace door handles. But there was only one door handle and one screwdriver, so we had to take turns taking the handle off and putting it on again. We had to take turns with the shovel digging a drain, take turns with the trowel putting down little squares of concrete. Most of the time you sat around waiting for things to do— some catch to attach or shelf to paint. For book work we had to draw different types of hammers and saws and hinges. It all made you feel stupid. One week's worth of stuff stretched out to twenty. And there were no jobs. All we could do at the end of it was go on other courses, graduating from one to another.

'Horticulture was a flash name for weeding gardens for old people and putting a few seeds in pots. Nothing to it really, except we flogged all the potting mix and plastic stuff and took it home for the tarutaru we had back here in the manuka—Shania, Taku and me. It was like it was all nothing, like messing about waiting for something to start.

'Arts Programme? We made prints using this method and that method, but always waiting for equipment or materials and having no use for the things we made. Not happening.'

All this and she'd only asked about the missing leg. She was standing now, making her way to the fire, stepping smoothly like a dancer so that she wouldn't make a sound, not wanting a stick to crack, dry grass to shift, not wanting to wake him up to the fact that he was telling. He watched her scoop water from the pot and return to the bank, rescuing her old teabag from where she'd left it in the grass and making herself another cup with it. She let the milk dribble in, concentrating on it, keeping her eyes off him so he'd go on talking—sipped, looking into her cup. He'd like her to know he wasn't fooled.

'The courses all had Job Search attached where you learned to phone up bosses, prepare CVs, go for interviews, fill out forms, all that. And Life Skills—visit libraries and supermarkets, one hour a week on computers and a pretending bit of bone carving with a tutor who turned up sometimes, sometimes didn't, useless hua.'

Talking too much, letting off steam about those courses, just talking. Boring stuff. Only asked about the leg, which could've been answered in a sentence.

It was something to do with fires he thought. Fires made talk, especially early fires and night fires, and it was when he had his fire going that he most wanted company. From the time he lit it to the time it burned out, whether it was his outside fire or the wood stove, were the times he wouldn't've minded having someone there.

Apart from those times he preferred living on his own. It's what he'd wanted to do ever since Nanny Blind had given him the place when he was a kid. 'You have it now,' she'd said. 'If my girl stayed, it for her. But gone, so you have it, for you.'

His aunties and uncles had never let him live there before, didn't like it even now, yet it gave him his physical life, that's how he thought of it. It was his physical life. Because what would there be to do now if he hadn't put himself in charge of getting people their fish, and who else to get fish now that Taku and Shania were gone? It had to be him.

And it was his physical life having to do things for himself—get his wood, nail up boards here and there, keep his water hole clear and his tank clean, grow his bit of dope and his pumpkins, shoot a few hares, catch his eels and his fish and keep the creek running. Once a fortnight he went out for supplies and once in a while Jase and Bones picked him up for a night out.

Life out front meant being trapped in front of infomercials, *Days of Our Lives* and Ricki Lake along with aunties, grandfathers and truants. It meant everyone running around after him not allowing him to do anything for himself. But back here he'd given himself a life.

'Then I got something, something I wanted. A mate of my father's had building work round the city, said he'd teach me but couldn't pay much. I stayed with him two years and learned heaps. Taku and Shania got hacked off with courses too and they managed to get enough seasonal work to keep them going—a bit of fencing, picking pumpkins, packing corn, picking grapes, shearing. The two of them were saving to go to Aussie to stay with my father and get themselves jobs over there. But me? This was always the place for me.'

Her eyes shifted from left—catching him halfway—to right, still dulled, wiped, Marmite. Must be hanging out for a smoke by now, hanging out for news on his missing leg too maybe, but he hadn't got to the leg bit yet. She asked for it. Made him feel like laughing—which he thought was probably also something to do with the fire.

'My two cousins came to meet me one Friday with their pockets stuffed full of their shearing money. We went off to the pub and got to drinking, playing some pool, drinking some more, then Taku pulls out a fistful of his dollars and says, "We never drink all this. We go and get us a car."

'So we went off to this place where people had vehicles parked up for sale, found one, bought it, put petrol in and off we went heading for home. Taku was checking out our car, what it could do. We come to a corner too fast and went flying, is all I remember. In hospital I found out Taku and Shania were dead, my same-age cousins. No shark got my leg. They chopped it off at the hospital. One broken leg I had, and one missing leg that left its ghost behind, giving me hell.'

She was watching him now, careful not to move. Marmite had picked up a glimmer from somewhere—from fading fire, from sun criss-crossing through leaves, from light coming off creek water or a tin roof, or . . . or, from a hot spot in her skull.

'It's buried over there with them. Never wanted it back.' True, not that anyone would believe it, so what made him say it when he'd never said it to anyone before?

It shifted her. She stood, sensing that he had gone as far as he would go, that 'physical life' may have been beyond what he'd wanted to say. Or was it that the fire was gone now and there was only a dribble of smoke coming from it?

Or that she'd got all she wanted?

He'd got away from *them*—the prying aunties and uncles who pulled all sorts of stuff out of you like they were big hot poultices. On you like hot packs, them, so you felt only comfort while they drew you out. Now he'd brought her here with his 'I know a place' and was letting all this stuff out, but he didn't care really, knew what was happening and he could let it happen—but ahh, only to a certain point.

'I did have a prosthesis . . .' He felt pleased with the word, which he'd never said out loud before. She took her plate and scraped the bones into the fireplace. Flies scattered, and the bones woke a spark. 'Supposed to get refitted after a year but I was living here by then, escaped my aunties. It was a nuisance taking it off all the time to get in the water, and even out of the water I can move round quicker without it. Didn't bother about the refit.'

She returned to her place on the creek bank and sat with her arms as struts on either side of her. He put a handful of dry stuff on to the spark and blew, poked in a few sticks and scraped his own plate out.

'So . . . so . . . I should get on my way,' she said. He noticed 'should'.

'The tide'll be down in another hour,' he said. 'I could go out through the hole and phone up Jase to come after work and give you a lift home.'

'I don't like to trouble anyone, even though I know I'm doing that already.'

'No trouble. Anyway I want to. I need a few things, batteries for my tape deck. Go crazy if I got no sounds.'

'Sing. Dance. They had you up dancing. It don't stop you dancing.' Her eyes narrowed as her mouth widened into her big teeth grin.

And it was the fire.

It was the fire. It was the flames, the way they flared orange and blue and waded through the wood chips. Or it was words, like 'physical life' and 'prosthesis', or cicadas racketing hard-out in the trees with the sound of waterfalls. Or it was the waterfall itself spilling down the hill behind them, or it was smoke up his nose.

Was it all of those things making him pull himself up onto his foot and begin singing and doing his stick dance, his hip thing, as he went towards the house, '*Whati whati to hope . . .*' Hand slap, '*Ringa pakia e.*'

Was it all of those things making her flop and laugh?

'*Waewae takahia, e hura o kanohi e,*' one-leg stamp and silly eyes.

'*Titiro whakarunga, titiro whakararo,*' look up, look down and haere whakamua, hoki whakamuri, making his way past clothes steaming on bushes to the house and taking the song up a note. She was laughing up on the bank out between her rocks of teeth, then singing along.

He took the half packet of flour from the shelf and put it in a bowl with baking powder and a tin of syrup and a fork, and when he went back out she was dancing back and forth along the creek bank in her fat and her towel with her face all beamed, her arms swimming, diving, circling, gleaming like seals or dark fishes. She came stepping down, picking her clothes from the bushes and went singing and dancing inside. Had a voice on her which came from down low, like it pulled up from her knees, up through her groin and stomach, coming smoky and ragged up through a crusty chest and out between the big teeth. It was out-of-breath, gutsy, kapa haka, god and all that. It needed, he thought, a different song.

'Now what?' she said, coming out in her dress that was snagged and crumpled and still steaming. 'Ah, fry bread, I'll do it.'

She picked up the flour and emptied it into the bowl, shook in the baking powder and took it to the tank for water. While she mixed he tipped hot water in the pan, sitting on the ground while he scrubbed it with a brush then wiped it out with newspaper which he dropped into the fire. For a moment as it burned the paper took the shape of a bird which, with the heat under it, rose, colourful and decorated with advertising words which said *Imported Fragrance. Where everyone gets. $3.99. Luxury of. Nationwide.* The bird settled, disappeared in flames.

'I suppose he came, asked around, found I'd gone. Probably thought I'd rung my father to come and get me. He'll ring my father and when he finds I'm not there, he won't have a clue where I am, and won't care really.

'The *other woman* lives down there, Wellington. Glamorous as. More his style, so I don't know why he doesn't just stay down there with her. More convenient as it is, I suppose, with me here, her there. I mean I wouldn't care. Or would I? He treats me fine when he's around—or does he? He's like a tricky baby. No he isn't. He's a liar, and a user and that's what makes me want to get my own back on him . . . But . . . not worth it, not really, because how much would he care if I wasn't there on Friday when he comes back. He'd care about an empty house and nothing cooking, care about no one out earning while he flies here and there spending other people's money. Bugger knows I always come back in the end.'

She whipped the sticky dough with the fork, beating the remainder of dry flour from round the sides of the bowl down into it.

'Before I met him—which was only five years ago, but it seems like we've been involved in ten years worth of *business* together—I had a good job in an agency where I got to arrange travel for kapa haka groups. I was just getting into a management area, you know, of kapa haka groups and their travel, which would've meant travel for me too. It's what I've always wanted—overseas travel, seeing the world, all that. Instead, off I went with him, escaping from this and that failed scam all over the country, and haven't had a decent job since.'

He spread the wood to lower the flames as she began pulling pieces off the dough, shaping them and letting them down into the fat that had become smoking hot.

'Telling you all this, things I never heard myself say before,' she said, shifting the bread around the pan. 'Landing it all on you, and here I am got a son about your age. Sorry about that.'

'It's the fire,' he said.

'Aaay? True?'

'True.'

'What's it got? Germs?'

'Something. For talk, sing, dance, laugh, whatever.'

'Aaay? Is that right?'

She lifted the first panful of fry bread out on to the plate. 'Well, whatever it is I could do with more . . . more letting off steam. It's a hundred times better than walking the floors at DEKA all day to keep him in fancy underwear and me in smokes. Got to work so I can smoke, ha ha, couldn't last another day. But hmm, at the moment, just right now, it'd only take cigarettes to keep me here 'til after Friday—long enough for him to come back from Wellington with his unfaithful washing and find me not home.'

'I got . . . other stuff.'

'Nah, it's got to be nicotine thanks all the same.'

TWELVE

DURING THE summer when he was fourteen, Archie had taken Taku, Shania and him to the far crayfish rocks, sending them down just to look the first few times, "'Til you can see, 'til you can see,' Arch had said.

And gradually their eyes had become familiar with the contours of the rocks, the movement of the weed, the positions of the holes and finally the shapes and sizes of the crays at the entrances. 'And a game plan,' Arch had said. 'You got to have one, got to know what it takes. Do it when you think so,' and he'd left them and gone fishing.

What it took was the deepest breath and getting down as quickly as possible, diving and pulling themselves along via the jutting pieces of rock and into the holes to grab, two-handed, the crays already backing away from their approach. It meant holding hard over the spiky backs of the crays and pulling them up against the rough cloth of the bush singlets that Arch had given them to wear. Then there was the hard push off rock, kicking for the surface, sometimes having to drop the catch if they were running out of breath and needed their arms to get them up quickly. But Arch was pleased with their five crays when he returned with the boat. 'Because it's up to you,' he'd told them. 'You young ones got the lungs for it, and who else is there now Jackson and his brother gone?'

It was that same day, as the boat nosed its way through the rip, that he'd looked out towards Cave Rock and decided to ask Arch the question he'd often asked before but never received an answer to. 'What's down there?' he'd wanted to know, but the only answer he'd ever received was, 'You don't go there.'

Not allowed.

Not allowed to go there and not considered old enough to know the reason, but perhaps now that they were old enough to be cray catchers Arch would consider him and his cousins ready to be answered. 'What's down there?' he'd asked again.

'Ghost of Parai Maaka,' Archie had said. 'A relation of ours. Went the wrong way in.'

Arch had turned the boat then slowed the motor, picking a way back through the skewing waves. 'You line up the top of the rock wit' the waterfall, and then you see the path. Watch for it.'

It was as Arch turned the boat, heading it along the track of the rip that the tip of the rock had become aligned with the waterfall, and there, looking across to Cave Rock he'd seen the narrow strip of quiet water that would've let them there. If he and Ani Wainoa had started out from the opposite side they would have come to it. 'Down there? The ghost of Parai Maaka, kina as big as plates and big fish feeding,' Arch had said. 'Never mind, leave it. Leave it to the fish and old Parai.'

It was four years since he and Ani Wainoa had gone seeking a way and a treasure, and though he knew that they would never attempt that again he'd gone to find her to tell her what he'd found out about this place of boiling deep and treacherous crossing.

These words of hers, from books she stole, that she'd eased him into four years earlier, were now unsayable. Also Ani Wainoa was different, there being nothing he could say now that would interest her in the deep, the high and the far, the hills and cove. She had other words to use, other things to do and other lies to tell.

'Turning into the rip, lining up the tip of the rock with the waterfall you can see the way,' he'd said.

'It won't be long,' Ani Wainoa had said, 'and I'll be gone from here forever. We'll be together he and I. We'll be as one, forever.'

That day she was wearing the top half of a singlet with white rugby shorts, and her arms and legs, shining, had reminded him of eels. It was Stefan she was talking about, who she'd met on Show Day at the bumper car rides.

'You wouldn't think . . . but if someone shows you, you can see,' he'd told her. 'Arch slowed the motor down, went slow through the high waves, and only from there you can see.'

'Every night he signals me with the headlights of his car, from far away on the hill road, and I go under cover of darkness . . .'

Hiding from Nanny Blind and a half blind dog? She always was bullshit, that Ani Wainoa.

'Until I come to the edge of the moonlit forest.'

Which meant that every single night there was moonlight, where this bumper-car Stefan hung about waiting to take her into his arms.

'He's coming to take me away. He's in love with me. I'm in love with him. We're so in love with each other.'

Words that would have made his voice crack and slide if he'd tried to say them—but still *she* managed to say them, words from some of those kissy books she stole.

'And what we do . . . what we do . . .' she'd said, taking off the singlet and the shorts and throwing them into the bushes.

People were trees, with trunks and arms and leaves. You could go up against a tree, put your arms around a tree, push up against, up against, a tree.

'But you wouldn't know,' she'd said.

Or trees were people, with bodies and arms and hair that you could climb up and into, where you could find a place, where you could straddle and hold. You could hold the tree. It could hold you. You could rock. It could rock you.

'You wouldn't know and you'd be so afraid.'

Rocking and riding would open the tree's big arms and heads out to glimpses of the sky. He knew that she knew he wasn't afraid, had never been afraid of anything they'd ever done together.

'Afraid and you wouldn't know.'

He wasn't sure if he knew, but he'd taken off his clothes and gone right with her as she slid herself to the ground.

And he did it, did all of it.

They'd done all of it.

It was only when they stopped that he didn't know what to do lying there still joined. Was there something else to do, something to say? What he didn't know was what came next.

Next was she'd shoved him, and as he rolled away she'd leapt up and put her foot down on his neck saying, 'That wasn't good. I didn't like that at all.'

At first he hadn't believed her because of the way she'd ridden under him, thrust under him, up and up and up, arching, breathing hard in and out, riding just like him. He'd seen her face.

'If you tell anyone I'll kill you,' she'd said pressing her foot down hard.

He'd upturned his hands beneath her foot and thrown her off, rolled away and stood. And then he'd believed her. He didn't like it either.

'I mean it, if you tell I'll kill you.'

Blood—on him, on her.

'And it's not allowed.'

'Course not.'

For some time afterwards he'd kept away from Ani Wainoa, and on the occasions when he was sent with bread and supplies to Nanny Blind's, Ani Wainoa was never home. Sometimes he thought she'd gone away as she'd said she would, then he would realise she hadn't because there would be her clothes drying on the bushes, her comb by the washbowl with strands of her black hair caught in it, a book open on the ground.

Occasionally on his way there he had looked across from the rise and caught a glimpse of her hurrying away from the house and into the trees because she'd seen him coming.

The weather had just begun to warm up when one day he left his cousins to their after-school practices and their spacie games at the Lotto shop and come home knowing that the tide would be down and the blowhole dry. He'd changed into shorts, put gear in a bag and gone running with his dog down on to the beach then round the curve of it and up through the blowhole.

The sun had backed away from the cove by the time he arrived there, but the warmth of morning and early afternoon had been enough to keep the chill away.

It was an in-between-moon time when there was little movement of the tide which was out as far as it would go. There was nothing cutting the surface of the water, the weed hung at a standstill in it and the birds had gone off roaming. An off-white light caused by a spider web of cloud had spun itself between the backed-off sun and the water, the edges, the ridges.

He'd broken all that, first with the swing and splash of his line from off the ledge, then with the perfect bomb he did from the plank. After warming himself into the water that still held a pinch of cold, he'd gone to explore the kina beds and the paua rocks thinking about what he would collect later, to take home. Every now and again he'd gone across to his line to see if there was a fish on it or to see if the hook needed rebaiting, and even though it wasn't the season for crayfish he'd swum out to the cray rocks, diving down to look into the hollows and crevices.

By the time he began making his way back there had been a further dulling down of the sky—grey light on the water as well as on the shore, where the bushy treetops looked like fallen cloud.

He'd come out of the water for a knife and bag to go and collect paua and kina, and on returning had to wait at a distance from a stingray which was making its way among the weed, one wing and then the other lifting out of the water, dark and triangular, as it fed and browsed.

It was while he was treading water, waiting for Whai to move off, that he'd looked towards the rise which was catching remaining light from the sun as it stepped down behind the hills, and had caught a glimpse of black and white that was like a flash, black-white, like a trick, a turning up and turning down of a hand of clubs or spades—a flick of Ani Wainoa, a trick of Ani Wainoa.

Going or coming?

He'd watched, and by the movement of the bushes, realised she was making her way towards the cove. But why so slowly, because Ani Wainoa was never slow? She was up to something, but what?

So he'd swum ashore, climbing to the ledge waiting at the end of the track that he knew she was making her way along, and eventually she'd stepped out holding something in her arms.

On seeing him she'd turned to go back, but realising it was too late for him not to have seen what she carried. She had come at him, thrusting the bundle into his arms, a bundle wrapped in a tee shirt of hers.

As he held it Ani Wainoa had picked up a lump of wood, then, holding it two-handed, had backed him along the ledge shouting, 'You. You throw it. Throw it or I'll kill you.'

Backing away from her, feeling for each foothold along the narrow track, he came to the place where the plank ledge began. There he'd turned and run out to the edge with what he held and jumped with it folded into him.

When he surfaced there was a wriggle and sneeze from in the wrapping, and up on the ledge in the dark that was now coming down he'd watched the curling away of blackwhite, which was like a seagull wing.

A seagull scream had echoed round the bowl of the cove. 'You tell and . . . You tell anyone and . . . And I'll come after you . . . After you . . . come after . . . after you with . . . with a knife, with a knife knifeknife, with a knife.'

He'd turned onto his back, held the bundle high on his chest and frog-kicked for shore on the blackening water. The edges of the sky were a cooked-cray colour where the sun had dropped behind the hills and he was thinking he should've done what she said, thrown it. He was thinking he could let it go now because it wasn't anything or maybe it was a bird.

Leave it, swim away, run off home.

Not because of the knife. He'd never been afraid of anything Ani Wainoa said.

As he came out of the water he'd unwrapped the baby, whose eyelids were shuddering, whose nose was bubbling, whose mouth had opened and begun letting out squeaky sounds, whose wingy arms had lifted as though to fly, then drawn back. On the ends of the bird-arms were little creepy hands.

He'd wrapped her in his own dry shirt and thought of leaving her there. She was a bird. Thought of handing her up into the arms of a tree.

But he found she was too warm to put down, too warm to be left in the dark, so he'd decided to take her to Nanny Blind's.

In the dark he'd made his way along the pathways among the threaded roots and vines, among all the heads and arms and hands of trees. The squeaking had stopped and there was a night smell of blankets, a breathing, a creaking, a taste in his mouth of kawakawa.

As he neared Blind's house he'd slowed his pace and quietened his dog, holding the brush and grasses aside to let himself through without noise, hoping Blind was asleep, hoping her half-deaf Toss would not alert her.

He'd found Blind sitting in her chair with a lamp on the shelf beside her. Her shut eyes were leaking and her glass-eyed dog was stiff at her feet. 'Ani Wainoa, Girl,' she'd called.

There on the bed, then run home.

'Me, Rua.'

'Boy, you got to bury my dog.'

Leave it and run, but it was too warm to be left.

'Go . . . get . . . get . . .' he'd said going back on to the tracks, stooping, holding the bundle into him as he hurried through the trees to the area of bare, packed earth where the path ended.

One more step and there'd be no turning back. One more, and he'd be in the place of wind, the place of eyes.

One step.

Night breeze, night light—white stars, a chalky piece of in-between moon, a white edge of water—a smell of weed, heaped on to the beach by a recent storm, an assault of midges which he snorted away from his mouth and nose.

The lights were on at the wharenui and he'd made his way towards it going in through the opened-out doors to where an argument about drains had come to a halt.

Into the nearest pair of held-out arms was where he'd placed the bundle—which happened to be the mean, yellow and bandaged arms of Lady Sadie.

All about him the meeting broke into questions, and he'd given out answers as ridiculous as No-one, A seagull, A bird, Screaming, Whiteblack, Flying.

People had put their arms around him as though they believed him. They'd helped him home, dried him and dressed him, as though he was two years old. Others had gone from one house to the next to the next, using phones, finding cash, preparing to go to the city and the all-night pharmacy for milk powder and nappies.

There were lights on all over, and above the talk and hurry he'd called out, 'Blind's dog's dead,' which had caused another clatter— torches, movement, voices in the other direction.

THIRTEEN

HE WONDERED if she, puffing along behind him with the torch, noticed the shells he'd scattered along the path. White shells and torchlight made it easy, or he thought it should be easy but she was gasping and the light from the torch was going all over the place. Gasping or laughing? He crossed through the creek and waited for her to step over on the stones.

'You mean,' she said, 'I came across there blind yesterday, step, step, step?'

'No,' he said. 'No step step step, you. Straight through. Water, water, like you didn't see, like you had your own path.' The thought of it stopped her, leaned her laughing against a tree.

He went on more slowly now as she stumbled along behind him in her wedding shoes and her asthma, or something.

'I mean . . . it should've . . . ha ha killed me. Never walked this far in my life.' The torch was doing nothing, nothing useful—treetops, undergrowth, everywhere but. 'Just shows . . . just shows . . . what a skinful can . . .'

They began to climb the rise. It shut her up and he could hear her scrambling. I could give you a hand if I had a leg, he thought of saying. When he came to the top he sat to wait for her.

'Don't believe this, don't believe. This'll kill me,' she said as she came up pulling herself from bush to bush, at last arriving and sitting breathless beside him with the torch stuffed down the front of her dress, lighting and shading her face, giving her the look of a big wife of Dracula.

'You got an alternative route?' she asked laughing the torchlight up and around from behind him on the track going down, 'Got a . . . got a Smoker's Path or something?'

'Supposed to be . . .' he said collapsing, strung up between his sticks and . . . buckling at the *knee*, he wouldn't have minded telling her. 'Supposed to be showing the bloody way, you.'

She fell into the trees and the light was gone.

'Haa, give you a hand if I had a leg.'

The car was coming, Jase giving the usual double toot and turning to shine headlights in on to the track. So he had to drag his bones back together, get himself out of this jelly, waiting while she smacked about on the ground trying to find the torch, but it was gone. He wiped off tears, pegged himself. 'How come wasted you never fell down?' he asked.

'All right for you with sticks,' she said. 'What about us?' She was up, crashing along behind him in the cracking-up trees.

Stepping out of trees he straightened his face to face Jase who was opening doors and looking pleased about something, or maybe his cousin was on an insulin high.

'Coming,' came from somewhere in there behind them, and a moment later there she was in the ragged light of headlights coming out of the shapeless trees calling, 'Wide load following.'

Jase plonked his foot down and wheelied them away in a dirt spray and bumped them hard over loose metal and corrugations, past the graveyard, the meeting house, the front houses, jolting ha ha ha out of them. On to street lights and tar-seal, along the road to the turn-off and on to the main road where something moved on the road-side, someone hid, and Jase said, 'Who's that?' bringing the car and ha ha ha to a stop.

Jase backed back along the verge, shining headlights into the high grasses, looking for the face they'd all seen.

Taking his sticks he got out of the car, swinging across the ditch where he called and Kid got up from her hiding place. Her clothes were torn and he could see she'd been crying. 'What you doing?' he asked but she didn't speak. 'Come on,' but she made no move, 'we take you back.'

'The kitten,' she said.

'Come, you got to come home . . .We take you . . .'

'Find the kitten.'

'Never mind the kitten.'

'Door locked.'

'What you mean? They can't do that. We take you home.'

'Can't, not allowed.'

'Bang the door down, us. Swear at them, give them heaps treating you like that.'

'Where's kitten?' Jase was out of the car standing there beside him.

'It went, run away,' she said.

'Come on, we look for your kitten tomorrow.'

'Dead,' she said, 'Run over on the road and threw it in the bushes. Chucked in the bushes there.'

'We take you home.'

'No.'

'To Aunty Wai's place.'

'No.'

'And Aunty Wai give them real arseholes locking you out like that.' He was shaking and his eyes were streaming.

'No.'

'Bring her,' Maina was saying from the car. 'Come on, little Kiri.

Home to my place first. In here by me.'

Kid made no protest when Jase picked her up and put her in the car.

'Bring her in,' Maina said when they arrived. 'She's cold, shivering, little Kiri,' and she went ahead of them towards the back of the house. He held the car door while Jase lifted Kid out and they went along the path to the front of the house where the lights had been turned on and Maina was opening the sliding door. 'On the settee,' Maina was saying.

Jase put Kid there while Maina tucked a duvet around her and put a pillow behind her. 'Little Girl, I'll change my clothes then give you a little wash, clean all those scratches and put some Savlon on. Then a cup-a-soup uh? You too Rua,' Maina said to him. 'Sit down in the chair by her.'

'It coulda been her,' he said.

'I get it,' Jase was saying. 'Soup? Put some water on. Whatever.'

'Through there,' she said. 'In the cupboard above the bench. And toast . . . but we'll have to get a loaf out of the freezer. Look in the freezer for a loaf.'

She went away and came back wearing track pants and a shirt, carrying a basin of warm water and towels, and began washing Kid's face and arms and hands, talking, wiping, patting with the towels, applying the cream.

'It coulda been her. Coulda been her run over.'

'Do you think,' Maina said, 'you should ring home?'

'Locking her out like that . . . in the dark . . . like . . . like a dog.'

'Do you think they could be out looking?'

'Let them.'

'There you are Girl,' Maina said when she'd finished. She took the wash things away and in a little while he heard her in the kitchen talking to Jase. They came in with the cups of soup and a plate of toast. Maina handed one of the cups to Kid and one to him, moving papers off a coffee table and pulling it over close to the settee. 'Well, there's more important things,' she said, 'Embarrassing really, shooting my mouth off to your whole whanau and then involving you in my domestic affairs when there are more important things.'

All that cooking, singing, dancing, laughing and crashing through trees? It seemed to have happened days ago, and thinking about it now was like looking back through a long tunnel of days to when he'd been someone else, someone he could never be again. What to do?

FOURTEEN

'I MEAN, I mean what're they doing right now?' he said after they'd told Wai. Wai, who had got out of bed after waking as the car drove in, opened the door for them then moved the cushions from the settee so that Jase could put the sleeping girl down. 'I mean what . . . Out looking? Getting up a search party?'

'God knows,' Wai said. 'Babs rang to see if she was here. Hours ago. Didn't say Girl was missing.'

'Car's still there. No lights on. Seems to me like they're in bed asleep, no worries.'

'Going to get it from me tomorrow, those two.'

He was disappointed with this response from Wai, expecting her to say she'd keep Kid there from now on. After all, there were only Wai and granddaughter Eva living in the house now that Uncle Morehu had died and all the family had gone. It was a house that had always been full of people, full of kids—her own and other people's, such as himself. 'Someone's got to . . .'

'Last time I kept her—had her two weeks—those two put the cops on me.'

'She can't go back there.'

'Got the Welfare on them once, but you see the girl's in good health, good enough clothes, everything. The Welfare talked to the school, found nothing wrong and they all end up thinking it's me being a troublemaker. What those two do, how they treat her's not bad enough, that's their way of seeing it.'

'Locking her out like that?'

'I keep her a couple of days. After that we got to keep an eye on her . . . but don't want cops, don't want the girl pushed and pulled, no courts. None of that.'

'Coulda been her run over.'

'We got to watch out, all of us. Got to do better. Should've done better myself when Babs rang, asked why she was ringing, but I let it go. Eyes on television or something. Brains gone walkabout.'

'It shouldn't be them. They shouldn't . . . Why them?' But he already knew the answer to that.

'We all let her, let Lady take her,' Wai said. 'That time you brought her into the house . . . you standing there like a wet pup, shaking, dripping all over the place, holding this baby. How long before we all understood what we're looking at? How long before we realise Baby could only be from Ani Wainoa? Then Lady held out her arms and no one could argue with that because she was Ani Wainoa's close relative, the elder relative. No one liked it, that's why we sat there quiet, that's why all that silence at first. We all knew how the lady was, how she treated her own two daughters. They were good daughters to her, Amiria and Babs, you know. Now Amiria and Babs treat this one how they were treated, hmm but not as bad.'

'On the side of the road, clothes all paru, scratches all over, crying, dark . . .?'

'Hard, hard for the girl. But also hard . . . to take away . . . to take anything away from Amiria and Babs.'

'Them? I mean . . . Asleep in their beds, no worries?'

'You two better bunk down here for the rest of the night,' Wai said. 'In your old room Rua.' She left them and returned to her own bed.

He was disappointed with that, upset with Wai who didn't seem to understand and didn't seem to care what happened to Kid, instead seemed to be siding with Amiria and Babs.

'I did it,' Jase said from the top bunk. 'Rung.'

He decided he'd talk to Arch the next day. If Wai wouldn't have Kid maybe Arch would, or there'd be someone else, because someone had to. Had to let people know what was going on.

'What?'

'Rung her. Tina.'

'If they were hitting her, if Girl was getting a hiding, getting hit, that's different,' Arch said the next day.

'Nearly nine o'clock and she's out. Locked out.'

'Mmm, nnn. My sister had a piece of them this morning. Chewed their ears.'

'Coulda been her run over.'

'Well, we all got to watch out, is all.'

Is all? Arch was hopeless.

'Have a meeting,' he said. 'The whole whanau. Get everyone together, tell them . . .'

'They won't interfere,' Arch said.

'Let everyone know what's going on.'

'You know they got their good points too, your aunties. Always been workers.'

Arch was hopeless just like Wai, sticking up for those two like they did no wrong.

'Touchy,' Arch said. 'And . . . and, we all got to live here you know.' That was Arch backing out, dropping the subject . . . then trying to make up for dropping it. 'And aah, have a chat with them. My sister got her way, I got mine. Maybe . . . Anyway, we go and find that poor cat? Give it a decent burial.'

Hopeless.

Later, he pitched his tent in the trees at the cove, fixed up his fireplace and collected wood, needing to get himself into water. Today the surface was saw-edged, saw-coloured where the sun reached, bruised-looking under the overhangs of ledges and trees.

On the sun side, shags, like part of rock on which they perched, had their wings out drying. Further out the gulls and terns were diving and the water was churning with kahawai, which he knew would soon make their way in to where he could get a line to them.

He entered the water with his dog, swimming towards the rocks to collect bait. The kawau turned their necks, shifted their heads, ready for flight if he or the dog came too near, but there was no need to disturb them. After collecting a few paua and kuku he returned to shore where he took his backpack of gear and began making his way around the base of the hillside and cliff faces, climbing to a place from where he could drop his line and float it out.

Wet pup?

And too silly at the time to know what the trees already knew. Kutu was a pup then too, he remembered, whimpering all the way home along the tracks in the dark.

Up on the bank looking down on the water he removed the sinker from his line, baited up and tied a plastic carrybag to the trace. He dropped it over, setting it to float, the light breeze ballooning the bag and taking the line out. He fastened the end to a branch and waited. The birds were moving closer, hanging, spying down on the shoals of small fish, diving, then coming up out of the water gulping. Kahawai driving through water were eyeing the fish from their own angle, leaping and snatching and making the water boil. Eventually they would come his way.

Ten years ago he'd brought her home. Wet pup days. Then one day, about five years later, while out in the water he'd allowed the truth to come to him—rejecting it at first, and then having to accept—allowing understanding to edge its way in, the secret for life that had to be left with the trees.

Now he couldn't be that wet pup any more. There were matters he needed to think about since it seemed no one else was going to.

When he left Arch's place he'd called in to Pop Henry's to see if he had any advice, but the old man wasn't with it, wasn't taking in what he was telling him.

'Past it,' Reggae had said. 'Gone up top, but not all the time.' It was a shock. He'd never noticed the old man loopy before.

After that he'd decided to talk to the younger ones, his cousins who had children of their own and who were all upset when he explained what had happened.

'We hear the way they talk to her,' Moana had said.

'Hear the names they call her.'

'Makimaki, nikanika, rat, cat, witch.'

'True.'

'But don't talk like that in front of Aunty Wai and them.'

'Stuck down at that Post Office everyday after school cleaning up.'

'Standing on a box morning and night doing all their dishes . . .'

'While those two shower and powder themselves . . . '

'Watch television, burn their oils, massage their faces.'

'I'd have her.' Moana had said. 'I could ask. No harm asking.' But he knew that there was really nothing the younger ones could do.

The birds and the fish had come in close and it wasn't long before the floating hook was taken. The fish broke water as it went for the bait, and as he took hold of the line he felt it plunging and rising, tearing away, leaping and turning, while he held hard, steadying himself against the bank and dragging the line in.

So who was he now that he couldn't be that wet pup any more, and what could he do? Could he now be who he'd taken five years to realise that he was?

The fish, as he brought it in, flipped up silver and green, and smacked down onto the water again. He pulled it slapping over the rocks, up the side of the bank where he sat, and removing it from the hook, heaved it into the sack.

The full dog? What the trees knew? The secret for life?

Rebaiting the hook he floated the line out again.

Or who?

And what to do?

Sometimes he thought of going away, leaving this place where it seemed he'd always be a child. Home from hospital he'd thought of it, wanting to save himself from all the over-the-top care that people thought he needed, not only Aunty Wai and Uncle Morehu, Uncle Arch and Pop Henry, Nan Tini and their families, but the whole whanau including Babs and Amiria with their puddings and cakes. People cooking for him, walking for him, deciding for him, almost seeing and hearing for him, telling him things he already knew.

Even a wet pup didn't need that.

But he hadn't gone because this had always been the place for him. He'd moved to the old house instead which had given him his physical life, he thought, let him do things for himself.

Or was that all humbug really? Kidding himself, because instead of being some kind of outer island, he'd found himself still attached.

What to do?

Hold hard, if you want to bring home fish. Now, more than ever he knew he would never go.

And now he knew he would have to give up the old place, return to the front into one of the empty houses so he could keep watch. Lose his space? But what was that anyway? Sorting out to do.

There were six good ones in the bag by the time the fish moved away and he climbed down into the water to swim his catch ashore. Salt stung his hands which had been cut by the line, and once back in water the fish went wild in the bag.

The tide was down and he knew that if he hurried with the cleaning of the fish he'd be able to go out through the blowhole to deliver them, then return before the tide came up again.

Home with fish, not with answers.

Tomorrow he'd go out to the cray holes to look for octopus for bait, and later in the week he'd go with Arch to deep water to fish for hapuku for the Friday night fundraising dinner.

Life as usual but nothing was the same.

FIFTEEN

THAT VOICE of hers . . . *world stop turning . . . sun stop burning*, as he went along the side of the house and round to the back door followed by Jase carrying the pillow and duvet . . . *only dream that matters has come true*, steel string uke going for it, *In dis life, I was lo-ved by you.*

'Come in, come in,' Maina said, out of breath as though she'd been walking tracks, crossing creeks, climbing, dancing.

'Just dropping these.'

'No, no, come in.'

'And we got to go, pick up a karaoke . . .' but she was holding the door wide, waving them in. 'I was just thinking of you, all you out there. I've been ringing. There's something, something you all got to know.'

She took them through to the lounge, moving folders from the settee so they could sit. 'I wanted to come, talk to Wai, Archie, or someone, but I'm stuck here without a car. I've been phoning, but anyway here you are. Get you something, a can?'

'OK, thanks.'

'Not me,' Jase said. 'Banned substance.'

'Ah, Mormon or diabetic?'

'Not Mormon.'

'Come in handy these diabetics,' Rua said. 'Driving us drinkers all over the place. Even if they do go to sleep, end us up in sand.'

'Coffee then.'

She returned from the kitchen with the beer and coffee, biscuits in a plastic container and turned the CD off. 'This stuff on the answerphone got me thinking,' she said. 'Then home by myself all week I started snooping round and a few cogs started clicking. Have a listen.' She played the phone tape back then set it on forward.

He listened to a man's voice giving name and details, then to a message about a late deposit that was in the post. This was followed by similar messages from people wanting to book sites. Didn't know what it was all about, but thought he and Jase should be on their way. They had to get round to Eddie's to pick up the sounds then get home to set it up before eight. Also he knew Jase was wanting to get back because Bones and Remelda were bringing Tina with them to the dinner. Jase all jumpy. The tape came to an end.

'Then all this,' she said. She was showing them long envelopes, some with foreign stamps. 'Cheques I reckon.' He didn't know why she was telling them all this or what it had to do with them and didn't want to ask. 'So I had a hunt around,' she said. 'Not that he hides anything. I mean, I mean I didn't have to look far. Letters, ads, photos—for the Internet I suppose. He knows I won't help him any more, so he does a lot of it himself, well . . . in the meantime. There's always someone who'll come to the rescue and do stuff for him. What he's done here is set himself up as an agent for the new millennium—an agency providing campsites for all these tourists who want to be first in the world to put their eyeballs on the sun on the first of January 2000. But he's got no land you know, not even under his big toenails.'

Man of perfect feet.

'So where's this land, these sites he's getting in deposits for, for all these campers? I opened a few more folders. Found these.'

She was showing them photos of the sun rising, waves rolling in on beaches, patterned sand, trees, flax in bloom, gulls in coloured skies. 'Here's your place,' she said, and she was right about that. There was their beach at dawn with the waves riding in catching coloured light. There was their meeting house, the big paddocks beside it, hills and trees behind. 'Yours, and others all up and down the coast. Already advertised. Money coming in already. Here look, a grid showing tent and caravan sites, list of highlights.'

Well it was true there was something going on, more than he could take in at the moment, and more than he had time for.

'I know him, know what he'll do,' she said. 'He'll do the rounds, persuading marae groups to lease land to his agency, just for the millennium spree. But won't tell what he'll really be charging for a site. People round these parts aren't used to city prices, tourist prices, don't realise the money value of a Year 2000 sunrise. He'll lie to you, rip you all off.'

It was all a bit too much especially when he hadn't been listening properly, and although he didn't know what this was all about he didn't think his aunties and uncles would be fooled.

'I think ah, Wai, Archie and them are . . .' On to him, he wanted to say.

'They won't know what he's raking off,' she said.

'I think they . . . don't think they'll go for it.'

'And he could . . . he could go ahead anyway without you all knowing. Get deposits and abscond. Won't be the first time, and . . . all these mad-as-hell millennium campers'll come waving their receipts under your noses threatening court. He'll be gone. You got to warn them.'

She was really spilling it on her old man. All this to get back at him? But he didn't think so. She was watching them from under a deep frown, really wanting them to understand that this was something serious.

'Better if you tell them,' he said. 'I mean . . . you know what it's all about.'

'It's got to be soon. I've been ringing ever since I got home from work but couldn't get hold of Wai or Arch, or Cass, or anyone.'

'All down the marquee working.'

'Ah, well . . . See, what I was thinking . . . I want to get this stuff to them, get it out of the house and into their hands before he gets home later tonight. Haven't seen him since the wedding, or heard from him. Don't even feel like speaking to him, even seeing him really. Not since I found all this, and don't know about the rest of it, all the other places up and down the coast, but at least this . . . at least you . . .'

'We could take it, give it to Wai.'

'Good.' The frown ironed itself, her face creased, lips parted on the rocks of teeth with smoke easing through.

'Or you could come with us now if you want to talk to them,' he said. 'You could bring the stuff, come to the dinner.'

'Dinner?'

'Fundraiser. Eight o'clock. We got to get the music set up.'

'I had a real good time . . . But I was haurangi then, or something.'

'Well, you could be again.'

'Ha, you.'

'Or maybe not. Bit of a dry do. A bottle of wine on a table might be it.'

'Anyway I suppose they'll be too busy for all this.'

'Stay over if you want, and see the aunties and uncles tomorrow. Still camping out, me. Don't need my house.'

'I couldn't stay but I could come to the dinner. I could bring the stuff, tell them a bit about it and leave it for them to look at.'

But when she came from the bedroom dressed for the dinner he noticed she had a bag with her. 'Well why not?' she said. 'Just in case there's no one to run me home, and there might be a chance to talk tomorrow. Just get what I need out of the folders, and a bit of bread and stuff. Don't forget smokes, don't forget walking shoes, don't forget torch. Did you find your torch?'

'On the blink it is . . . And, all right if we take a few of these?' he asked, holding up a handful of tapes.

'Help yourself,' she said. 'I haven't . . . I wanted to ask about little Kiri.'

SIXTEEN

A QUARTER of a century on from when Ngarua crossed the inlet, followed by supporters and everyone's dogs, there were three sisters who were her direct descendants. They were named Ruahine, Tunia and Harinia, who came to be known in their later lives as Nanny Ru, Nanny Blind and Lady Sadie.

There were three brothers too, who despite their patience, their importance to the family and the fact that the youngest lived long enough to have children, don't need to be named.

It was the father of these three daughters and three sons who first built the falling-down house in the trees that Rua was now giving up for the Friday night so that Maina could arrange a meeting that would put her husband's pot on, and, she hoped, teach the no-good crook a lesson.

The father of the three daughters was a sullen man, who in spite of having a great deal of land, far more than anyone else in his family, decided to build his house apart from the homes of his relatives in order to keep his wife away from the front places and therefore from the society of his brothers, sisters and cousins, who in his opinion were far too fun-loving. Even when first built it was a mean house made of corrugated iron, odd pieces of timber and manuka brush. The falling-down house of today was far more substantial.

He was the eldest in his family and all the responsibility of this had made him brutish. Being a seasonal worker he was often away from home, and though he was a hard-working man he never brought money home, spending it instead on drinking and betting and cards.

His wife, in his absence, had gardens to tend, a house to patch up, water to carry, wood to chop, babies to give birth to and to look after. What the man didn't know was that she also had a life of her own, and that in spite of him she enjoyed herself.

While he was away she would bring her children out of the bush to the front houses and spend mornings, afternoons, whole days, whole nights, sometimes days and nights on end, with her husband's sisters and cousins. In the mornings, after their chores were done, she would gather along with them in one house or another to listen through the crackles and whistles to the wireless serials.

In the afternoons they'd garden or go through to the cove for shellfish and when the weather was bad they'd stay indoors with ukes and mandolins and sing. At night they'd go floundering with lamps and toasting forks or table forks tied to sticks or wire forks that they made with number-eight borrowed from fences. On other nights they'd go eeling or fishing for sharks.

They sometimes went to town on the back of an uncle's truck, she wearing a dress, hat and shoes that her husband didn't know she had. On occasions she got drunk along with everyone else, if someone had money.

Everything would be fine when the man came home. He would find the gardens had been cared for, the wood cut and stacked and the children well behaved.

His wife would be looking dull and beaten enough for his satisfaction.

The man had never been present during the births of any of the children, except that when the sixth child, daughter Harinia, was born he happened to be at home. That was when the man seemed to go soft in the head, or heart, or maybe stomach or spleen or liver or bowel. Somewhere changed.

As she was born little Harinia's eyes locked into his, or that's how it seemed to him, and his liver or spleen melted. Harinia was no more beautiful or astonishing than any of his other children, but the father could only go by what his heart, stomach, liver, bowel told him, which was that she was the most wonderful child ever born.

She was quite wizened really, like an old apple. Frightening, but not to him. He was in love for the first and only time in his life.

His wife only lasted six months after the birth. It didn't matter because he had his two older daughters to be mothers and servants to this wonderful baby—to wash and dress her and cook up special dishes. He had sisters to make her clothes and buy her shoes and had sons and nephews to carry her wherever she wanted to go. He filled the girl with sugar, bringing home blackballs, boiled lollies and jubes that she didn't have to share.

From a wizened apple, Harinia grew to a smooth round apple with a dark complexion for which the father blamed his late wife. He bought Harinia large sunhats to wear and made sure she kept in the shade. She became beautiful in a softened, pale sort of way. Eventually there was no sign of the apple, old or new, and Harinia became the colour and consistency of a mock-egg sponge. She was cushiony, droopy and her teeth were never any good.

The father died when Harinia was eleven, but Ruahine and Tunia and the brothers were in the habit now of doing everything for their young sister. A lot of responsibility fell on Ruahine because Tunia's sight was quickly fading and later the brothers escaped to war in Africa where two of them were blown to pieces. The rafters have it that the man died of his own home brew after someone had got into it while he was away, making up for what they'd used by tipping a bucket of creek water into it.

Tunia, the sister going blind, never married or had children, nor did the two older brothers who never returned from the war. The youngest brother, before he left for the war, had two children, Arch and Wai.

Ruahine, the oldest, with all her responsibilities, married late in life, leaving time for the birth of just one daughter, Ramari. Later she took her granddaughter, Ani Wainoa, from Ramari to bring up as her own.

Harinia married and gave birth to Amiria and Babs.

Genealogy is never easy to keep in the head and it can be tedious. It can choke you too unless taken piece by piece at the right moment, perhaps in snippets pulled down from the rafters year by year, along with an accompaniment of gossip and a chance of embellishment. But taken a little at a time, if you get to live long enough you get the hang of it.

Tunia, or Blind, was brought down from her house in the trees the night that her dog died. An hour or two earlier Ani Wainoa had left and Te Rua had come into the wharenui with the baby, putting it into the nearest pair of held-out arms.

Blind couldn't give slight to her family by not accepting their care now that her dog and grandchild had gone so she allowed herself to be taken to live with Arch in his new, warm house where she was able to have a room of her own.

Arch's previous house, along with two others nearby, had been broken up by wind and taken away by water and mud during a cyclone a year earlier. Also demolished at that time, as already mentioned, was the wharekai, which was a wooden structure with roof and walls of corrugated iron. It had been fitted with rough-sawn timber benches, had its own water tank, and a supply of electricity rigged up via extension cords that was adequate for lights and a refrigerator. Across one end of the room was the long open fireplace with its wide corrugated iron chimney and its lengths of railway line mounted on concrete blocks, under which the cooking fires were built, and up on which the big pots and water tins sat. In one corner was an old-style copper that could be stoked up to heat water for washing up.

In the main body of the room enough trestle tables and long forms could be set up to seat a hundred people. From time to time, where occasion and weather made it necessary, marquee extensions could be made, leading out from the double garage doors.

At the time of its demolition by Bola in 1988, people were not too unhappy to see the old place go, and in fact were too absorbed by more urgent matters to give it much consideration.

Eventually, the street preachers and singers that came into the township once a fortnight to the vacant section between the butchers and the Lotto shop were able to take advantage of the phenomenon of Cyclone Bola to show people their own unworthiness. It was the state of their unclean, unsaved souls and because they lived the life of Hatana that made them all deserving of such a disaster. The reason that the everloving God was handing out this punishment was all to do with sins of the flesh. People had brought it all on themselves.

In Ngarua's time, water coming off the hills had combed down through thick forest, among rootworks and undergrowth that bound the soil, then down into the equally as densely forested valleys and riversides. It delivered into the waterways only what was light and loose in the way of soil, seed, leaves and old wood.

In her time, whether fishing, swimming, playing or making a crossing, except in extremely deep places, people were able to see the river bottom through clear water. Everything that was there, was known to their eyes. It was a place where they could see their own faces, where on looking up from sandy or stony contours or from fish swarms they would be able to find these reflected, up-flipped, in each other's eyes.

But Ngarua lived to see the clear felling and burn–offs that bared the hills and revealed their fragility. She saw hills turn brown in dry summers, where grass had been shorn down by the two front teeth of too many sheep until there was only dirt left. She lived to see the browning of the waters, the heaping of logs, the blocking of waterways and the shifting passages of creeks and rivers.

She lived to see lands and livelihoods dwindle and even Ngarua, pioneer as she was, was unable to prevent it from happening, could only do what they all had to do, struggle to survive.

Each winter floodwaters broke over the land and the new coursing of water made it necessary for them to move their houses and gardens and threatened the meeting house they had built. They began to prepare a site on higher ground away from the edge of the inlet for the wharenui, and then to dismantle this first house in order to rebuild it. This was still the old house. The present one was built on the same site years later.

Ngarua lived to see the first ferry, which was attached to each shore of the inlet by ropes. She lived to see the building of the first bridge and then to see it taken away after a few years by dark and now unpredictable waters.

In all the time throughout this clearing of trees, the erosion of land and the changing of water routes, the resulting mud was being taken down through the inlet and belched into the ocean.

It seems unlikely, having witnessed all of this, that Ngarua would've blamed the hand of God if she'd been around at the time of Bola.

What had gone on up until then was the softener, setting up conditions over the years, priming the land for the big event. Bola was the Big One when the hills came sliding into the valleys and became the rivers. Not water bearing loads of soil as in previous storms, but hills, farms, pastureland, that had become infused with enough water to push them down and along the river pathways, taking with them everything that had already been weakened and loosened by wind—that is, trees, roads, sheds, houses, power and telephone lines, gardens, vehicles and machinery.

Throughout the district, crops, vineyards and orchards were flattened and water went through paddocks taking animals out over the top of fences and floating them away.

As the water rose round Arch's house and neighbouring places, the people came to see what they could do. They pulled the baseboards off the houses in the hope that the water would flow under them. This worked for a while but the water and mud kept coming, eventually breaking up the houses and taking them off. Those houses that remained had metres of silt dumped into them.

Arch and others had to take their clothes, an army of shoes, photographs, a few chooks and their dogs and go to live in the least affected places, including the wharenui. They were without electricity and had to empty out their freezers and use what they could of defrosting food. The only clean water they had was what rain they caught in buckets and drums. Once their road became impassable, and because the sea was tossing up ten-metre swells making it impossible to go anywhere by boat, they became isolated.

What a laugh.

All they could do was entertain themselves watching the devastation, marvelling at the might of Tawhiri Matea.

The clean-up lasted for many months, though it had never really been completed as far as the waterways, gardens and pasturelands were concerned. The sandy banks of the inlet, as well as the beds of the creeks and estuaries, were now mud, and every time there was heavy rain, wood and debris had to be cleared to get the waters flowing again. In many places where silt had covered the land, though plants began to grow again, the ground underneath was as soft as porridge and those places had to be abandoned. Arch had to leave his old house site and rebuild further back on his land. He had to make new gardens and set up new places for his chickens and pigs.

The few places on Dogside that had not come to any harm were the wharenui which stood back against a treed hillside, the cove, where there had never been any removal of trees, and the property of Amiria and Babs. Theirs was the very best of land, handed down by the melted father to the daughter Harinia who became known as Lady Sadie.

People had already spoken of the need to rebuild the wharekai and had planned on having something that was much better than what they'd had previously. It was when Blind died four years after the cyclone that they had first felt the lack of the old building, when cooking had to be done under tarpaulins in the wet and boards needed to be put down over mud in the marquee where the tables had been set up. The new kitchen and dining room was to be large, modern and all-electric.

Arch was still in employment when Blind came to live with him, and was into the twentieth year of his widowerhood. He hadn't yet met Cass and had been living alone since his children left home. Each morning as he left for work he'd deliver Blind to her cousin Henry's for the day. Blind's sister Ruahine had died eleven years earlier, as had her remaining brother. Her sister, Harinia, Lady Sadie, was still alive but Blind didn't like her. It was her own choice to go to her cousin's place rather than to her stinking sister's, but she grew tired of being delivered and of having everything done for her. It was a useless life, really.

One morning while her cousin was in his kitchen coughing, leaning on a chair, she took up her stick and headed for the bush at quite a good pace considering there was only the memory of a dog padding along beside her.

The only ones about were little kids playing on a pink trike and a red horse. Older children were away at school. Aunties, uncles and fathers were away at work, or asleep, while others were inside looking in cupboards and fridges to see what was left.

'Nanny Bline, Nanny Bline,' the little kids called as she went by on her balloon legs floating off to her own place.

By the time Henry was through coughing she was well on her way. He busied himself cleaning his fireplace and only after he'd completed that did he begin to wonder where she was. He went from house to house looking for her but it was only the riders who could tell him she gone, Bline-eyes, Nanny Bline-eyes, gone.

So she was brought back to Arch's but soon afterwards made the decision to go off after her dog. What else was there to do?

Blind died with her eyes open, whereas in life she'd mainly kept them closed. It's all recorded in the rafters.

SEVENTEEN

KID.

By the way Kutu lifted his head and put his ears up, and by the smile on his dopey face, he knew it would be her coming. The dog stepped towards the blowhole swinging his banana tail.

She wasn't alone, there were voices and other dog sounds now, amplified in the cavern. Kutu was beginning to yelp and turn himself.

He'd been looking forward to them coming with the midday tide, had been expecting them once the water went down because it was just the kind of extra-low, full moon time that made you hungry and that you couldn't ignore. The further the water pulled back the more it drew you towards it. And it was the right sort of day, nipped by coming winter, clear and breathless, so still that he could hear the snapping beaks of piwaiwaka vaulting among the puffs of insects rising out of the manuka behind him and the wingbeats of birds and their sharpened calls as they crossed overhead in bunches. You had to get out in it, break it up, colour it, crack open its paths and surfaces.

Kid came through with her two same-age cousins, she and

Hinewai carrying bags and Georgie carrying Dirtyrat. They'd been running and their faces were the colour of dark plums. Behind them were Eva and her mate from Polytech, then the rest of the cuzzies with kids and all the dogs—all their food and water and pots and bags and clothes. None of the aunties and uncles were with them, he noticed.

It was company, company that he often longed for but wanted to be able to do without, as though all these trees, all this water, all this physical life could fill him while he looked for his grown self. But there were only so many hours you could spend in or around water getting people their fish, only so much time listening in the trees because he wasn't a bird or a fish after all. There were always the fire times.

But huh. Just think how much more of a physical life being one-legged gave him. Great. Two-legged and he'd have all this wood collecting, fire making, food finding, cray diving done in half the time. All that more time on his hands, ahhh. Then, if he had no legs at all, ha ha. Hard out, day and night with all this physical life.

More coming through. Bones with Remelda's baby in a back-pack and handfuls of bags. Remelda following with more stuff. No aunties, no uncles.

'All having a hui with that Maina,' Bones said when he asked. 'Some sort of hush-hush korero. Yack yack, so we took off, left them to it.' He swung the baby-pack down looking pleased or embarrassed or something.

'And Those Two?' he asked

'Ahh, *Those Two*?' Eva said. 'At the meeting too, them. So Nan Wai said go and get Kid, bring her over, said it in front of The Aunties and they didn't say a thing. Sent Georgie to get her.'

Bones lifted the baby out of the pack and handed him to Remelda. 'Her and Georgie Boy and Hinewai took off—run all the way here,' he said. 'Dirtyrat after them, but legs too short ay? Had to carry him.'

His cousin was talking a lot, pleased or embarrassed or something, about Remelda and some other man's baby, some jailhead's baby, his asthma singing after the walk and the climb. Remelda had her tit out and the big blackberry knob plugged into the piggy baby.

Dogs were moving in and out of the trees, some sniffing and yapping along the cove paths, breath sawing against the dark rock and banks, others twisting and turning themselves round kids who were scrambling here and there picking up wood to pile above the high water mark. He strapped on his knife belt, tucked a Pak'n Save bag down behind it and waited until there was a fire going before getting down to the water.

Eva was already out in it even though she was two-legged enough and the tide low enough for her to get paua from rocks round the shore. But, like him, she wanted to be in water. She was calling her mate to come in but it was too cold for Makere who was standing up to her ankles. 'No way, cold as, bloody freezing.'

He jabbed his sticks into the sand and lay down in the shallows, pulling himself along until he reached deep enough water where he ducked under out of the nicked air, under and up, under and up, breaking it. Eva was doing the same ahead of him, cracking and colouring all the surfaces.

Back on shore the kids were peeling off and running in too, even though parents didn't want them to and were echoing at them, *You'll you'll freezefreeze, and get sick and, you'll and you'll bark freeze barkbark all all night like bloody, like dogs.* But the kids weren't listening.

In the channel he went down and sped along under water to the weed and the low edges of rock for a fast pick of paua to put in the fire. He wedged the knife, cranking the fish from the rocks, and after a while was joined by Kid, Hinewai and Georgie who looked after the bag for him. Eva worked round the higher edges of the rock ducking down every so often to keep the water round her.

After the fundraising dinner he had taken Maina back to the

house, remembering to go along at a slower pace this time. He'd lit the lamp for her and set the fire for morning. When he left he'd wanted to take his transistor with him, but thought he should leave it for her. It's what he'd missed this morning, a bit of music to light his fire by. He began making his way back feeling hungry and realising he hadn't eaten since early morning.

The cousins had put their jackets, towels and bags of clothes into the forks of trees away from wet kids and dogs and had water on the boil on his camp fire. They'd taken one of his tarps and put their food and cups out on it. Remelda's baby was asleep in the mingimingi wrapped in a rug, and now Jase had come through with Tina who was looking uncomfortable, a bit pissed off—not sure of this dorky Jase, not sure of the clothes she was wearing, not sure of dogs. Her two children clung to her. Jase was proud, or something, as he came down to the water to get the bag, taking the paua from it to put in the fire.

'You, Rua,' Kid said, sitting down next to him in the dark at slow song time, Eva on guitar.

'You, Kid,' he said.

'You got to.'

'You don't say "got to" to your aunties.'

'Got to. You know.'

'Know what? What do I know?'

'You know I cracked out of an egg.'

'Porangi. Who said?' But he knew who said.

'Or a seagull shitted me.'

'Don't listen to your aunties, they're porangi.'

'But you know, you know.'

'And you been told.'

'Cracked out of an egg. Shitted from a seagull.'

'You know your mother called Ani Wainoa lived with an old woman, a nanny who was blind. You know your mother gave you to me to bring home to mothers and fathers.'

'Or, I cracked out of an egg. Or, a seagull shitted me.'

'Porangi telling you that.'

'So how?'

'Ani Wainoa . . . '

'So how I got there? In that Ani Wainoa?'

He put his arms round her and pulled her against him, his eyes watering on to her head, ask the trees, ask the trees. Her cousins were playing on the grassy slope in the dark, while his own cousins, with friends, by the light of the last bit of fire were beginning to collect their things to go home, or with loves were off tangling in the trees.

Soon they were gone, torchlight ebbing, the blowhole empty, nothing answered. The one-eyed fire was all that was left, and, nailed up there, the far, unloving stars.

Music was what he wanted and a smoke was what he needed. It was late, but now that Maina had gone he'd go back to his house for his tapes and sounds and a bit of weed from his stash, and he'd sleep back there until it was time to fish the high tide in the morning. The weather was going to break in a day or two and he wanted to get whatever fish he could before he packed up camp.

And he had to decide what he was going to do. It was up to him now, no one else.

He called Kutu, sent him ahead on the track and followed the dog's white backside with the flickering light of his torch. It was cold and he and the dog were moving too slowly through the trees in the dark to get the juices going, but once at the house he'd light the fire and put some music on. Porangi as, Those Two, telling her stuff like that.

But there was singing coming through the trees, Maina and Englebert—whose father was Maori and that's why he could sing, everyone reckoned, ahh. Full blast. He called out so she'd know he was coming.

And . . . all his candles. Candles all over the bloody place. Burn his house down, her.

'I just ah . . .'

Well what? He couldn't walk in now, just take the tapes and the player and go. 'Well didn't ah . . .'

'And neither did I,' she said. 'Sorry about that.'

'Nah, it's okay.' She'd washed the dress she wore to the dinner and it was there hanging near the fire, rigged up somehow—on wire from his hinaki by the look, dancing there, like a thin one of her.

'Cass was going to take me back,' she said. 'But she's going in early Monday. She can give me a lift right in to work Monday. I didn't . . .'

'Nah, I'm going back down. Just . . . wanted stuff, bit of weed.' The fire was going for it, eating up his wood but he was getting warm.

'I could've stayed there with her and Arch,' she said. 'But I wanted to come back here, just be on my own for a day and Cass didn't mind. I got stuff, baggage to sort, my whole life to sort, even if the walk nearly killed me. I got to be away, away from him, away from all that shit, just while I sort myself. But I should've . . . '

'Nah, sweet as. I'm not stopping.'

'Cass said you wouldn't mind, so I thought . . . God I never walked so much. There and back in one day? I got the fire going and . . . and found the bath, did what you said. It was . . . it was . . . Then come in here and couldn't stop lighting candles, sorry about that. I been sitting here reading books from schools and shops and libraries.'

'That Ani Wainoa stole.' He'd got rid of most of them. Bugs had had a go at some, mice too.

'Ah, Ani Wainoa, the little one's mum.'

So she'd found that out.

'And, been playing tapes, some of yours some of mine, using up all your batteries.'

'I got spares.'

'That's what you come for I suppose, your tapes, your sounds?'

'Nah, its OK.'

She was wearing a Hawaiian tee shirt and a seashell sarong, stretched, and her hair was wet and springy. She started talking about the meeting, saying what the aunties and uncles were going to do, that is, tell her old man where to get off then take up the idea themselves—tent sites, caravans, camper vans. Far out. The fire was going for it, he was warming up and Englebert was winding down.

'This one,' she said, ejecting Englebert and slotting a new tape in. 'I saw you listening to it the other day when you called. Iz.'

Awesome and high up. Flat out, wired up high on the neck of the uke and real, real, coconut style. 'You been to Hawaii?' he asked, to keep himself there a bit longer by the fire and because he wasn't really interested in what happened at the meeting.

'No. There was a group that came to Tauranga when we lived there, came over from Oahu for a festival then travelled up. We swapped tapes, swapped shirts, swapped songs. But mm, I want to go there one day.' She began singing along deep underneath Iz with her good voice.

He leaned and picked up the poker, let the stove flap down and stoked, putting in more wood, keeping himself there. Easy once you listened to the words, all those aas and uus, so he joined in, couldn't help it, high up there with Iz while she burrowed along beneath both of them.

Him'n Iz up there, her down there, ha, her hands gone all hula because she couldn't help it, her face crumpling up, and her big teeth, big voice, awesome, and saying to him, 'Ha, ha. Dance then.'

It was the fire.

And she was just like his aunties and cousins, who he knew would've left him alone if he was two-legged, come come come. But he always got up when they said, couldn't help it. So he did what she said, got up on his sticks, it was the fire.

It was the fire that had him swinging in the bit of space between the bed and the fireplace by that skinny sister dress of hers, a bit of hip, he couldn't help laughing.

She was up too, knocking over two candles, set his place on fire her, bending and picking them up, one out, one not, dancing in the left-over bit of space and relighting the gone-out candle from the other.

Dancing with candles, ha, ha, no room to move and trouble with his stick, couldn't help it. So close she couldn't help but know, looking at his face then blowing out the two candles, taking his sticks away and holding him.

Hardly dancing like that, hardly moving at all.

Trouble, or no trouble?

Grown and no trouble.

Grown and going down no trouble on his busted bed. Finding her and holding—locked, folded, shaped and his eyes leaking. Climbing a long time, unlocked and easy and just sweet as.

In the morning he sat on the edge of the bed, pulled on the shorts and tee and couldn't think at first what he wanted to say. He pulled himself up and went to the stove, rattled the poker in among the embers and put in a handful of kindling before moving to the doorway, propping himself there looking back at her sitting up smoking.

There was light coming in. Kutu was out there pushing through the long grass.

'I suppose,' she said, 'suppose . . .' Half a finger of ash balanced there on the tip of the tailor-made. 'I shouldn't . . . I shouldn't . . .' Burn his house down, she could. Frowning down on the tailor-made. 'Shouldn't be . . .' Frown ironing itself out. 'Using up all your batteries.'

'Ha, I got spares.'

Rocks of teeth, ash dropping on the pillow, bashing at the ash with her hand flappy as a fish and awesome.

The nip had gone from the air, there was a bit of wind from the north-west stirring, warm and gusty because there was a storm coming up, but not today. Soon the tide would be full and the fish biting. Later, at low tide, Bones and Jase would come through to collect the fish from him to take home and give out, but before they came there was a whole morning.

'Come down the cove with me,' he said.

EIGHTEEN

IT HAD taken a couple of trips back through the trees to get all the gear home and then he'd had to get his shelter down and pack up quick. After that it was a race to get his wood in before the rain came.

From the ledge he'd seen the storm coming from out over the sea, at first nothing but a blurred, humping horizon with whipped up water climbing to meet the bags of rain. He'd packed up his bedding first, got most of it home in the backpack, then gone back to take the covers from the frame he'd made in against the trees. Out there it was coming, the sea beginning to roll in, climbing the rocks and banks. Bags of rain, tarps and sacks of wind he thought of telling her.

Thought of telling her that after seeing her to the end of the track in the early morning he'd managed to get home dry, get his wood in, put his bucket out under the broken spouting to catch water, and that he'd packed his tent and gear back where he usually kept it, propping up the broken side of the bed.

After he got the fire going he'd put the tapes on and followed along with the guitar in the company of cockroaches that had crept in out of the weather, sitting round the walls like medals. The lightning was fish-flash putting him in spotlight and there was thunder set up on the synthesiser breaking breaking breaking, ha, alone at his own disco with a stack of wood drying in the space between the bed and the fireplace.

'Don't think of me,' she'd said walking behind him on the track in the early morning in dinner clothes that had been washed, then dried, looking like a dancing sister, on wire of his. Old shoes for walking the track, dinner ones in her bag for when she got to work, even though, as she'd said, they weren't suitable for a day walking the floors of DEKA.

Don't think of me.

It was Kid he ought to be thinking about.

The next morning, when he saw how much the creek had filled, he'd gone to the place where he had only partly cleared his dam following the dry summer, getting into the water and pulling away mud, stones and debris to free the flow. It had been an easy creek to live with before the days of Bola, clear and easy in its passage all the way to the estuary. Now it was full of silt, its course had been altered and there was still debris being carried down from the hills eleven years later, catching in its curves and piling against the banks, damming the flow.

After he cleared the dam he had pulled his way upstream through the muddy water clearing the narrow necks and tossing out broken branches from the wide pools that had formed, knowing if he didn't get the stuff cleared there'd be flooding out at the front houses, the gardens would be ruined again and there'd be mud everywhere. The rain was still falling, and though sheltered from the wind he'd been able to hear it, see the heads of the trees on the hillside rolling and tossing like waves. Down at the cove the breakers were coming in like trains.

He could go to DEKA, find her he thought, with her face made up for work a little bit less than for a wedding or dinner. He'd watched her do that, working a squirt of cream one-handed with her sharpened fingers, the other hand holding a mirror the size of a playing card.

Could have a conversation with her as if he were a customer. Do you have one-legged pyjamas and track pants, haa, half a pair of socks or shoes, a couple of left-foot gumboots?

He'd slid himself out onto the wet banks dragging the wood into the cover of the trees from where he would recover it later, working as quickly as he could to try to keep the cold away, and he'd thought of Archie, with his smoked lungs and pickled liver who he knew would be out shovelling, clearing shingle from the mouth of the run-off. But who was there at home to help Arch now—a few old ones, a few young ones with babies. They wouldn't be able to get any Council workers in to help because they'd be away clearing slips off the main highway.

Ace of diamonds.

There was a pack of cards up on the shelf with Ani Wainoa's books, one joker having to be the missing two of spades, the other the missing ten of hearts. In a storm you could lay them out and play euchre or five hundred, or matchstick poker with the stakes increasing.

Over the top of it all with a piece of sponge, then a bullet of lipstick drawing lightly over the blackish colour of her lips.

Don't think of me.

There was his own backside to think of. He'd kept working until he couldn't ignore the cold any longer then had gone back to the house and stoked the fire, taking his clothes off to stand out under the spouting and wash the mud away. He decided he would cook up a couple of fish heads with a load of onions and pepper and think about that. In a day or two the storm would blow itself out and once the sea had begun to flatten he'd be able to get into water and swim hard through all of this, hard and far, concentrating on not drowning, not being pulled under or taken away, not breaking his head or his ears—swimming, swimming, knowing how far his breath would take him, how long before he might freeze. No space for anything else. He'd come out and shake himself dry, and maybe after that he would be free to think of what it was he had to do.

'Don't think of me,' she'd said from back on the track, behind him in the dinner clothes and old shoes. 'I shouldn't't've . . .' with her face made up for work, her hair brushed and plaited, twisted and tucked and tied.

'Don't think of me. Shouldn't't've . . .'

Frowning along on the track behind him?

'Lit all my candles?'

'Aa . . . you . . .'

Face creasing he'd thought, there behind him, drawing up and bunching, eyes screwing to slits, lips curving and parting over teeth, 'Ha ha, aa, you . . . Look you, don't want . . . want, fall in the bushes again you know . . . torches.'

'Torch busted ever since.'

The car was coming, Cass.

'But don't. At the end of the track, that's me, gone. You shouldn't . . .'

'Shouldn't, like, come there stoking up fires?'

NINETEEN

IN THE story of ancestress Ngarua and the crossing of the inlet, there's mention of a wharenui built by the people as a statement of their authority in this new place. This house, it was believed by its planners and builders, was better in every way than the one left behind in that country on the other side.

It is true at least that this house was larger and stronger.

It was a modest house really, a house of its time. The walls were made of sawn planks lined on the inside with kakaho. Bundles of manuka brush, wired against the outside walls, kept some of the cold out. It had a thatched roof and a packed dirt floor. The few feet of overhang at the front kept most rain from the doorway, though not the rain coming in from the east.

Decoration was minimal. The front overhang had at its apex the carved head of the ancestor, while ancestral arms outstretched at either side, though mostly of plain, painted wood were carved on the ends, that is, on palms and fingers.

From behind the carved head, going through to the back inside wall, the backbone of the ancestor had been painted in thin white lines of kowhaiwhai decoration, as had the ancestral ribs. But apart from this small amount of carving on the exterior and the scroll-work on the beams, the house was unadorned.

Retelling would have it that defections were numerous at the time of The Crossing. In fact those that crossed from north to south numbered about twenty, with as many dogs. Though life was never easy the land and sea were good cupboards.

Thirty years later numbers had grown to about a hundred but lands had dwindled because of government legislation, men had gone to a world war and most had not returned, the country was in severe depression and there was no work. Nor was there finance available for land development and this situation continued until people's remaining land shares began to be consolidated into blocks and partitioned into farm-sized units. All the shareholders were to receive dividends from these blocks, but the land did not provide work for many of them.

The situation worsened over the years and it became impossible for everyone to survive on the land that remained.

People left home to find employment, to go to the next war, or to go into tuberculosis wards and sanatoriums. Those who were left behind scratched for a living, took in the orphans, brought home the sick, disabled and traumatised. People were thin and dazed and their dogs were even worse.

When the situation in the country became a little better some were able to find work scrub cutting or shearing. Some were able to take out mortgages and replace the old Crossing time homes and shelters with timber houses that had corrugated iron roofs, glass in the windows and outdoor washhouses in which home brew rigs were likely to be found.

Those without work made do with patching up the Crossing-day shelters, or they slept with rats and birds in cow sheds and out-buildings—but also in the meeting house which by then had gone beyond people's means and energy to repair.

Numbers decreased even further over the years. Even though

there was now a road only a short distance away, and small-time development inland, most of this development passed them by. More and more people left to find work or to join gangs, or because they had been able to do some comparisons and now thought their turangawaewae was a hole, the pits, the backwater of the universe, and should be left to the manuka and the dogs.

Now in 1999 there were not too many more people living on Dogside than in The Crossing days. There were fifty or so people living in fifteen of the houses, that is, counting the falling-down one where Rua lived. There were four houses that were unoccupied and though the area of available land had reduced considerably over the years, there were pieces of land either side of the wharenui that were also unoccupied. That was the land that Piiki Chiefy, the rogue husband of Maina, had his eye on.

However, though there were only fifty people now living there, there were those from elsewhere to whom Dogside was turangawaewae, and who had the same rights as those in residence. Dogside was their place to stand, their place to speak and give voice. Shares from land incorporation were owned and dividends due to them just as much as they were to their on-site relatives, and they claimed descendency from Ngarua in the same way as their home relatives did.

Some of these exiles had moved only as far as Turanganui, the near city, while others had gone to the far cities of Whangarei, Auckland, Wellington, Christchurch, Dunedin, Invercargill and everywhere in between. Others had crossed seas to Australia, Europe, America. Many of the children of these exiles had never seen home.

All of these demographics have been researched by one of the family doing hapu studies at university. There are figures available and all sorts of information, including the fact that dividends from shares in the amalgamated blocks now stood at: one free mutton per person over the age of fifty-five, once a year at Christmas, as long as the person was registered and on hand to collect it.

But never mind that. The study was useful when Wai and her helpers needed to contact the whanau to get them to come to a meeting regarding the new dining room and Y2K activities.

The exiles were always moved by news from home. From a distance their turangawaewae sat warm inside them like carbo-hydrates and gravy, and when the call came the employed of other places began scheming as to who they could get to cover for them at work, or what they could say to bosses that would enable them to lengthen their weekend by at least a day. The unemployed borrowed money or a vehicle, or got out on the road to hitch home. This didn't happen for those from the far south for whom travel to the North Island was too expensive, though they did contemplate it. They did wish.

Of course those who lived in Sydney, Melbourne and beyond couldn't even contemplate, but would've been offended if they hadn't been notified. They were able to send koha—usually one or two hundred dollars. Anything less would've seemed mingy, especially when everyone at home believed they were making it big in these far cities of the world. Along with koha the exiles sent messages that they were saving to come for Christmas, or that they wanted to send nephews and nieces across for a holiday, or that one day they would return for good.

'In a box.'

'In a wooden overcoat,' was the response to the latter from those at home who didn't believe a word of it, having once too often brought their relatives home from afar, for burial.

Not all this warm spuds and gravy stuff applied to everyone. There were those who had pulled their feet out of home ground and would never plant them there again.

The wharenui where this meeting was to be held is twice the size and more strongly built than that erected by Ngarua and her followers. The old one was eventually pulled down and burned, the only pieces kept for incorporation into the new one being the ancestral head and the arms from the outside, and a short section of the ancestral backbone from the interior.

It is not one of the grand houses of modern times. It has a veranda large enough, with enough depth from front to back to shelter a coffin, and enough space for widows and other mourners to keep the dead company for a few days and nights. There are hooks on high from which to hang the awnings that provide shelter for the mourners during their vigil and to keep the sun from playing havoc with the carefully made-up face of the dead.

Inside, the ancestral backbone and wall poles have been carved and the ancestral ribs painted in kowhaiwhai patterns.

In between the carved poles are plain plank walls, except that in recent years, on the back wall, young artists on a Maccess scheme have painted a mural depicting The Crossing, Te Whakawhititanga a Ngarua. In it you see Ngarua, in full daylight and bright sun, standing large in a great carved war canoe, prow feathers and all, striking downward with her ornamented paddle, the waves mountainous on either side of her. She's dressed in a kind of leather-look battle dress with a piupiu over the top. Her eyes are gold, her face shining and her black hair fills the sky.

Behind her on a far shore is Maraenohonoho on the back of a knock-kneed horse wielding, not a lump of driftwood but something resembling a jousting lance.

Some like the mural.

Others think it modern and hideous and say that ancestress Ngarua has been made to look like a gang member or a bikie. They're awaiting an opportunity to paint it over.

The reason for the piece of tahuhu, or ancestral backbone, being kept from the old house to be put into the new one is because the wharenui is the repository of talk, and rafters are its storage place: Ko nga kupu e iri nei i tara-a-whare mau tonu, mau tonu. It was a way of transferring the old stories into the new house for safe-keeping.

At the meeting Wai knows that there'll be a great deal of talk to get through before they'll be able to get to the business of the day. The house is full, which means that the initial talk that connects them all, the nostalgia, the catching up on what is happening in all their other worlds, will probably take most of the morning. It can't be hurried because it's one of the main reasons most of them have come—which doesn't mean they're not interested in this project of Wai's. Wai is just hoping the talk and the in-between songs won't take too long.

Pop Henry, the one whose mind has gone ahead of him to meet the ancestors, is being helped to his feet to begin. No one can make head or tail of what the old man's talking about, except that once in a while something connects with what is already in the house hanging from the rafters.

But at least the old man is there for them to see, to look at, and now that they're all comfortable it doesn't really matter how long he goes on. Those who haven't been home for a while and didn't know the old man had gone funny, take the opportunity to lean sideways to ask what's up.

They discover the old man is being looked after by a grand-daughter, Reggae, one of Beano's kids. She's a single mum with two children who's good to the old man but not old enough. Looks after his clothes good, feeds him good, but there's no life for her. Now and again she takes off somewhere without telling anyone.

Sometimes it's the old man who takes off and it's difficult for Reggae to keep an eye on him all the time. Off he goes along the beach in his slippers, halfway to the blowhole, raining, tide coming in, and they all have to keep a watch out. Archie goes along to see him once a day. Rua gets him his fish. Old man's got a suitcase full of new pairs of socks under his bed because it's what everyone's been giving him for his birthday and Christmas for ten years. Go there with your present of socks and he rips off the paper, pulls out his suitcase, opens the lid and slings them in. Bagful. But no one can think what else to give him apart from lollies.

And his sister Tini. She left her house to go and live in the city closer to her kids and grandkids, but at least today she's there for them to see. Her grandson has brought her from Turanganui for the day.

Once the old man has sat down there's an interruption in proceedings from Atawhai, by the far door. He wants permission from the gathering to leave his cellphone switched on because he's on call.

No problem with that.

Atawhai is the doctor in the family, born on Dogside, who left there on scholarship at thirteen to attend boarding school, and was sent from there to medical school. He's spent thirty-five years in city hospitals and in private practice in South Auckland where the most difficult thing for him to do was to close the doors of his surgery in the evenings. But after thirty-five years he began to think more and more about flounder in the estuary, crayfish in the cove, and about growing corn and cabbages.

Retirement.

It wasn't easy to leave people's illnesses, beatings, rashes, malnutrition, iron deficiencies, diabetes, impetigo and running ears, but once he'd made up his mind he quickly sold up and came home. He built a house just across the bridge in the township and bought a boat which was hardly ever taken out by him though his nephews over from Sydney made good use of it.

It wasn't long before Atawhai found it necessary to convert one of the rooms of the new house into a surgery. He was the only doctor within a forty kilometre radius and was on call twenty-four hours. Though he didn't have time to fish he never went without crayfish or fish of any description because all varieties were brought to his door as payment in lieu.

Atawhai had come to the meeting because it was to do with all this millennium sunrise business and he was concerned that if there really was to be an influx of people at new year he might have trouble coping with all the extra fishhook injuries, motor and boat accidents, fevers, sunstroke, sick babies, drownings and falls from bridges.

However he didn't get a chance to bring up the matter because halfway through the morning his phone rang and after answering the call he opened the door behind him and went out, for a moment removing from the painted mural the down-stroking paddle of Ngarua, a wild wave and an ancestral thigh.

Two others present were brothers Jackson and Joeboy who knew plenty about making deals and money. They'd ridden down from further up the coast on their Harleys, taking time out from cannabis plots and drug dealing to come and see what the meeting was about. They were dressed like cowboys with cellphones on their belts like guns—but saying they had phones slung like guns isn't saying these two were armless. They did have a real gun, carried on the back of their ute, that they used mainly for hunting. But in business like theirs there was always a possibility of it being needed as a deterrent or a persuasion.

It was afternoon before Wai got to outline the project and her scheme. Her idea was simply to use the planning already in place, that is to remove it all from the original planner—'your relation' she called him—and carry it through themselves, using the skills of those present. To raise all the money they needed in one major effort, then to build and equip the wharekai, was the aim. Wai had a broad idea of how they would reach the goals she was outlining but her most special skill was in knowing who she had in front of her and how to delegate.

What she knew she had was a voluntary work force of people who could do what was needed, or people with the contacts that they needed for the task. They'd have to have everyone there working for two weeks over the new year, or for part of that time.

No holidays, no celebrating until it was over. As well as that they'd need some people working from now on, doing bookings, preparing the grounds, extending and improving their toilet and shower block, and whatever it was that had to be done for all that Internet business. They were going to have to use the money already raised to bring it all together.

Her biggest task at the moment was to persuade them. She knew that without everyone agreeing it wouldn't work, for although the people in front of her were workers and people with contacts, that wasn't all they were. They could be objectors too.

As she spoke she looked around reading the silent language, which is a language that works its way into the rafters also. She saw that there were some who sat with eyes fixed on her, or even with eyes averted but who she could tell were listening and interested. Others were hunched, averted, while others sat flat up against the wall, their eyes sideways, uncommitted, suspicious, whispering behind hands, eyebrows up, eyebrows down, waiting for her to finish so they could leap up.

Her eyes, nail drivers that they were, told her there was going to be division, perhaps a bust-up. She knew if it happened it couldn't be diverted and only hoped there'd be time to work through it by the end of the day, that is if they were going to be able to work through it at all. She knew it could all fall down round her ears, and if that was the case they'd have to count her out as the main fundraiser from now on and find someone else, because she'd already made up her mind she wasn't going back to raffles and dinners, which were too much work for too little return and meant money coming from the same people all the time.

She reminded them about that. 'It's tourist dollars we want. Just this once then thanks and goodbye. Haere ra mo ake tonu. OK that's it,' she said. 'Over to you lot. If you want it, think what your role can be. Or, have a go at me if you want. The only thing I'm asking us not to waste time on today is slagging off our big-chief relation. We been screwed by our own relations before. Hei aha. Deal with him when we get him here for the takeover, hmm, after we thank him for the idea of course.'

So the talk started.

Not in the following order, because there are protocols to do with order, which though imprecisely followed on this occasion, were roughly adhered to. Well, it was all in-house anyway. Most of what came at first were objections from those Wai had already seen were waiting to leap. Nothing would nail them.

'All this 2000 business. What is it anyway? It's a Christian celebration, that's what. So why are we celebrating it. What's "New Year" to us—nothing to do with our people, our culture. If we want to be celebrating then we should celebrate our own survival in our own Matariki star time. Never mind all this other rubbish dumped on us by missionaries and colonisers—all eyes to heaven while they take the land from under your feet. We got to decolonise ourselves, unpick our brains because they been stitched up too long. We need politicisation and decolonisation if we're going to claim tino ranga-tiratanga, otherwise nothing's gunna change, gunna keep on being bad statistics, our kids are gunna keep being kicked out of school, keep going to jail, keep killing themselves. Babies are gunna keep on dying, people are gunna keep on being sick, poor, kicked around. Shit-all happens unless we get rid of this shit out of our heads. We been messed with long enough.'

So hang that in the rafters.

Dion was getting off the track, some people thought. You know, parents make sacrifices to send their kids away to become teachers and lawyers, but all the kids are doing is shouting around the place about everything instead of getting on with their studies. You can't switch on television without seeing this niece or that nephew march-ing down city streets with a lot of untidy mates waving flags and holding up rude signs. Families paying for all that. Waste of money.

But some agree with Dion that they've been messed with long

enough. 'We keep letting it happen, letting our own do it to us too, our own relations. The sun's going to come up on the first of January with dollar signs all round it. Already in Turanganui thousands of dollars are being spent doing the place up—face-lifting the city—new paving and palm trees, doing up the clock tower, soundshell lights, digital calendar all lit up counting down the time. It's all gearing up . . .'

'Well but, so what? I mean . . .'

'All that money being spent, but people are still poor. Airlines, hotels, motels all doubling their prices so everyone can come and hoon around and be first to watch the same old sun come up. Poor old Te Ra. People letting their houses out for $1000 a week, leasing out their backyards to campers—all for nga Merikana, nga Hapanihi, nga Tiamana, nga Wiwi. He aha te mea nui? He moni.'

'Well, we might as well be in too, I mean . . .'

'And what about our fish?'

'And what about tourists all over the place, lighting fires and being a bloody nuisance, tramping all over the urupa.'

'There's enough robbing of paua and crays as it is without more and more people finding out it's a real good spot.'

'Well now, while we're on the topic of fish, and rip-offs, have a look at what our own Runanga's doing to us. Never mind what a few strangers might do. It's selling its cray quota to our own fishermen for seventeen dollars per kilo and our poor fisherman only getting twenty bucks. That's it, making three dollars a kilo—don't even cover expenses. Yeh, making money for themselves to fly here and there in aeroplanes, sleep in flash hotels, set their kids up as consultants and managers.'

All recorded in the rafters.

'Well you know, you let strangers on your land you never get them off. They stick there. They start off as campers and end up sticking there. I remember when I was a kid running round in the toitoi and strangers started coming with tents. Later, our parents and grandparents let them build baches. No rent, no nothing. These people had flash boats with motors and didn't even give us a fish. That's how some of them got in further up the inlet where there's good launching for boats. Now this here's the same thing.'

It wasn't easy to get back to the topic once people began on land issues, and it may seem there wasn't much support for Wai. But there was plenty of support really. What has been recorded is selective and, what's more, without lunch.

Anyway they weren't celebrating the new year, or century, or millennium Wai reminded them, only taking advantage of it. Year two thousand or year sixty thousand was irrelevant, and she didn't care if it was a Christian festival, pompom girls or mice poop. 'Come home Christmas, you won't be on holiday, won't be celebrating, you'll be here to work if we agree on this here today,' she said.

This is not Wai losing her cool here, she's just dishing out a few reminders and nobody objects to that.

'True. And anyway who cares how we get it, as long as we get it. It'll only be once so why not go for it?'

'Well there's other ways.' This came from Jackson who was sitting under the window with Joeboy. It got everyone laughing. Wai was relieved about that but took the opportunity to reiterate what she'd mentioned earlier, that if they did take on this idea they'd be coming home to work—no holidaying, no alcohol, no celebrating and none of that electric puha either. 'While we're at it no patches, no insignia, not if I got anything to do with it,' Wai said. 'And remember it's not the ones living away who cook in the rain, feed people in tents and who could still be doing that in the twenty-first century—if we're allowed to call it that.'

There wasn't much hard disagreement by the time the meeting adjourned for lunch late in the afternoon. They all understood the necessity to rebuild the dining room, which would need to be fully equipped and easy for the home people to manage, all knew they had to get the money from somewhere and that Wai had outlined a good way to do it. Their crook of a relation was no worry because they knew they could deal with him easy. However there was some initial disappointment among those who had been planning on coming home at Christmas to get away from all this Y2K hype.

If there were some who were still not quite convinced that they were doing the right thing, the smell coming from the pots as they went out to the fireplace for lunch was so good it kind of melted them. Dion, who'd been one of the ones blazing at the beginning when Wai had first put the proposal, felt himself cooling. He dug his food out on to his plate and while eating began putting forward his theory that the closer food was to the fire the better it tasted. He reckoned that food cooked on fired stones in the ground, or food put in ashes, had the most flavour. Next best was food cooked in pots over an open fire like what they were eating now. One-pot soul food tasted great, stayed hot a long time, sat hot in your mouth and swallowed hot. The next best thing, according to Dion, was kai cooked on a wood stove. On from that you were getting on to sad stuff—electric, gas, bloody microwave. Sad food. Those around him thought he was gabbing too much, thought he liked the sound of his own voice, but he'd always been the same—way-out ideas and always going on about something.

'And people. People get sad the higher they get off the ground. People with the beach and trees around, and a little house flat on the ground laugh more. You go and live in a suburb, squeezed in a house or flat where all the paths and roads are concreted over, then your mouth goes down a bit at the corners and you get a wrinkle on your head.'

'Ah, shut up Dion.'

So Dion kept quiet for while, used his mouth for eating, then helped with the cleaning up. He'd made up his mind he was coming back in the holidays to help raise this money even though he didn't agree with some things. In spite of his theories about fire-cooked food he knew he couldn't expect everything to go on as it was. The home people were all getting older and fewer, most with one sickness or another. Anyway, it seemed they were all keen to keep the open fire since there was always plenty of wood but were going to have all the sad food machinery as well.

It was easy after lunch.

What the heck.

They all wanted to be part of it, and there were enough of them around to be watchdogs regarding any of the concerns they might have to do with fish. Anyway it would be unlikely to be visitors who'd be out stealing crays.

TWENTY

HE DECIDED he'd hear Pop Henry through then go out and find Kid, talk to her—but what to say? A good thing about being one-legged was what you could get away with, people always believing you had good reason for leaving meetings, falling asleep in odd places or going up creek to live by yourself.

Rolling banks and breathing trees.

Fire time he'd told Maina what Kid had said. Cracked out of an egg. Shitted by a seagull.

Earlier, in the water by the weedy shelves he'd crumbled bait in his hands, fine enough so it floated, and the fish had come swimming about them collecting bits, flicking away and returning. She'd said she could bloody drown.

Old Pop was seeing kehua, talking to the old ones and thinking he was back in the old place.

'Wants something, little Kiri, something from you,' she'd said and he'd had to look away, lean back taking his face out of the light of the fire, out of the way of her watching him.

'There's things . . .' he'd said from back there out of light,

'Things can't be told. Or . . . could. Could . . . There's something
. . .' Back there against the tree shadow, against the quiet of trees.
'But what if it's bad?'

'My first husband was a jerk,' she'd said at the stubbing-out of
a cigarette. 'He was also father of my kids. I didn't want my kids to
know they had a jerk for a father, that he was the one who I'd let
be the father of them—a drug-dealing wife-basher in an Aussie
prison for killing a man. Kids had nice photos of him and thought
he was great, though they'd never seen him since he slung his hook
and were too little to remember. But they kept asking, just like little
Kiri. Didn't want to lie to them. Well, I would've lied, but thought
they could go looking for him one day and find out I lied. Didn't
want to be caught out, so I told them everything. You know they
were devastated at first, and it was like they were mad at me for
telling them, but after a couple of weeks they ditched him, shoved
the photos away under clothes in their drawer and one day Pare
said, "Anyway we got Koro. That makes up for it."

'We were living with Dad. Dad made up for it, was how they
saw it. And he did too, Dad. They were the best days, those days
living with Dad. He wouldn't let me take the kids with me when I
remarried, but anyway they were older by then and made up their
own minds to stay. I was pleased when we shifted back this way
because it meant I could be near him and the kids, who are off
flatting now but still around. Made up my mind I don't want to
move again, won't move again . . . You know, bad, but there was
something to make up for it.'

Pop Henry was sitting down, and he was just about to leave when
Atawhai, beside him, stood to ask about the mobile phone. As
Atawhai sat down and the talk resumed he got up onto his sticks,
opened the door behind him and went out to where his dog was
waiting, face on hands, eyes rolling up.

What would make up for it?

Looking out he could see the tide was down. The kids were along by the blowhole, some up on the banks or in and out of the hole, some on the beach and the shore rocks. Georgie was climbing the hill face, turning and calling something down to Hinewai. Behind Georgie were the twins and Te Mana.

Kid wasn't on the hill, nor could he see her among the older children at the hole, poking around with sticks. Not there.

Down on the beach itself he tried to name the kids off as they appeared around rocks, from among dogs, from in and out of the poles and arches of the wood they were carrying to make a tunnel or a house or whatever it was going to be. But there were too many of them and he decided to go along there even though he thought she was most likely at home cleaning up after Floss and Minty's baking. The Two Aunties had arrived at the meeting armed with cakes as usual.

'Home, mus' be,' the kids said looking him up and down maybe wishing they were one-legged, wondering if he would give them a go on his sticks or lay down on the beach and give them a chance. No one had seen her outside her house or going to the shop, or anywhere.

He found her on her bed with her arm, as though it was something separate from her, resting on a towel. It was like a small fish that had been thrown there dead, cooked and cray-coloured. Her dark skin had paled, her dark eyes had darkened. From the doorway he could see she was damp and shaky, and he felt his breath leave him.

'Tell me,' he said.

'Hot water on the stove.' Her voice crept out of her, heavy as though she was bored. 'My arm in because . . .' Eyes bored, looking at him, 'Arm in because, I felt like doing it.'

Had to swim, swim up until he found breath. 'Get Atawhai,' he said going to the door, then remembering he could ring, he phoned the doctor's house for the mobile number.

'Darling Girl,' Atawhai said when he looked at the arm. 'We taking you round my place for a little jab. After that it won't hurt so bad, then we take you to the hospital. Get Girl a bag,' he said. 'Get her pjs, toothbrush and things . . . a bottle of water. Her aunties?'

'She don't need aunties.'

'Those Two . . .' Atawhai said as he helped Kid up, gathering a rug and pillow and taking her out to the car.

'They're fixing her up, then they'll take her to a ward,' Atawhai said. 'She'll be in a few days then have to come back for dressings.' His phone was ringing and he spoke into it. 'I have to get going,' he said when he'd finished. 'You . . .?'

'I'll stick around.'

'And The Aunties?' Atawhai closed the phone and dropped it into the pocket of his track pants.

'OK, I'll let them know.'

'You can't always be sure,' Atawhai said, his marbly eyes rolling upwards as though he was seeing him on ceilings, 'where the problem is.' The long hairs combed forward from the back of his head to cover the varnished top had come unstuck and were flopping to one side. Doc sticking up for Those Two, just like everyone else did.

'All I know, she's not going back there,' he said, which he could see left Doc with words in his mouth that he was unable to say. Instead Doc asked about money.

'It's OK, Jase'll help me out. And, sleep down Nan Tini's tonight.'

After Atawhai had gone he realised he should've used the cellphone. Jase and Nan Tini were both back at the meeting and he needed to get hold of Jase before he left there, get him to go back to his place for some gear and his bank card. It meant he'd have to find someone home—one of the kids to go and dig

Jase out of the meeting to answer the phone.

Later, when he knew Nan Tini was back at her flat, he'd ring her so she'd know he was coming and wouldn't get a fright with him turning up there knocking in the dark.

Once they got Kid settled he'd be able to use the ward phone to make a couple of calls.

When he returned to the cubicle after ringing Jase, Kid was lying back against a pile of pillows, her black hair in loose strands against it. Black eyes, spider lashes above full cheeks which had some colour in them now. The dressed arm was hooked across in front of her.

What would make up for it?

But it wasn't the time to talk, the spider legs tangled, separated, tangled and soon she was out to it. He sat down to wait by her until it was time to ring Tini, thinking how bullshit he was making out he had to live on his own to stop people doing things for him.

Bullshit, when he knew he really had people to turn to any time he wanted, places to stay anytime, TV to watch if he felt like it, Jase to run round after him.

Water? Fish? Physical life?

One-legged bullshit hero. But what had he done for *her* apart from nut off now and again about other people's neglect, other people's unwillingness? Now it was time to get real. Now he needed what he could've had long ago—something to fill the gap below the knee—because now he was going to fix up one of the front houses and needed two legs so he could do it. There were windows and weatherboards that needed replacing and rooms that needed painting. He'd get a car and use some of the bloody ACC money he had stashed away. Leaning forward he removed two pillows from behind Kid and let her head down. It had taken this to move him.

A baby in a cot in the corner with bandages over his head and ears was starting to cry and the mother was lifting him. Shadows were entering the room, lights were going on round the wards and it was almost evening visiting hour. He went to ring Tini.

'Be back in the morning,' he said to Paula at the desk when he'd finished.

'Have fun, Rua.'

He made his way along one corridor and turned into the next, and at the other end of it, coming towards him, was Maina. There were voices coming from reception, a trolley ticking along, a monitor beeping. There because of Kid, because of him?

'It's Dad,' she said. 'We brought him into A & E this time yesterday. They took him to theatre and he's still critical.' He could see how tired she was and thought of being away from there in among fish, among rock and weed, up on grassy banks by fire, in under tarps and sacking and in among trees.

'I could wait with you,' he said.

'It's all right, my brother's here. My kids. So . . . ahh . . .'

She turned to walk towards the exit with him. Night time visitors were entering through the sliding doors, making for the lifts and stairways.

'It's Kid,' he said. 'A burn on her arm. Be here a few days.'

'Little Kiri.'

'Asleep. Knock-out dose. Going down Nan Tini's for the night, me.'

'Can I drop you off? My car.'

In a car, going somewhere . . . away.

'Only down the next street,' he said. 'But . . . be around in the morning. Ahh, come and see how you're all doing.'

The inner door was open and he was standing in light coming through the steel mesh of grand-aunt Tini's security door.

'Grandson Albie got it for me from demolition, yeh, a hundred and fifty dollars,' Tini said as she turned the lock. 'Come in Rua . . . And security window fifty dollars, well you never know. On the back door just a lock and chain and I keep this inside door open on some nights so I can watch the old man three doors down who been putting his rubbish in my bin. Mmm, caught him putting his stuff in. I said, "Look here you get your own rubbish bin." He been going along the rows putting his rubbish in this one, that one, this one, that one, poor old thing. His family come along and take things off him, you know. I reckon they took his bin. Got a bed for you Rua. There. Sofa bed. You pull it out to sleep. From the Warehouse. Finish my payments next month, automatic out of my bank . . . We get some kai.'

'Should've got milk and bread but come without money,' he said. He was empty, hadn't eaten all day. 'Jase calling in here on his way back with my gear and my bank card. Tomorrow I'll have money.'

'All right, I got blood pudding and bread.'

'Haa, you got tomato sauce?'

'Tomato, Lea and Perrins . . . Who is she, that one with Jase?'

'Tina.'

'Two kids?'

'True.'

While she cut the sausage and put it in the microwave with a piece of cooked potato he sat and sliced the bread.

'Why don't he find a new one, make his own kids?' Tini asked.

'Bones too. Remelda and a baby.'

'You don't say . . . Ahh Rua, your young cousins leaving you behind. When you getting yourself a girl?'

'Mm, true.'

'Aach, never get you a wife living way back there in the bush. You want to come to the city and live, like me. Never mind back home there. Look here, I got everything—electric stove, microwave, television, washing machine, electric blanket, telephone with call-waiting . . .'

She was putting teabags into the teapot and waiting for the jug to boil and he wondered if she really had forgotten that it was all electric back home too and had been ever since he could remember, or did she just enjoy showing him her stuff, pleased to have some-one to talk to, like him at fire time. Tini was another one living alone, choosing to in spite of others not approving.

'And town water,' she said. 'No tanks. No more running out of water in the summer, washing in the creek and can't have a decent bath. No mud. All concrete paths, lawns all nice and don't even have gumboots. No gumboots. Each flat got its own little garden, bus stop a few yards down. I go to flea market every Saturday, five o'clock in the morning, to sell my crafts. Seven dollars for my own stall.'

She poured two cups of tea, left them on the table and began throwing things on to the sofa bed from behind it.

'See here, bath mats, cushion covers, coat hangers and this blanket,' she said. 'See here. I sold one already.'

'Give me it,' he said. 'Keep me that one.'

'What you saying?' She moved to the sideboard then to show him what he could already see. 'My clowns, poodles, dolls,' which were sitting and standing among photos, calenders and Get Well balloons. More in the glass cupboard among cups, coasters, glasses, jugs and sugar bowls.

'And a doll, hmm.'

'Ahh, which doll?'

'You say.'

'I give it.'

'Nah, I buy it. Doll and blanket.'

'And slippers?' She was tipping knitted pairs, all colours, from a bag. 'Taking all my crafts back home for New Year too. Plenty of campers there might want dolls and blankets, townies and tourists, plenty money. My mate, my mate sometimes share a stall with me. Crochet hats from bread bags, her. I told her you never know, all those Hapanihi coming for the millennium might need hats so they won't get sunburn. Sun might be too hot for those Merikana, those Hainamana. Plastic bread bags, yeh, cost her nothing.'

A green-faced doll was looking at him out of button eyes. It had hair of all colours, a hat of all colours and yellow clothes. 'That one,' he said pointing his stick, giving it a poke. 'And red slippers, mm.'

'Nephew, nephew,' Tini said. 'I could knit you one. A slipper, haa.'

'And one for the stump, what you say?'

'True, true. Keep you warm . . . And how's that girl anyway?'

'There a couple of days, then got to have somewhere to stay while she goes back for dressings, or might take her with me.'

'Yeh, bring her here. We get a mattress from Judith.'

TWENTY-ONE

'WAITING IN the water for a stingray to move away from my possie I saw black hair and white clothes, someone up on the hill. I knew it was Ani Wainoa. Ani Wainoa went into the trees so I watched, saw the way the trees moved, it's how trees talk.' Telling her all this when he should be getting straight to the point, right to what it was she wanted to know.

'Ani Wainoa had her own tracks that she'd made through the trees and I could see the tops moving above one of those tracks, just moving, one treetop and then another, real slow. I didn't know why slow like that because Ani Wainoa always runs.'

Kid didn't seem to care for the doll. She'd taken it from him, looked into its green face and button eyes, touched the hat, lifted the crocheted frill then put it on the locker beside the bed.

'I thought Ani Wainoa might be looking for something or following a cat or a bird, but why would she keep to the path if she was doing that? So then I thought she could be carefully carrying something that was secret. It's what the trees told me, moving their heads here, there and hardly at all.'

Using too many words, and Kid was lying back as if she wasn't listening, because maybe she didn't believe he was going to tell her anything different from what she already knew. Or maybe it was too late and she didn't care any more.

'Carrying a secret and I wanted to know what it was. I got out of the water, went round the cove bank without making any noise or disturbing any birds, and climbed the rocks on the other side to the ledge. Waited by the track where I knew she'd come out, waited a long time while she came slow, slow, slow with this secret.'

And now he knew he had to lie, leave out some of what had happened that day and what was shouted into the trees as he backed away watching the two hands holding the lump of wood. Watching, watching, watching, throw it or I'll kill you. There could be another time when he'd have to tell it all, but for now the trees would have something to keep.

'At last she came out from the trees with her secret. You were her secret. She came out of the trees with you, but got a fright to know that I knew her secret, held you out for me to take. I took you, had you there. Freaked out, me—freaked out big-time, and so I stepped back.

'Tripped and stumbled, then had to jump to save us from falling onto the rocks, folding you into me with water all round. My feet touched the bottom, pushed me up and when I reached the surface, swam like an upside down frog with you on my chest. Seagulls were flying.'

You tell and . . . you tell anyone . . . after you . . . after you with, with a . . . knifeknife. It wasn't that that had scared him.

'Out on the bank dried you with my shirt but you were hardly wet at all. Like you'd been oiled. Ani Wainoa was gone, running—away through the blowhole and gone. I knew she would never come back so I took you to Nanny Blind's, but it was no good leaving you there, Nanny Blind was crying and her dog was dead. Took you home.'

It was what she already knew.

'She gave you to me. Ani Wainoa gave you to me because it was me. It was me, how you got there in that Ani Wainoa.'

Watching him tell what had been meant only for trees.

Watching him.

And he watched her, watched her understand, watched her eyes picking up light, watched her high cheeks pick up the colour of plums.

'I was fourteen, too young to be your father and didn't realise then that I was your father. I took you home.'

She reached for the doll, put it in the bed beside her with its head on the pillow and its green arms out over the bed cover.

'Your father, but it's not all.' He could hear lunch coming. The trolley was out in the corridor, footsteps in and out of the ward rooms.

'It's not all and . . . and, if there's something bad, something bad . . . If there's something not good . . . well . . . what will make up for it?'

Because there was something that was known not only to trees, that anyone could tell her once they knew he was her father. He knew he had to be the one to tell and knew he had to do it now. She was watching him.

'What will make up for it?'

The trays were coming in and he could smell cauliflower cheese.

She sat up. 'That you never leave me,' she said.

He leaned and propped the pillows behind her, helped her balance the tray.

'You're living with me now. Going to have the house next to Pop Henry's so it's easy for you to go to school.'

Had to stop talking about that. All of that was for later. Bread rolls and butter, wet salad, cheesy steam. 'I was eight when my mother died,' he said. 'Her name was Ramari, your grandmother. My sister Moananui, who is your aunty, was four. Before my mother got sick we used to go to Nanny Blind's once a week to take bread.

We'd see Ani Wainoa there and my mother would say, "Come and live with Mummy now." My mother was Ani Wainoa's mother too.'

He watched her as she unwrapped a knife and fork from a paper napkin and peeled back the foil lid on the butter. 'Ani Wainoa is my sister, that's what's bad.'

She broke the roll, smeared butter inside it, pulled a lump off with her teeth. 'Who cares?' she said.

'What's bad is Ani Wainoa is my sister. What's bad is you're not allowed to do that with your sister, not allowed to put a baby in your sister. A sister isn't allowed to get a baby with a brother.'

'Who cares?'

'Well, you don't want a daughter to know some things . . . about a father.'

Daughter. Father. The words had been said.

'Who cares?'

'Or people to know wrong things about a . . . girl's father and mother.'

'Keep it a secret then, who cares.' She was scoffing the bun. 'Who cares if my mother is your sister?' Chomping on the cauli-cheese and downing the soggy salad. 'Who cares if that Ani Wainoa was going to drown me. Don't give a stuff, Rua.'

The mother of the bandaged baby in the corner cot was spooning mashed food into its mouth, tasting it first, eating half of each spoonful before giving it to the baby. He'd seen other mothers do that, eat half the baby's food and always wondered why they did it. It made him feel like laughing.

'We're going to Wellington to get me a leg,' he said. 'You know, artificial, so I can walk good. We're staying at Nan Tini's while you have your dressings done, or we might just go to Wellington if they say you can get your arm done down there. Getting a car and furniture, beds, a blanket from Nan Tini.'

He thought he should stop talking, let days happen a piece at a time, thought he should leave now and get a cab, pick up Tini and go to Pak'n Save to get a few supplies—and there was phoning to do. But he didn't want to leave and decided he'd wait until someone else came in—Wai, Archie, Cass, Floss and Mint, Eva. In the morning he was going to buy a car, automatic, and good-looking enough so he wouldn't get stopped by the police and asked for his licence.

But it was Maina who came in. She'd slept, he could see.

'How's this Kiri?' she asked. Kid held up the doll to show her. 'Where'd you get that?'

Kid tipped her head in his direction. 'Him.'

'Nan Tini makes them, sells them at the flea market,' he said.

'Well . . .'

'How is he now?' he asked.

'Stable . . . and OK . . .' a smile, a glance his way, into his eyes quick and out again.

'His sister and nephew are with him, arrived last night so I went home for a sleep.' She was seated opposite him, her hand on Kid's forehead stroking back hair. 'Are you allowed up?' she said to Kid. 'Have you had a coffee, anything to eat?' she asked him. 'I was on my way to . . . to have a smoke to be truthful, but coffee and a sandwich at the caf would do.'

'Sounds good,' he said. He took the knitted slippers from the locker and put them on Kid's feet which were already dangling over the side of the bed. It was a shock seeing her feet, a copy of his own feet—narrow heels, wide fronts, wide gap between the big toe and the next one, the same pattern of toenails. Felt like mentioning it.

He tied the strings and draped the hospital gown over her shoulders. 'Dressing gowns,' he said. 'You got dressing gowns down there at DEKA?'

'Let me get it. I'm calling in to work this afternoon and I get a discount . . . I know what . . .' She left the room and returned with a wheelchair. 'Here, so you won't bump your poor arm.' Kid got in and the two of them were off and out in the corridor waiting while he reached for his sticks and followed.

'Fix you up tomorrow,' he said. 'For the dressing gown.'

'Get back to work as long as he's OK,' she said. 'And be in lunchtime and after work tomorrow. His sister and Tony are staying 'til Sunday . . . Now, now . . . this dressing gown . . .' she said to Kid. 'Pink, pale blue, dark blue, dark red?'

'Dark red.'

'Like the slippers. Dark red'll just suit you won't it, Girl?'

'She's OK,' Maina said, looking to where Kid had manoeuvred the wheelchair through the arrangements of brown tables and orange chairs to the windows overlooking the car park and outlying buildings, 'She looks ah . . .'

'Told her what she wanted to know,' he said across the table.

'How was it? Was it OK?'

'It was. It was OK. Going to Wellington, her and me, while I get the prosthesis.' There was his money to see to and he had to get to the supermarket then go home to Tini's to ring Wellington for appointments before they closed down for the day. But he didn't want to leave.

'That's good then. Is it?' A glance and then away.

And he felt like saying something to her, something loving, something out of his heart, but didn't know what it could be. Didn't know how to say something loving and out of his heart.

Kid was up out of the wheelchair, pushing it, making her way back in and out among the tables.

'I think of you,' he said, breaking open a packet of sugar, shaking out the grains and looking deep into coffee.

'But don't.'

When they arrived back at the ward Wai and Cass were sitting by Kid's bed waiting, and he noticed the look that passed between them when they saw him and Maina together. It told him that on the morning when Cass had come to pick Maina up, the trees had told. It told him Cass thought it was funny and Wai didn't think it funny at all. Not that he cared.

He left Cass and Wai there with Kid and went to the elevators with Maina, poked the elevator button with his stick.

'Because,' she said, 'I'm not the one for you. There's someone out there for you. Someone young, someone without all this . . . baggage . . . I shouldn't . . .'

The lift was making its way up stopping, starting again. Red light, red light, green.

'Someone who'll want to have children. I mean, I shouldn't . . .'

The doors opened, an orderly came out pushing a trolley.

'I have a child,' he said as she stepped in.

She turned, looking into him as the doors closed.

TWENTY-TWO

HE KNEW he should've called in to see Arch and Wai to tell them what he was doing but he was still wild with them. He'd gone in to see Pop Henry instead, brought him out and showed him the car and told him he was moving in next door when he came back from Wellington. Promised the old man a fish.

'I know you,' Pop Henry kept saying. 'I know you, you're Ru's boy.' There was a heater going and Reggae's two kids were hot and grizzling.

Now he'd come in to have a quick look to see if there were any repairs needed round the house and to try out the taps and switches. He thought about what he would have to get in the way of beds and bedding and other furniture, and measured up a space in the kitchen where he could put a fridge. Later he'd go over to the cove to get fish for Tini and the old man then get up to the old place and pack a few things.

Instead of going over to her aunties' place for clothes for Kid, he decided he'd get her new stuff before they left for Wellington in the morning. But how did you do that, buy her clothes?

Maina had come into the hospital with the dressing gown. Kid was pleased with it, and it was really true that the colour suited her, but how did you know things like that? He had a child, but would he know what to do? Did he know how to be a father?

It was near the end of the lunch hour and Maina, who had already been to see her father, was hurrying to get back to work. 'Don't think of me,' she'd said again. And he'd wanted to say something to her that would let her know he understood.

'It's OK,' was all he could think of saying.

'There are things . . . and I want to live with my father.'

'Nah, it's OK.'

And it was right, had to be OK. He had a daughter and wanted to be her father now, wanted to do that himself even if there were things he wasn't sure about. How did you stroke a forehead, put back strands of hair, have the right words to say? How did you have what a girl needed, such as . . . Such as what? A good house and dresses, was all he could think of.

Wai and Cass were out there looking at the car then coming towards the house dawdling and talking, coming to find out what he was up to. How to tell them what he had to tell? But he guessed it would all fall out of his mouth somehow.

Wai came in with Cass following, both blinking coming out of the sun. 'I'm moving in,' he said. 'She's coming to live with me.'

The look that passed between them, Cass trying to look serious, Wai looking wild, told him they thought he was talking about Maina coming to live with him. Made him mad. 'Kid,' he said, louder than he meant to. 'She's coming to live with me.'

The words rattled in the empty room against wood walls, wood floorboards, wet plaster and dirty glass.

'Ahh,' Cass said.

'Well aah . . .?' Wai said, which meant she didn't think so.

'Clean it up, get what we need and we're shifting in when we get back.'

'Well . . . don't know . . .'

'Moving in.'

'The Aunties . . .'

'Got no say. Kid's coming to live with me.'

Wai had begun to move about the room, stopping every now and again by old lino tacks with scraps of lino still attached, touching each with her toe. 'They won't give up easy,' she said.

'Coming to live with me because . . . I'm her father.'

'Brought her home that time.'

'Because I'm her father.'

'Ani Wainoa . . .'

'I'm her father.'

'Watched out for her ever since then . . .'

'And I'm her father.'

'You were . . .'

'I'm her father.

'A boy.'

'Fourteen.'

Archie had come in and was standing with his back to the window, sun all over him and blossoms from a pear tree outside snowing down behind. Cass leaned against the bench, watching with her mouth shut down. This was family business. Wai was pacing and toeing.

'Who else but me?' he asked. 'Who else could it be?'

'She told us herself . . .' Wai said, but then she stopped speaking, stopped pacing, her eyes filled. 'We believed her,' she said. 'Seen her with that Wiwi, that Dutch, that Swedish, whatever.'

'But what?' Archie said. 'Come to think, what did we see? Saw her riding round all night in bumper cars, that blondie giving her free gos, that's it. Never went off wit' him, nothing like that.'

'She been meeting him, she said. We rang her father's mother after she left, Tawai. Ani Wainoa wasn't there when we rang, but next afternoon her father got hold of us. She was there. I talked to her. "Stefan's the father of the child," she said. "He is my lover and we are soon to be reunited," that way she talked. "I'll never return," she said, so we believed. You were a kid.' Wai was pacing again, sniffing, tears of hers splashing on the floor.

'Fourteen.'

'A kid,' Arch said. 'And we didn't watch out, didn't look after you good. Didn't look after *them* good, letting them live up there going funny in the trees, old Blind and Ani Wainoa.'

'I was looked after good,' he said. 'And I knew . . .'

'You were a kid,' Arch was looking down on shoes. 'But it happened and now . . . '

'And now we know . . . we know, but it can't be told,' Wai said. 'Can't be told that there's a daughter come from a brother and sister. Outside of here it can't be told.'

'I'm her father,' he said. 'If people got to know . . . If I got to put it over Iwi Radio then I will.'

'Listen. Let Sis and me go to Babs and Amiria and we tell them you want to have Kiri now because . . . because . . . she was given to you,' Arch said. 'Claiming her now as her closest relative, as the brother of Ani Wainoa. They got to be on the back foot those two, after what they let happen.'

'They won't.'

'They might.'

'If they don't?'

'Then we got to tell them what you told us, you might be her father and so you got the right. We tell them they got to shut up about it.'

'Ahh, might as well ring Iwi Radio.'

'Try, have a go.'

Which they could've done before now he thought of telling them. 'OK, but I'm having Kid anyway. No way she's going back there. Tomorrow, off to Wellington and taking her with me. Staying with Dion while I get me a bionic waewae, then back to fix this place up for her and me.'

'Got you a driver's licence, Son?' Arch asked.

'No, but I put my name down.'

'Got you a pretty good car.'

TWENTY-THREE

'AT LEAST it's cheap,' said Dion from above. 'That place I had last time you came was too expensive, and I had to travel into Vic every day on the bus. Cost me heaps. All I have to do now is run up the side of the hill and I'm there, run down and I'm home.'

He'd expected something the size of a showground or a stadium but instead found that Te Aro Park was a small grassed wedge with tiled pathways, prow-shaped, with tiled pools set into it like peep holes from underground streams. At the bottom of each pool were painted swimmers that seemed as though they could have surfaced from the underground places and were now locked there, minding water as if it was the only bit remaining. Seagulls and pigeons stepped about in slow dance.

But they hadn't seen all this on the first day when the taxi dropped him and Kid off after shuffling them from the railway bus depot through the late afternoon traffic.

It was as they moved through the city by taxi from the bus depot, stopping, starting and swapping lanes that he'd felt relieved he hadn't driven down, as had been his intention when he bought the car.

'Nowhere to park, Cuz,' Dion had told him over the phone. 'Nowhere unless you want to pay top dollar in an overnight place.' So he'd booked seats on Intercity instead. 'Tell the driver Te Aro Park. Get out and look up, Cuz, you'll see our flag.'

After getting out of the taxi they'd looked up, turning themselves until they spotted the flag on a pole hanging from a second storey window above a deli. Also at the window was a little face that he'd thought at first belonged to a child, then as they crossed the road the woman whose face it was came out of a doorway onto the pavement.

'I'm Miraana,' she'd said. 'One of the flatmates. Dion's working late up at Student Union and asked me to watch out.' Her hair was like pop-weed tied up in a high bunch and she was wearing tight black clothes and high shoes. She'd led them up a steep stairway.

'But not for too much longer,' Dion was saying from up there. 'Graduate then get me a full-time job. Well . . . I hope . . . Near home maybe. I want to find somewhere to live that's level with the ground.'

At the top of the stairs Miraana had taken them into the lounge and kitchen where the concrete walls were painted pink and purple and where there was a square pillar in the centre of the room covered in yellow, green and blue patterns. She'd sat them down on an old sofa and stood with her back to the flag window asking questions about the bus trip. He didn't know how much Dion had told her about why he had come, didn't care.

On the wall opposite were old band posters—Dread Beat and Blood, Lee Scratch Perry and Roots Foundation. Music from a tape deck mingled with the sounds of booming waves of traffic below. Low down on the same wall was a map marking out he didn't know what, and on an adjacent wall were photos of street marches, demonstrations, protests and occupations all featuring the flag.

Miraana had told him about the different events, the different key figures, but he wasn't able to keep up with what she was saying, thinking of food instead, wondering if he should be getting Kid something to eat or if they should wait for Dion.

In the kitchen was an unused stove with pot plants growing down over it and a stainless steel bench that had a split in it as though it had been chopped with an axe. But on a little table, beside a set of silver painted cupboards, were a two-plate camp cooker, a toaster and a jug. There were people coming in, being introduced, going off to rooms then going out again banging their big shoes on the stairs.

'At least I got a few mates here and it's only one flight of stairs, one storey. Seatoun? Way up there, six floors and living on my own. People forget where they belong when they live high up, and the ground keeps on trying to remind them, pulls at their feet, takes colour from out of their bodies making them greyer and greyer and pulling all their corners down. They have to keep looking out to see where the ground is. It's down there but its all concreted over with no rain or sun touching it, so they keep frowning down trying to look through those layers and their eyes get tired and their faces get lonely. The higher you go in buildings the grumpier and more faded you become.'

From the flag window they looked down to Lunar Park and The Faultline Bar, Loading Zone, Wicked Charcoal, Hair Afrik, Kwanzaa, IKON, Karaoke, Great India, Kebabaholic. There was one big pohutukawa tree and a wind-beaten ti kouka; paste-ups and papers, and alleys and car parks where workers were allowed to go and smoke. People, stretched out on seats and on grass, ate from boxes and paper bags. They wore big shoes, big jackets, black clothes. Trolley buses trundled by.

When he asked Miraana if there were any takeaway places still open she'd directed him to an all-night cart, and on asking if she wanted anything she'd answered no, so he'd guessed she didn't have any money. He and Kid had gone out for chicken and chips bringing enough for Miraana and Dion as well. It was ten thirty by then and Dion had arrived not long afterwards, grateful for food.

'It's unfood day,' he'd said. 'Tomorrow we get money, put in for ten dollar meat packs and two dollar bags of veggies, put something into the flat account for tea and bread. By this time of the week there's only tea and bread, sometimes.'

'People long for the earth. Even if it's concreted over they still know it's there somewhere because they see it sneaking out of cracks. The higher you go the less of a person you become. You become a kehua, but sometimes you don't know you're a kehua, you feel you're wearing a mask instead. Try to take it off but you can't. So after a while you realise it's you. Earthquakes rattle you and your bones start coming to the outside. Well it's bad enough here, up a storey and sleeping on a shelf.'

It was a room of white concrete with an ungibbed wooden wall that had been erected as a divider to make two rooms from one. A platform had been put up and that's where Dion had his mattress. A bed lamp provided the only light for the room. 'The ceiling light is in the other half, on the other side of the partition,' Dion told him.

Underneath the platform was a sofa and a small formica table with Dion's books on it, and across one corner, balanced on jutting screws, was a broom handle where he hung his clothes.

It was when they'd gone to bed on that first night that he wondered if he should've left Kid with Nan Tini instead of bringing her with him. The noise of traffic hadn't stopped and every now and again a siren or alarm would sound, or when a bus or truck went by the whole building would shake making the windows rattle. But Kid had quickly gone to sleep on Dion's sofa, pleased with the new sleeping bag he'd bought her. He'd unrolled his own bag on the floor in front of the sofa, which was the only remaining space on the piece of old carpet which smelled of damp and rot while his sleeping bag smelled of fish. Dion had climbed the wall and got into bed.

The next day he and Kid had taken a bus to the hospital so that she could have her dressings done then they'd walked over to the Artificial Limbs Centre for him to begin his physio treatment. Most of that day had been spent in waiting rooms, or in one of them having treatment, and it had been much the same every day. Again on that first day he'd wondered if he should've brought her, yet knew he couldn't have left her for six weeks—or however long this was all going to take.

Before the shops closed that day he'd gone down town for a foam strip to put under his sleeping bag to get himself up off the rotten carpet. After a few days he became used to the noise of traffic, the shaking and rattling, and would go to sleep listening to Dion's voice, thinking of water, thinking of *her*, managing to sleep at least until the street sweeper trucks came grinding through at four in the morning.

After a week he became used to that as well. He'd wake, think of home, of her, and go back to sleep again while Kid slept on.

'We're all trapped in some way. Me here, you there. Me so I can graduate and "work for the people", which'll mean I can never live at home again until I'm old. You, you're stuck there in among all the home politics where you can't even fart without everyone knowing and having an opinion. You, getting people their fish but not knowing what else is going on in Te Ao Maori.'

On the days after Kid's last dressings had come off and when he had early appointments at the Limbs Centre they would spend the afternoons down at the waterfront, by the sea with all its edges trimmed against jetties, walkways, wharf sheds, cafés and markets, walls and breakwaters. They'd watched the fishing boats, the day trip boats, the people coming and going, the row of men sitting with their fishing lines over the side waiting for bites that never seemed to come. He'd thought of stripping down and getting in for a look around, but the water looked oily and lifeless, and he thought he'd better take notice of the warning signs.

There *was* life down there though.

One afternoon the fish were biting and the fishermen, who on most days had looked like nothing but sad, bent statues, had pulled up small kahawai one after another. At last they had become people, men pulling up food to take home, the fish flashing white out of the thick water.

Sometimes they'd gone to the big museum on the waterfront though he didn't really like it there. On going in the first time it had seemed like a big expanse of shiny floor, a dark shop and stairs. Up the stairs there were lit-up information stands, lights flashing, lights everywhere, yet it had seemed dark. Other people all seemed to be going places—he didn't quite know where—in their walk shoes and fishing hats, their sweatshirts tied to them, backpacks on their backs.

In a darkened area with lights set into the floor, there were glassed-off birds, and forest sounds mixed with wind and sea and tapes of kids' voices, yet everything had seemed dead and still. There were glassed-off fish, a good-sized cray with its tail tucked under, rows of shells, skeletons, skulls and numbered bones of dolphins and whales, seabirds strung up above.

Kid liked it.

On the way out he'd bought her a blow-up dinosaur, and some packets of bugs and insects to take home for her cousins.

'There's more, there's more,' Dion and Miraana had told him that night. 'There's Bush City, Maori Exhibition, Discovery Place, Marae. You have to go up and go out.' So they'd kept going back and he began to enjoy it after a while. Well, he began to enjoy being a father taking his daughter places.

One night after they'd been there a month there'd been a phone call from Archie. It was a Wednesday, two-dollar night, when all the pubs around were selling cheap drinks. People were out on the pavements yelling and laughing and some of them were trying to sing. There was someone screaming up the outside stairway and someone swearing down, so much noise that when the phone rang it had sounded distant. 'I wouldn't mind being out there two-dollar-nighting. Wish it was me out there pissed as a pukeko,' Dion was saying as he left the window to pick up the phone.

'It's for you,' he'd said. 'It's Uncle Archie shouting so loud he doesn't need a phone. Just get up the top of Puketoi and call out, him.'

'They filed for custody,' Archie had told him. 'Couldn't talk them out of it, and reckon they charging you wit' abduction you don't bring her home soon. But keep talking and I reckon they give up in the end. Don't worry Son, we all help you wit' your daughter, help you keep your daughter, you're the one she wants. Don't know why they want her back actually, don't understand that. My sister been giving them a hard time, but ah . . .'

Archie'd had a lot to tell, shouting over the phone about the millennium project—the bookings, the ground preparation, where they'd be getting the water in from. 'Water trucks in every three days to keep the tanks topped up and Bussy's bringing a refrigerated truck in from the removal firm, for food supplies and cold drinks. Bookings, deposits coming in from all over,' he'd said. 'Mostly from Kiwis, some from overseas as well. Got you and Dion down for Waste Management, ha ha—taking stuff to the tip. Jackson and Joeboy too. We got trailers lined up. All go.'

He listened to all that but what he'd really wanted to know about was the weather, the tides, the fishing, how Pop Henry was doing. The millennium business would be two weeks out of his life, then it'd be over and there'd be plenty of good tides after that.

Building the wharekai would be a good buzz, something he'd be able to help with once he had his limb.

'Your cousin brought Remelda and her baby home to live in the pink house,' Arch had told him. 'That ex of hers done his time and she reckons he be after her, out to get Bones, so keeping out of his way. Well our mate Jase is a bit low and he's back home too, travelling to work from here. Never worked out with him and Tina. Gone. Anyway good to see the houses filling up again.'

Wanted to ask about *her*.

'Maina been here with Cass, going over receipts and things, tidying up after her old man. Holding on to $7000 of people's deposits she reckons. Ha, tell you later. Anyway they sorting out who all paid and Maina reckons she's selling the car to pay it back. Ha, you know, when she left him she took the car and hid it at her mate's place. Well, ah, she paid for the car in the first place and put it in her own name, haa. We told her don't sell the car. Wasn't her who pinched the money, and we got a fund. Anyway my sister having a go at getting it off him.'

Later that night when he told Dion that The Aunties had filed for custody of Kid, Dion had become concerned. 'You have to file too,' he'd said, 'otherwise you'll have no power in court. You have to file straight away and it doesn't matter where. I'll take you tomorrow. And you have to get hold of Ani Wainoa, get her to name you as the father. No one needs to know the relationship, but it's dirty business. You have to try and settle it out of court, otherwise the court makes all the decisions, often based on who's not fit to be a parent rather than who *is*.'

Time to go. The final adjustments had been made to the limb, and he'd packed everything ready to head for the station the next morning. Dion, from up above, was saying on this last night, 'So who's going to look after us now on unfood days? All back to our normal starve-o. Anyhow not long and I'll be home eating fish.

Home to the Y2K Christian celebration, big fat Christian sun coming out of the sea bringing us dollars, ha. You could've stayed on a bit Cuz, waited for me. Miraana would've liked that—as you must've noticed. But you . . . Well, if that was me . . . if that was me . . . but she's not interested in me. I used to dream of her and me climbing up my wall together. Suppose I talk too much, suppose she prefers the strong silent type.'

Home.

Back to new millennium.

TWENTY-FOUR

THERE WERE some who reckoned Piiki Chiefy wouldn't have the neck to turn up to a meeting arranged especially for the purpose of stripping him down. They thought it a waste of time setting aside a whole afternoon when there was so much work still to be done.

These disbelievers were the ones who didn't know the man, either because they came from elsewhere and had married into the whanau, or because they were too young to remember the time when PC had made a run for it thirty years before with funds from local rugby.

Others, who knew him better, knew he had plenty of neck, and thought he would probably come to the meeting just to see what he could make out of it. These ones had grown up with him. He was a relative of theirs, and even though he was brought up on the other side they'd all gone to school together, been in the same teams and leapt off banks and bridges into the same water holes. Every now and again when they were kids, a Dogsider had dealt him a biff, probably because he always brought shop bread to school for lunch instead of home-made rewena, and because he always wore shoes. He was never too unhappy about the hits.

There were other kids, always Godsiders, who had shoes too, but they had the sense to remove them and hide them in the bushes as soon as they were out of sight of parents and grandparents. These ones would spend the days barefoot and get the shoes back on their feet before they arrived home at their back doors. In this way they didn't get picked on. It also meant the shoes were seldom worn and could last as long as one wearer and the next could squeeze feet into them. There were some, both Godside and Dogside, who now and again took shop bread to school, but this didn't happen as regularly as with little PC.

Another thing that earned him a slap-down or part drowning every now and again was the way words came out from between his teeth. He had a smart mouth, grew up swanky and gum-chewing, and had long pants by the time he was fourteen that had been handed on to him by a short uncle. He left school at fifteen and got an oily job, which he didn't like, in his uncle's garage.

At about this time he had a girlfriend who used to get up in front of him on his horse on the way to the pictures. He'd let her down in the horse paddock behind the picture theatre, they'd kiss behind the backside of the horse, then she'd join the cousins she was meant to be with and go into the theatre. In there, as well as other kids, would be uncles in cowboy outfits with butcher knives in their belts, aunties in old dresses and broken shoes with babies wrapped in blankets.

After six months at the garage he moved on to work in the dairy factory. He didn't like that either, but he liked having money, which he spent on tight trousers, big jackets, crepe-soled shoes, string ties and oil to stick down and slick back his particularly jumpy hair.

In other words he dressed himself up like a city boy. The dairy factory wasn't for him, but it took him a few years to realise money could be available some other way. He was married with two children by the time he got himself into a position of responsibility in the Rugby Club.

Easy.

Away he went in a new car, with a new woman, leaving Neta and his children to be looked after by his relatives. The ones that set out looking for him to teach him a lesson did so not because of the money he'd stolen but because of Neta and the kids. They never found him.

After some years his name kept coming up in connection with one scam after another, but none of this seemed to make any difference at all to him being given responsible positions in government departments and on advisory boards. It was a laugh, really. Those who'd grown up with him and knew him well couldn't help but have some sneaking admiration for him and thought those who employed him were so stupid that they deserved what they got.

Among those who knew him better and thought it likely he *would* turn up to the meeting, were some who thought such a meeting a waste of time anyway. He'd never part with the seven thou, which had probably been spent already, and they didn't need anything in the way of information from him because they'd been given everything they needed by Maina, who, once she'd decided to put her husband's weights up, had done it in a big way.

In his absence she'd downloaded everything she needed from the computer, picked up a bundle of envelopes containing deposits, emptied the letter box and had all their mail redirected to her father's address. What more did they need?

She'd vacated the house, taking everything she wanted and locking the car away in a friend's garage, because she knew her husband had a spare set of keys and would be looking for it.

Maina hadn't always been a shop assistant. She was trained in office management, had knowledge of the tourist industry and travel and had held down some good jobs prior to marrying this Joe Fingers. It was because of having to uproot and move from place to place that her career and travel plans had been interrupted. She enjoyed her work at DEKA, but was looking out for a position where she could continue with what she'd started out to do. Now she was pleased to be back living with her father and close to her children and had already made up her mind that she was staying put, and that she wasn't ever again going to be a party to any scam, or be supported in any way by crook money.

Not long after their arrival in the city, PC had talked his way onto several committees and had been taken on as a kaumatua in a health project, for which he received a retainer. This work didn't take all his time so it gave him plenty of spare hours to look round for some new venture. He'd always seen opportunities and had good ideas, which in the early days he would outline to Maina with great enthusiasm.

Maina had picked up on those ideas when they first met and had been able to commit them to paper and come up with impressive information leaflets and brochures, for which work he'd led her to understand she'd be paid. She accompanied him to evening and weekend meetings where he introduced her to clients as his business associate, but the operation had ended for clients once money had been taken in, that is, prior to delivery of goods or service.

Instead of a payout he married her and they'd absconded together, though she hadn't realised that they were absconding. Whatever they were doing they were doing it in a beautiful car and she was having a great time speeding about the country living in flash hotels all over the place with this great, new, flash husband. Choice. Every few days she'd send postcards to her father and children telling them what a good time and a great life she was having.

After they'd been on the road for three weeks she'd found herself in a new city looking for a new job. There was no money, nothing in the bank to pay the rent with, so they'd had to sell the car.

It took her a few more years to realise how deeply her husband believed he was entitled to other people's money in exchange for pieces of paper, along with eloquence in any setting, in either or both of his two languages. She'd supported him even after realising what a rip-off he was, because she liked him. Most people did. She loved him actually.

But she had standards. Though still wanting to be his wife there came a time when she wouldn't be his business associate any longer. She insisted on moving into low-rent houses and always paid for everything with money she'd earned herself. He'd had no problem finding other skilled and attractive new associates who would work without being paid and who would go through their own marriage and partnership break-ups in order to enjoy the high life with him for a while.

There came a time too when she didn't want to be his wife any longer, and in anticipation had made a couple of good moves on her own behalf, such as registering the car in her name and making sure she always had access to computer files and data. He wasn't at all unhappy about this because he trusted her—or trusted that he'd always be irresistible to her and that therefore she would always remain attached. She'd left him and gone to her father's on previous occasions but had always returned to him, so it was days before he realised she'd gone for good this time.

He didn't mind too much at first, but he realised once he found the files gone and that the mail had been redirected, that he'd been done over.

At that point he could've done a runner with the seven grand worth of deposits, but decided he should stand his ground for a while, attend the meeting he'd been told by Wai he'd better attend and see if he could salvage anything.

So those who knew him best were right. He had plenty of neck. He came.

It was a warm day, juicy from previous rain, so that in the end even those who had thought it all a waste of time were pleased to leave the work they'd been doing to sit out on the marae for an hour or so in the shade of trees, looking out over rollers free-wheeling in, unbreaking until right on shore. They knew there could be a bit of excitement with Wai in the mood she was in, determined to get those deposits off this relation of theirs, determined she was going to make breakfast of him.

He came accompanied by his new associate who was unaware that, though he had other irons in the fire, this particular iron of business was now non-operational as far as his involvement went.

The new assistant was small with a little, pinkish face and clipped-back, brown hair—pretty and pleasant looking—who laughed every time everyone else laughed even though she knew little of what was going on and nothing of what was being said. She was dressed in a tight fawn jacket and a small skirt, suitable for sitting behind a desk in a quiet office but not for sitting on old seats of rigged-up beach logs out on a marae atea. Not suitable either for an afternoon in the sun. She carried a case containing an electronic notebook and though she didn't get a chance to use it, it wasn't long before she was named for it.

In other words, when people looked across the marae atea to the gate where the two were waiting to be called in, someone standing behind the kaikaranga said in a not-too-quiet whisper, 'He's brought his laptop with him.' This caused the kaikaranga to choke on the first syllable of her call, which is very bad form indeed.

As the two proceeded on to the marae there were some gathered who were getting a good look at him for the first time. From what they'd heard they could've been expecting to see someone shifty or seedy looking, old and falling apart from the weight of sins, maybe someone anxious and uneasy, given the circumstances.

They could have been surprised and would have been impressed by this straight-backed, good-looking man walking towards them. His skin was an even, dark brown, the jumpy hair, dyed black, had been sculpted up round the back and sides of his head and shaped high and flat across the top. At fifty-nine, which was sixteen years older than Maina, he was fit and muscular looking, as though he worked at heaving bricks. He had his swank under control.

When Archie got up to make the welcome speech he said the equivalent of: Greetings, indeed, greetings. We all welcome you with open arms and open hearts. He paid his respects to the dead after which he recited PC's genealogy for the information of everyone, and gave a little of the history re the boy with shop bread, shoes, teddy-boy outfits and how they nearly drowned him. Even those who believed this whole meeting to be a waste of time were pleased they'd come along for a bit of entertainment.

Arch warmly welcomed the new business associate, then spoke of the intention of the meeting in general terms. But as he concluded he became more specific and told PC he was there so they could turn his pockets inside out, turn him upside down and shake him, do him over. Good laughs for all including PC and the associate. And so welcome to you on this beautiful day, welcome, welcome, indeed welcome was how Arch concluded his greetings.

After the formalities were over they moved into the meeting house and during the course of the afternoon PC had it explained to him what had been done with the information that Maina had given them and where they were up to with preparations. This was all by way of warm-up. After that had gone on long enough they came to the main reason for the meeting.

What they wanted was the seven grand worth of deposits that he had pocketed.

He wasn't giving it.

'Just think of it as payment for the work I did,' he said when it was his turn to speak. 'It was a lot of work getting site plans out of local council, making the grid, setting up promotions, advertising on the Net, keeping it secret. And there were expenses too. I'll tell you what, I could send you an invoice and you could write it all off, paid. You'd be getting a bargain.'

'But who did all that work anyway?' someone asked. 'You or your associate?'

'Ideas,' he said, 'are the most important ingredient in any new venture. Unless someone has the idea, nothing happens. People pay good money for ideas.'

'Not these people.'

'And I could do more for you,' he said without even one drop of sweat running off him. 'I can offer experience, expertise . . .'

'And an opportunity to get your hands on . . .'

They were brown polished-looking hands that placed themselves palm upwards in different spaces about him as he spoke. They flew up sometimes, flew out sometimes, sometimes up and out. Or they rested, lightly knuckled, on hips, or came together quite close to his chin or to his heart, though nothing was too overdone. Anyway it was his face people were all most interested in, and his lit eyes. He seemed to be having a good time.

There were some, as they listened, who came to believe he could be useful, mainly the ones who didn't know him. They liked his clothes and his teeth. It was true he had ideas and experience, and they needed every bit of help they could get. Even some of those who knew him well began to wonder if he should be given a chance.

'To what?' Wai asked. 'A chance to what? No. There's help we can use, there's help we can do without.' Then she said, 'He's in, I'm out.'

No one wanted that. OK, out with him. But to return to the matter of seven thousand dollars, what if they went to the police? 'I'm not illegal enough,' PC said with teeth, but not too overdone. 'You'd have a job pinning anything on me. Besides it would cost you money to take me to court . . . anyway you're too busy. You wouldn't have time.'

All of this talk was being sent up to the rafters on fits and blasts of laughter, looping up and around and hanging there. 'I mean give us a break, you're going to make sixty thousand clear if you do it right, jeepers have a heart. I could've got off with most of that after giving you your cut if I hadn't trained my dear ex to be so smart. I mean you've probably got your fifteen thousand dollar millennium venture grant from the Runanga for setting up, that is for your toilets and tank and site preparation. You're probably going to provide food, have stalls, hangis etcetera, that you'll charge good prices for. You'll do sixty or seventy, eighty if you do it right. You got a free work force. No, no, gimme a break. You don't need to strip me down, my wife already did a good job of that. You've got my wife working for you and she's one of the best. I reckon you should pay me another seven. I'll send an invoice.'

This was all attaching to the rafters and fattening them, and it was also attaching to Wai's ears. There was plenty of useful information in that lot, and a few good ideas too. So even Wai seemed to be chilling out, had a few teeth showing there, couldn't help it. She knew it had gone as far as it could and that they weren't going to get toenail out of him.

'So when are you leaving town?' Wai asked in recognition that the discussions were over and to get a last crack at him.

'When I get me a seven thousand dollar car, ha, ha.'

And because the time had now come for his waiata he stepped across and took the guitar from Jase and began to sing 'Release Me', which was yet another reason for rafters holding their sides.

Release him?

Let him go?

Haa, OK. At least they'd given him a bit of going over, a run for his money—this Joe Fingers, this tangata whai haere panekoti.

Or had they?

Well at least they'd all had a good time, and anyway there was one thing their crook relation wasn't going to get away with, not if Cass had anything to do with it. They could see Cass having a word in the ear of the business assistant, giving her the message to take herself off, release herself from this no-good crook.

Let him love again?

Doubt it, or not this time. Cass was actually walking Business Assistant out the door to make a getaway. Ha, good one. Good day.

As PC took the song up a chord they all joined in.

TWENTY-FIVE

THERE WAS no one round when he and Kid arrived home ahead of a carrier bringing furniture and a fridge from the furniture mart, but on going into the house he found it had been cleaned. All the floors, walls, cupboards and benches had been washed down ready for his arrival.

All done, so he went off down to the marae where he knew they they'd all be working. It was a long time since he'd gone there on two feet—not even a limp according to Clarrie, the limb fitter at the Centre, wheeling about, eyeing up this angle, that angle.

An office had been set up in the wharenui. A few old tables had been brought in for a computer, telephone and other office equipment.

'Paper, paper,' Wai said. 'Not my thing, paper. My office? All up here,' tapping her head.

'Maina helped us with all this,' Cass said. 'Mmm, it's Maina who got all this up and running,' planting her eyes hard into him.

'Trained Eva up,' Wai said. 'Set up a system and Eva doing most of the computer stuff now she's finished at Polytech for the year.'

'Left her job,' Cass said, 'Maina, to look after her father and help us out. She brings the old man with her when she comes, Hani Silver. Hard case.'

'So we got all this in here in the meantime, crossing our fingers we don't have to move it . . . So don't anyone die,' Wai said raising her voice from the conversation they were having to include those around, 'otherwise we got to shift all this stuff out. You all keep healthy 'til mid January, you hear.'

'Yourself,' Arch said, 'you and your triple bypass. Keep going like this your ticker'll do for you. *You* making us shift all this. *You* face up out there on the veranda.'

'Not 'til I see this dining room up. Nice roof. All having the hakari for me in a nice wharekai after you put me under. Nice windows. Nothing out in tents, no cooking in the rain. Out of the heat, out of the cold, all gas and refrigeration. No melted jellies and no fly blows.'

Over at the paddocks the existing ablution block had been renovated and extended and a new block was being built on the far side. There was groundwork being done for two new water tanks to be installed.

'Then we need a few good downpours to fill 'em,' Archie said, 'or we be buying water in . . . And, ah, give you a day or two, Son, and we could do with another builder round the place, someone knows which end of the hammer.'

'Got our stuff coming this afternoon, carrier on its way, and first thing tomorrow got to go and have a talk with the lawyer. After that . . . '

'Plenty time, when you ready.'

'Get the beds and stuff into the house, later go and get our fish. Thinking of fish while I'm away and thinking how the weather must be warming up . . . Anyway before all that, before I go to the lawyer got to go and have a talk to those Aunties, see if I can talk them round.'

'Ahh, we been missing our fish. Too busy. Atawhai's nephews

come with a few fish one day. But mmm . . . don't know about those two, Brad and Horomona. Out a lot in their uncle's boat but . . .'

So what was that supposed to mean? Arch with something on his mind but then changing the subject.

'We come wit' you when you go have your korero with Babs and Amiria,' Arch said. 'Humbug those two.'

Pop Henry was there sitting on a chair under a sun umbrella his old face lit up by all the energy around. The carrier was arriving and Kid was coming up from the beach with Kutu.

Home in water, into the channels where fish moved about feeding in the stir of full tide—moki in and out of the dark places and maumau rising in bunches and dropping again, red and blue among the boulders and anemones the colours of gardens. Moving in close he pointed the tip of his spear to the gills of a large moki, loosing the spring then thrusting upwards to take the weight of the fish.

From the rocks, as he climbed out to put the moki in the bag, he could see that Kid, Georgie and Hinewai were doing well pulling in maumau on his handline. Two more big moki and whatever the kids got would be enough for them to carry home along the tracks.

There was still enough daylight left when they'd cleaned the fish so he left the kids on shore and put the spear gun down by the limb instructing it to keep guard. 'Ha, ha, ha,' the kids clutched their speared, leg-stealing hearts and fell down dead in the shingle.

He went into the water again exploring the bases of the rocks and the crevasses before breaking out of the channel and heading for the deep, swimming like he had gills, small fish churning the surface about him. On to the far cray rocks where only the tips showed above the high water, he came across crays that had been lured from their holes, their pale undersides spotting the water that had already begun to darken.

On the far side of the rocks he discovered the buoys, and when he went down saw that the pots were already full—too deep and too heavy for him to be able to do anything on his own.

It was already too late to get help and by the time the tide went down it would be too dark to see. All he could do was speak up tomorrow when Brad and Horomona came with the crays, knowing the brothers would only bring a few of the fish not wanting anyone to know how many they really had, or to know they'd been setting pots in the cove.

Other things to do before that. Get Kid and her cousins home, then after tea go and see The Aunties. School in the morning for his daughter, and into the city for him, to meet Heke Norman. And while he was in the city there were a few more things he needed to get for the house, but he'd have to go easy on the spending. The stay in Wellington had eaten into his compo.

More, at the moment, than water, but there'd always be water.

TWENTY-SIX

'WELL, WHERE is she?' Amiria asked after he'd greeted them, given them their fish and talked for a while about the leg and the millennium. The two were preparing for one of their meetings. Chairs and cushions were ready in the lounge and one of the oil burners had been lit, giving off an essence of he didn't know what. They were in the kitchen with their knives and chopping boards.

'With her cousin at Moana's,' he said. 'We got to talk about her, about us . . . all this business . . . '

'Our lawyer's all geared up,' Babs said. 'All we got to do is give her the word and there'll be abduction charges. If it hadn't been for Wai . . .'

'No need for it.'

'So that means you're bringing her back then?'

'Ah, no, not what I meant.'

'Well?'

'Look, Wai must've said . . .'

'You, her father? You're a little liar, Rua.' Babs was whipping up dip, scraping cream cheese and yoghurt out of their containers into the kitchen whiz with a spatula, turning the machine on then sliding chopped peppers and onions off the board and into it with her ringed fingers.

'And a thief, just wanting something that doesn't belong to you and no business of yours.' Amiria was spooning savoury filling into bread cases.

There was something he wasn't understanding here and he was now regretting he'd decided not to bring Arch and Wai with him. Liar and thief? They must know, laying out celery and carrot sticks, pulling apart a difficult plastic packet to tumble chippies into a bowl, that he wasn't lying.

'Look I don't know . . . I come to tell you I got a lawyer. I come to tell you I've gone for custody too, but we don't need . . . look here we can sort it.' He was grateful now that he'd taken Dion's advice because there was something funny going on. Why would they think he'd make up something like that? He made himself keep calm. 'We could ring Ani Wainoa,' he said.

'Who is a liar and cracked in the head,' Babs said.

'Look, look, we can sort it.'

'Yes, easy. Bring her back here.'

'Look . . . look I'm her father and she's staying with me. You go to court, you lose.'

'She belongs to us. She was given to us. It's in our mother's will. You're the one needs sorting.'

'She's not earrings,' he said, which was all he could think of saying just then. He could feel his voice rising which was not what he wanted to happen. 'Not earrings to be dished out like when someone dies. She's a . . . daughter, my daughter.'

Amiria pulled down the oven door, shoved the trays of savouries in, banged the door shut and began clawing the trimmed crusts off the cutting board and into the scrap bucket for Archie's pigs. The dips and platters were away in the fridge, dirty dishes in the sink and Babs was washing the table down in large swoops with a wet cloth.

'And, and it's not right for *her*, arguing, scrapping over her,' he said, 'We can sort it.'

'Up to you.'

'Otherwise, all out of our hands. We got no say if the court decides.'

'You don't want a scrap you know what to do.'

Worse than he thought.

'Ring Ani Wainoa,' Wai said when he told her about his conversation with Babs and Amiria. 'Get her father's number from Directory— Lance Wainoa. She keeps in touch with him, or used to.'

So he was given the number by Directory Service and when he rang it Lance Wainoa was able to give him the number in Norway. He listened to the call going through knowing Ani Wainoa could lie to him.

What Ani told him was that she'd named him as father on the registration form and that his name was on the birth certificate. 'I found it more difficult to tell lies when filling out a form,' she said. 'I was going to enter Stefan down as the father but didn't know his last name, and anyway all we'd ever done together was ride bumper cars. I could've put "unknown" but didn't think of it.'

She told him about Harald whom she'd met in Auckland and fallen in love with. 'We journeyed to his homeland on this other side of the world,' she said. 'I'll never return to Aotearoa because I love it here so much. I adore this salted land, the black mountains and the deep cold water that is too mysterious for me to ever step into. I love the snow and the dark winters and the way people make light. I love not knowing the time of day. The sun in summer chases itself in a little circle, just like Toss going after fleas on his tail, and there's all the rush and excitement to be outside when the sun comes. I'm in a story here. This is my story now and I shall never return, but you are my true sibling, my utmost companion and friend deep in my heart. You would be welcome here if you would like to come and bring my niece with you.'

Her niece? He thought of Ani Wainoa ten years earlier, imagined her in a dark room in a white dress filling out the form in her perfect handwriting—Wainoa, comma, Ani. Tapaerangi, comma, Te Rua. After she'd gone there'd been something missing in the water, echoing spaces in the cove, something gone from in the trees.

Some months after she left her father she had rung Wai to say she'd gone to Auckland to meet up with Stefan. He hadn't heard much after that except that she'd married—Harald, not Stefan—and gone to live in Norway. That much had turned out to be true.

TWENTY-SEVEN

KID.

Her face came round the door as he woke. Black candle eyes and spider lashes.

'School,' she said, damp hair clipped back with hearts and diamonds.

'Up already?' Her lips parted, showing the tips of her teeth and her shoulders went up until her neck disappeared.

'You better get your leg on,' she said.

He hopped about getting what he needed, went to the bathroom and when he came out she had their cups and plates on the table, the Weetbix box on the bench and was making toast. Didn't take much looking after for sure. Kutu was out whispering in the porch.

Clothes, shoes, clips for her hair, a lunchbox and pens but didn't know about books or money. 'Go down Aunty Moana's and ask Georgie what else you need,' he said when they'd eaten.

'A note,' she said. 'Got to have a note for being away.'

Well, he didn't know what the teachers had been told about her absence from school and thought he'd go along to Moana's with her to see if he could find out.

Then he decided he would drop Kid and the others off at school on his way to Turanganui so he could call in and explain her absence to the teacher, find out if there was anything she needed. He could see Kid was pleased that he was taking her to school, maybe because she liked to ride in the car but maybe because she liked having a father who could take her.

'Get a copy of the birth certificate,' Heke Norman said, 'and I'll get your Aunts' lawyer to talk them out of laying the abduction charges. If you're the father as you say, and as the mother says, then maybe it won't be a problem . . . but it would be good to have a letter from the mother too, agreeing that you should have custody. I'll leave that to you. We don't want this getting to the main court. If you can't sort it between you we'll try family conference first, where people are brought together with their respective lawyers and whanau support. We'll try and talk things through, try to come to an out-of-court agreement. Family conference works pretty well, especially if there's no deep animosity. Do you think The Aunties'll come round?'

'I think so. Not too worried. My girl wants to stay with me, and others support it, so . . . '

'I'll get things moving. You get the letter from the mother and we'll see if we can arrange a session before Christmas.'

He left the lawyer's office and drove through a city that was preparing to make its mark on the new millennium. Couldn't be bothered with it. Also couldn't be bothered with lawyers, family conferences or any of that and believed Amiria and Babs would give up once they understood they had no one on side. They'd have to, especially once they knew about the birth certificate—unless Ani Wainoa was lying, but he didn't think so. After all, they didn't really want Kid. It wasn't as though they showed any love for her. So what . . . Why?

As he drove past DEKA he thought of Maina who'd left there now, but wondered how it would be if he called in to see her at her father's place. The turn-off was only a couple of streets away—someone to talk to about all this. Or it could just be an excuse to see her, wet pup stuff?

He passed the turn-off thinking that he needed to sort his head out himself, find a place in his head, like a water place, a place of suspension where he could begin to pick his way along looking for what was missing in his discussions with Amiria and Babs who had called him a liar and a thief. He could think of *her* if he wanted to for a while, but mainly he had to be a father and sort out about Kid. It's what he'd decided and what he was going to concentrate on once he'd dealt with one other matter, and that was just to get it into someone's ear about the cray pots.

When he walked into the tent where all the workers were having lunch he saw that Maina was there sitting up the far end drinking tea with Cass, and though people kept doing what they were doing the voices quietened as he went in because of what they *knew*, because of what the trees had told on the morning that Cass had come to pick up Maina.

Her father was sitting just inside the tent flap tipping his head back laughing down past his tonsils at something he and Arch had been talking about.

No crays on the lunch table.

He went to greet Hani Silver, bending so they could press their noses together.

'See there, Son,' Archie said, 'you couldn't a done that without your bionic, not without falling in his lap.'

'True, it's true,' he said.

'Come on show us then, give us a demo,' Hani said.

So he pulled up his pants leg and did a knees bend and waewae takahia, 'And see that Matua,' he said, 'no toe-jam.'

'That's a fact,' Hani Silver said.

'No go for kina prickles, no stone bruises.'

'True, no prickles, no bruises, ah.'

'Raupa.'

'No raupa, true.'

'Plastic fantastic,' Arch said with a great deal of pride.

Making his way round the inside of the tent, he stopped to greet two cousins who hadn't been there the day before when he arrived. It was hot away from the open side, and now as he came nearer to where Maina was sitting with Cass everything was getting quieter because they were all waiting, watching him.

'So it was you started all this, all this Y2K stuff?' he called to her, needing to say something to break it all up as he went towards her.

'Blame me, blame me.' She stood and they hugged each other quickly while the noise and talk got back to normal. Bones brought him a fresh bowl of food as he sat down at the table opposite Maina and Cass. No crays.

'How is she, little Kiri? The arm?'

'Healed up. A few scars, but going to fade they reckon.'

'And tell us,' Cass said, 'you been to your lawyer. I was telling Maina.'

So he told about his morning. 'Heke wants us to do some more talking to The Aunties. Got it in for me those two, but we don't want it to go to court.'

Maina stood up to go and refill her own and Cass's cups. Eyes were on her, on him, but people were beginning to move, pick up their dishes, swing their legs over the long forms they were sitting on.

'I want youse all to know,' Hani Silver said for them all to hear, turning on his chair so that he could see everyone. Those sitting at the tables turned their heads towards the big voice. The ones on the move, scraping dishes or standing at the tubs, stopped talking, stopped rattling and kept their ears open, uh oh, here's a go.

'Want youse to know it's not me. Not me stopping them.'

Maina, who was turning away from the tea urn with the cups, stopped and put them on a nearby table, sat and propped her elbows, resting her head on the tips of her fingers getting her face out of the way.

The old man was patting his heart. Here's a go.

'Nothing to do with this here, this here ticker, why she stops with me, why she give up her job, all that. If we want her to be a nun we send her to a convent, ne? Just because she give that relation of yours . . .'

'Ha, have a go Hani.'

'. . . that relation of yours the shove . . .'

'She did true enough.'

'Don't mean she got to be a nun.'

'A fact, Hani Silver.'

'So why not? She don't have to stop with me, no reason, free any time she likes. Or he can come down our place anytime. There's a home there for him and his daughter anytime, else the works gets rusty, ne?'

'True, it's true.'

As Hani went on the heat was getting up through his neck and into his head and he wanted to be in water striking out for the deep, knew the old man wasn't really joking. Maina had stopped leaning, wasn't sure what to do but he could see she wanted to put an end to it.

'Come on, come on, I'm offering . . .' Hani went on.

'Well Dad you see, there's others . . . could be . . .' Maina said.

'Offering my daughter . . .'

'Or there will be, should be, for sure. I mean . . .'

'Not interested,' he stood and said to save her, but also because he meant it. It popped clear out of water, clear out of his mouth and clean into silence.

Silence, when there should've been noise. Should've been five-ups, ten-ups and noise but there was something wrong. He realised they'd got him wrong, thought he meant he wasn't interested in *her*, like throwing the old man's words back at him and insulting his daughter.

'I mean . . . I mean . . . in them,' he said, 'not interested in those . . . those whoever . . . those other, or whatever.' His heart was knocking and he wasn't saying it too good but they got it right this time and there was hee yoo, yoo hee, ha, ha, banging on the tables. You said it, slapping themselves, trestles crashing, faaar out. Up fives and tens.

'He's like that,' she said as he walked back with her to her car, Hani following behind them with Cass and Archie. 'You never know what he'll come out with. Just one of those types . . . doesn't hold back. But I was always happy living with him. When I was a kid, and when my kids were kids those were the best times. The rest? All full of mistakes and bad decisions.'

He didn't say anything. He'd told her all he wanted her to know, a way having come for him to do it in front of everybody without it being all wet pup stuff, without it hanging anything on her.

'Don't trust myself any more,' she said. 'And for you . . . I mean . . . Also there are things I need to do, always wanted to do, just me. I reckon it's time.'

He wanted her to know it was all right. 'Me too,' he said.

Arch and Cass stood with him watching the car as it went along the road and turned the corner, then they all began making their way back to the paddocks where the work was going on.

'Couldn't help it,' Cass was saying. 'Couldn't help knowing. The two of you come out of the trees that other morning lit up like birthday candles.'

'Where's all the crays?' he asked.

'Out in the rocks and weed getting fat, you think?' Arch said.

Cass said, 'What crays?'

'Two pots set out in the cove yesterday. Both full. Tried to get to them but too deep, too heavy. I couldn't . . .'

Arch stopped in his tracks, then turned, swearing mouthfuls, heading for a telephone to ring Atawhai.

TWENTY-EIGHT

HE HALF listened as Clive Redding pointed out, in the pink room where stacker chairs had been arranged in a part circle to keep them all in eye contact with each other, the reasons for a family conference such as this.

'Opportunity for discussion so that hopefully the parties come to a satisfactory point of agreement where arrangements can be made in the best interests of the child, or children, as the case may be,' Clive said.

Waste of time.

Clive was small and brushy. He had thick, standing-up hair which was white specked with black like seagull shit; clumps of black eyebrows; eyes close together like a flounder with a good-sized honk in between. Fit and tanned, a serious boaty in his spare time most likely. Get on with it, Clive.

'The court option of course removes the power from concerned parties.' I'm a party, my own party. 'Once court proceeds, decisions are taken out of parties' hands.' But he had to make himself listen, get serious, get the hang of all this . . . all this waste of time.

Amiria and Babs were wearing their best outfits, Amiria in her dark clothes, good shark's teeth hanging from her ears and a new curly hair-do; Babs done up pink, the colour of walls, gold bells on chains hanging from her ears and the same curly hair-do as her sister. There were rows of rings on the thin fingers of Amiria and the tube fingers of Babs, and these fingers were clutched over tops of handbags as though they clung to the tops of walls.

All adding up to serious. Ready for a fight. But why?

Wai, Arch, Tini and the rest of them were all togged up too, though not quite so wedding-looking as Amiria and Babs. Party, party. They were there to support him, so why were Babs and Amiria keeping all this up when they could see the support he was getting, when they'd been told by Arch and Wai to let Kid go. Why let it all go this far?

'It's about families owning decisions.'

You already said that, Clive.

But serious. He wished he'd worn better clothes, hoped he looked serious enough in his tee shirt and jeans, but then this wasn't a court they kept being reminded. It was them as a family sorting it out themselves, but they were all having trouble getting used to the idea that it was in their own hands for now.

'About power remaining with the families, keeping in mind the best interest of the family member under discussion. In this case the concern is the custody of Kiri. We need to bear in mind at all times the best possible outcome for the child.'

All that, all that, but they could've sorted this out at home. And even if they did have to go to court Heke Norman didn't see a problem, not with evidence so far.

'It depends what else comes out,' Heke had been careful to say, but what else was there?

'In front of me,' said Clive, 'are reports filed by Cath Wyman, solicitor representing Miss Amiria Rapira and Miss Toi Rapira, by Heke Norman representing Te Rua Tapaerangi, and there's a brief statement from Martin Henderson for Kiri Te Rina Wainoa. While

I am not here to present cases, but rather to act as a facilitator, my suggestion is that I give a summary of the three documents by way of beginning discussion, if that suits everyone?' He had a good big smile and he was doing his teeth in all directions. Rolled sleeves, a happy tie.

'It's all for user-friendliness,' said Dion at the tea break. 'All this too. Tea, coffee, Shrewsberry biscuits.'

'In brief,' said Clive, 'Rua has taken exception to what he sees as poor treatment of Kiri who he claims is his daughter. He has presented evidence of fatherhood in the form of a copy of the birth certificate which names him as the father of Kiri, as well as a letter from the mother.'

'A liar all her life,' said Babs out of her duck-bum mouth, with Amiria glaring her down.

'And now wishes to claim parenthood and to have custody of his daughter. The report from Cath Wyman points out that her clients, yourselves, Miss Amiria and Miss Toi, have had full care of Kiri since her birth when your mother first brought her home as a newborn baby. There's a statement regarding the relationship of yourselves, Miss Amiria and Miss Toi, to the child, which I believe is known to you all. So . . .' He put his eyes around, put his smile around, 'so I don't need to . . . Amiria and Toi have given reasons why they believe Kiri has been well cared for by them.'

Since when? He wants to call it out but is aware of Dion's hand on his arm.

'And the interim statement from Kiri's representative, who however has not yet had the time to make conclusive judgments, does not contradict anything that they have claimed so far.' But that's not the opinion of Wai, Arch, Tini, Atawhai—or anyone at home. He wants one of them to say something.

'I have to emphasise that the discussion is over to you. My role is as overseer. I can help in matters of law interpretation, and I'd like you to know I have had several years' experience in matters of custody and in meetings such as these. I'm not here to make judgments.'

User-friendly teeth.

Now Arch was up on his feet thanking this Clive on and on, thanking him first, then remembering this building from the old days when it was Maori Affairs and he used to come to visit his uncle who worked there. Brought eels in for his uncle's lunch, his uncle who is still alive today.

Life of uncle.

History of the building's insides, which have all been refurbished now. Refurbished, refurbished, he could tell Arch liked the sound of the word. Big noisy fans in the ceiling back then. Clive was waiting, nodding, showing user-friendly. Arch walked along the riverbanks sometimes with uncle during lunch time, this uncle chewing eel.

Come on, Arch.

One time the river came up and crossed the road, Arch remembers. He remembers the winter of which year, but came back at last to thanking User Friendly and getting to it, getting to it at last.

'I want to talk to our nieces here.' The two were looking down at rings. 'We know, we know, all of us older ones here, it was you two done everything. We know that. Everything for your mother, everything for the baby she come home with. Even with your mother still alive it was you two.'

On and on praising them up—their sick mother, their cooking, their cleaning, their life history. They could've done all this at home without Clive and his palmy tie. 'Always you.' Praising them up, all that, then at last, 'Now we think it's time she went to her father.'

Babs and Amiria looked up from rings, not looking at Arch, but staring hard instead at pink walls, and at the floor that had been sanded down as far as insect tunnels.

Hard as boards.

Wai spoke in support of her brother. Atawhai spoke in support of his two cousins. Nothing at all was said about the burnt arm, about Kid being left like that, or about her being locked out in the dark. Tini was peering round at faces but saying nothing, there to support him but it was all half-arsed as far as he could see. Made him wild.

'We see she's happy with her father,' Arch said, which was more like it, more like it.

'We see he's serious, able to look after her,' Wai said. More like it, but nothing they couldn't have said among themselves at home. 'And we're all here to see to it.' OK but didn't need to be in a place like this to tell it.

'No way.' The Sisters' eyes were up off floorboards, away from walls and latched hard onto Wai. 'No way.'

'Her father, we all know it,' Arch said.

'A snatcher and a thief.'

Atawhai's hand was on his arm keeping him quiet. Dion's mouth was by his ear shutting him up and Clive was butting in. 'One of my roles of course is to help keep discussion on track, not that we want to prevent talk from taking place. If you think the pathway that we're on at the moment needs further exploration then . . . go there by all means. I'll just point out that allegations of abduction could be set aside from matters of custody, could be separate to final outcomes regarding Kiri.'

'Given to us,' Babs said.

'Now *he* wants her,' Amiria said.

'Thinks he can, thinks he can . . .'

'Your mother . . .' Tini said, speaking for the first time.

'Was dying,' Amiria said. 'And she brought the baby home to us. Kiri was given to us.'

Given to me, given to me, but he wasn't being allowed to say it. Atawhai was talking hard in his ear, telling him to bite his tongue, but how could he?

'My nieces, my darlings . . .' Tini said, which meant she was about to say something hard into the hard faces of Amiria and Babs while they all waited, waited, waited, 'Your mother treated you the way her father treated her sisters.'

'She loved us, she loved us,' said Babs out of her round mouth while her ball of fist hammered against her chest.

'She gave us everything,' said Amiria with her teeth unclenched and her throat opening. 'Ai-ii, Ai-ii Ai-ii,' came off pink walls, off insect floors, off the ceiling where the fan used to toddle round and round.

'Now look what you've done,' Babs shouted, accusing Tini, accusing Clive, accusing them all.

But why?

Then Babs sagged onto the handbag and rings joining in the Aii, Aii, Aii, while Tini and Wai moved to put their arms round the two of them. Nothing about Kid, nothing at all.

'I suggest,' said Clive, 'a break for lunch or . . . or . . . we could call it a day.'

Waste of time. And anyway if he wasn't allowed to say anything he might as well go home.

TWENTY-NINE

THE MURAL Te Whakawhititanga o Ngarua, much to the annoyance of some of the people, had become a noticeboard. Weren't there other walls, plain walls, that could've been used for the display of calendars, timetables, brochure samples, lists, budgets and rosters? And now today a big drawing had been put up which had coloured spots all over it and which covered most of the canoe and half of Ngarua.

'Ah shame you know, all that painting, all that good work done by our tamariki,' someone said. 'And now look—Sellotape, pins. One stuck right in the bum of Maraenohonoho's horse.'

'Ugly horse anyway,' someone else said.

'Nnnn, come to that whole thing's blimmin' ugly.'

'Paint it over after this I reckon, mmm, after all this lot comes down.'

'No way.'

'Look here, that there's work done by our own kids.'

'Had it. Scabby.'

'Well, a bit flaky. Mmm, cracking up but just needs doing up that's all, her face, her hair, all that whole door.'

'Uh not if I get there first with a big paint brush.'

'Look here . . .'

But these were only mumbles, nothing rafter-worthy, nothing much different from what had been expressed from the time the painting was completed twenty years earlier. It was just people talking, settling themselves while waiting for Wai to start the business. Since when did they need all this paper anyway? And what *was* this latest sheet, taking up half the mural, all colours?

'Site plan,' someone said. 'Stickers showing all the places that's been booked up already.'

'Aaaay?'

'Well that's something.'

'All them coming here?'

'Is that right?'

'That's something.'

During the meeting with PC on that Please-release-me-day, the day the hui went huri haere, Wai had picked up on some of the things that the crook relation of theirs had said about bringing in extra funds. She was a little concerned because registrations had slowed down recently and later she'd talked matters over with Maina.

'See, looks like there's a bit of resistance at the moment,' Maina said. 'Maybe all the hype, all the advertising about bringing people from all over the world to this part of the world so they can be the first in the world to see the Y2K sun, or dawn, or whatever, is scaring some people off.'

Wai thought this might be true. Talk of huge crowds, inflated prices, everybody drowning, being in slow traffic, having car accidents, being mugged by yobbos at midnight could be keeping a lot of people at home.

So they revised their plans, deciding to keep the registration prices down but to think about what they could provide on site for the holidaymakers.

'Get them here first, then fleece them, you mean, like our relation told us?' someone asked.

'Well, more like, if we have the stuff for them here they won't have to bring it themselves or keep going off somewhere else for milk, bread, whatever,' Wai said.

'Ah, so we could order in, keep it cheap, sell to them.'

'You got it.'

'We could cook.'

'Put a hangi down.'

'Live music. You know, get Eddie's band along.'

'Fishing contest.'

'Barbecue.'

'Bonfires.'

'Well, ah, in that case,' Maina said, 'I think we need to sort out a new message.'

The building of the toilet and shower block was now completed and all the cleaning and weed-eating and site preparation had been done. All looking good, and the least of their worries, Wai thought. There was to be food available from the refrigerated truck—milk, butter, eggs, bottled water, drinks. But also there'd be space in there where campers could keep their own supplies.

Frozen goods, such as meat packs, packaged ice-cream and ice-blocks had already been delivered and stored in Arch and Cass's freezer, which they'd set up under a canopy with a lead running to it from the wharenui.

In other freezers, cut up and packed down for the hangi, were two of Archie's pigs, mutton that had been donated by the Confederated Land Block, and chickens that a nephew had been able to get cheap from the factory where he worked. All of this didn't leave much space for the bait packs that Rua and the kids had made up ready for the fishing competition, and they'd had to stop collecting at least until after hangi day when there'd be room again.

Later that day stalls were to be put up for the sale of crafts, hotdogs, Amiria and Babs's cakes and bread. The Two had been hard at it baking and freezing in case 'fresh daily' supplies ran out. All this made them smile and rush about, wheelying round the place in their gold-top car.

The new Internet advertising that Maina did for them showed a picture of a full sweep of the bay with breakers coming in in loose curls onto a shadowy early morning beach, and the red-eye sun coming up out of the sea winking stripes across the water and blood-shotting the whole big sky. This is what visitors could hope to see on the first new millennium morning, that is if it didn't rain. New information sheets made known the privacy and safety of the location, the availabilty of refrigeration, good facilities, food and meals as well as planned family activities. There would be no inflated prices.

There hadn't been a lot of time to get the new message out, do all the preparation and find all the help they needed for the added services they were providing that would bring in dollars. Well, Wai's point of view was to bring in dollars. Everyone else, it seemed to her, had forgotten about fundraising and the dining room and were all buzzing about their cakes, their bonfires and hangis and fishing, and everyone having a good time.

'The putea, the putea,' she kept reminding them. 'Of course run a good show, give them all a good time, but don't forget what for. Dollars. We're not doing all this for nothing.'

Now, with Christmas Day behind them and only two days to go before the arrival of the first lot of campers, Wai was hoping they'd get through this last meeting, this nuts-and-bolts stuff, without too much time being wasted on unimportant matters. However right now an argument had sprung up about whether or not to charge campers for fridge space for their kai. The home people wouldn't hear of it and they were stuck on that when there was so much else to be discussed.

'Charging our guests for space. Space is nothing.'

'And the truck cost nothing.'

'Except petrol to get here. Except power to run it.'

'All you ones from the city, what you need to do is come back home for a while and get your ideas straight.'

'Nobody said overcharge but . . .'

'Look here, it's our visitors we're talking about.'

'Fine, long as they know they're our visitors, which makes us their hosts, not their servants, running round after them for bugger all.'

That came from big-mouth Dion who had no respect for elders, people thought. He had some support from round the room though, mainly coming from city cousins who all had funny attitudes. No aroha.

On and on, all the usual stuff, but although Wai wanted to get on to some of the more major items she was wary of cutting anyone off, needing to keep everyone on side.

'How about koha then?' someone said. Ah, compromise. 'Put out an ice-cream container. Those who want to give something will give, others won't. Write "koha" on it . . .'

'But, you know, these people coming are mostly Pakeha, Hapanihi, Merikana, Tiamana and don't know about this koha business, don't even know the meaning of the word.'

'Well write "donation". . .'

'But, but, but why? Why should we compromise our language . . . ?'

Usual stuff. Wai waited.

'Ahh, come on man.'

'Compromise our language . . . for Americans, for . . . '

'Give us a break, Cuz.'

'But he's got a point.'

'Yeah, come on, give us a break. Half the morning gone and we're stuck on refrigerated truck.'

'True, kei te haere te taima.'

'Let's agree on koha,' Wai said, taking her chance, 'Koha, and whoever's organising the space, whoever's looking after the fridge truck can decide what gets written on the box. OK?'

'OK.'

'We move on. Barbecue packs. Another hundred?'

Nothing too rafter-worthy in all this. Ah um, from rafters, with two days to go.

It was like watching a great and animated version of the coloured stickers, which over the previous weeks had gone up on to the site drawing in the wharenui. Caravans, trucks, camper-vans and cars of all colours, some dragging boats and trailers and loaded to the windows, made their way along the beach road, through the newly formed gateway backing in between the pegs that marked out the sites allocated to them. Out of the vehicles came people in this summer's shorts, tees and hats, with their shades, sandals, sunblock, insect repellent and water bottles. There were kids taking up boogie boards because indeed there were waves, yesss.

Who were they all?

Well, while it was true that a few of the visitors were from Japan, America and Germany as the planners had mostly in mind and who they often mentioned, most were from Auckland or Wellington or somewhere in between. These were regular campers, some of whom had been annoyed to find that the free beach sites that they'd been going to every summer for many years were now being charged for. They got huffy about that and decided that if they were going to pay they'd pay elsewhere, and had come across this place on the Net, which looked great, sounded great and wasn't too expensive. They had come to sus it out. Now they were here and it looked as if the advertising was all true so far. Great bay and surf, good loos and showers, cool storage for your beers and stuff.

Tents of all shapes and sizes and colours grew, along with the additional awnings, windbreaks, umbrellas and gazebos. To furnish all of this, out of boots, back seats and from off roof racks and in no time at all, came stretchers, tables, chairs, camp stoves, chilly-bins, bowls and buckets, cartons, and lamps on poles.

By New Year's Eve the camp ground was full of geared-up families all looking as equally colourful and crowded as the sheet of paper in the wharenui that represented it.

Among the arrivals were twelve-year-old Leanna and her eleven-year-old brother Max who weren't Hapanihi, Merikana or Tiamana, but who had come up from Palmerston North. Arriving at the same time in an adjacent camp site were eleven-year-old Ryan and his eight-year-old sister Tamsin from Papakura.

While the adults were busy unloading and setting up, these two sets of kids were sniffing at their parents for bringing them all this way, all day in the car to *here*, to *this place*, and there was *nothing*, not even one shop, not even one street (where they could walk up and down in their hibiscus shorts and tees and hats, their cargo pants, their Body Glove outfits).

'The beach,' their parents reminded them.

'So what? So what when we're not even allowed to go swimming,' was the general moan.

At the same time as they were expressing all their dissatisfactions, the three older ones in particular were eyeing each other up across camp sites and luggage making noises and speeches meant mainly for each other. 'Faaar, when are we having tea, when are we going swimming? Gaaar.'

'Later, soon. If you stopped moaning and flopping about and gave a hand for a change everything would be done a lot quicker,' their parents said.

That got rid of them. The four ended up together out on the path of trampled grass between the rows of tents and vehicles. They talked and made noises together for a while, keeping an eye on where their parents were at, then gave up on parents and went off spying.

The three older kids had something itching, creeping round inside them that was airy and not quite there most of the time, though at other times there was a specific vegetable or animal feel about it. It was like plantlife putting out sticky clamps and climbing one two, one two, through chest and arms and head, or putting down hairy roots in a way which wiggled down through lower torso and legs. It was as if they were about to sprout green. Or it could have been something animal—leggy insects scuttling about and taking up spaces, could even have been legless and wormy making tunnels and funnels, tickling all over and keeping the three all the time on the move, all the time gabbing, giggling, hooting and crashing, all the time awake.

Max and Leanna were serious lover-spotters who soon infected Ryan. Tamsin was a pain, a cling-on who couldn't be talked down, bribed, or threatened with anything to make her stay behind. They couldn't even lose her in hide-and-seek games, so she had to go with them.

Not that there was much to spy. People were still busy fixing up their places, carrying cartons and dishes and food, establishing their lamps and stoves and barbecues. There was no one *at it*, not even in the trees, where they'd found a track leading through scrub towards the sea. No one there. Just trees.

They made their way along until they found themselves looking through a fringe of manuka down on to the beach. What they could see from there was people swimming, kids playing in the sand, kids coming in on boogie boards, which reminded them they'd better get back because sometimes their parents changed their minds if there was no one to keep nagging at them.

But just as they were about to return to camp they saw two people coming their way, so they shushed each other and waited. What came by was an old, freckly man with a bare, freckly chest wearing old man shorts and a towel round his neck, and with him was a dried-up, orange woman in a two-piece outfit, walking right past under their noses. The two were joined at the hip and had their arms round each other.

'Lovers,' yelled Leanna.

'Lovers,' yelled Max.

'Lovers,' yelled Ryan, getting the idea.

The kids turned, crashed into each other on the narrow track, fell, got up and ran with Tamsin behind calling out to them to wait, complaining she didn't see, threatening to tell their mother.

Before they came to the camp they slowed to a walk. There wasn't much doing but they decided they'd have another try later when it was dark, and as they came out into the clearing and walked towards the tents they straightened themselves and their clothes getting their faces ready to whinge.

That night while parents were meeting neighbours and relaxing with their wines and beers, the kids set off with a torch. They were going for a walk along the beach, was what their parents half heard them mumble as they strolled off in that direction. They walked until they knew they were out of sight before making their way round behind the furthest row of tents and caravans that were in against the trees.

From there they began their snooping, with no need of torches, creeping close to see in tent windows, or rolling themselves up against tent sides, lifting flaps to look in.

Nothing.

Spare it.

Empty mattresses or babies asleep.

Everyone was out front talking, inspecting each other's set-ups and caravans, some recognising each other from some place last year or the year before or five years ago.

The kids left the camp site and went down to the beach where people were walking at the water's edge or up on the sand. They spied out couples who they thought might be likely to have a go, followed them at a distance with their torches turned off, but there was nothing doing. They followed a man and woman as far as the inlet where there were high banks of driftwood, tufty trees, sandy mounds. The creeping four lay in cold grass watching, waiting for the two to drop, or even kiss.

But nothing happened.

The couple sat on opposite pieces of driftwood talking, talking, and after a while went down and dabbled their feet at the edge of the inlet, talk, talk, talk, before returning along the sand where two girls came running towards them calling out.

Nothing doing. There was more going on in the streets of Palmy and Papakura they reckoned.

They went up to the row of houses but couldn't get near for dogs, except for one place where they got close enough to look in a window and see a creepy old man sitting by a fire with his jersey on, his dog beside him, and two kids asleep in the bedroom.

It was on their way home and keeping to the shadows at the top of the beach that Max, who was in the lead, tripped over what must've been lovers, who probably were at it, who yelled and swore at them. The four ran for it, yelling, 'Lovers, Lovers,' dragging Tamsin who was again complaining that she didn't see. Leanna and Ryan hadn't seen either, nor had Max for that matter though they all made out they had.

But Tamsin, despite all her disappointments and complaints was getting the hang of this lover business from listening to the talk of the older kids. Lovers were a man and woman holding hands or having their arms round each other, or kissing, or in bed together kissing or sleeping, or hiding somewhere in the bushes naked and kissing, or humping, or something.

By the next day, which was New Year's Eve day, the kids had forgotten about lover-spotting. There were waves coming in and no one was stopping them going in the water anytime they liked. Cool.

It was choice. They forgot their hibiscus and Body Glove outfits and their cargo pants, dropped them on the floor of the tents and spent all day in their togs. There was wood being stacked along the beach for bonfires and they helped with that in between swims. They had fireworks stashed away for after dark and they were going to be allowed to stay up all night.

It was primo.

THIRTY

HE WOKE on New Year's Eve morning to hear boats going out knowing that if it hadn't been for Operation Dining Room he and Arch would be out there too pulling in a few big ones. Even before he got out of bed he knew the day was right for it—overcast, windless, the tide at half, which was making movement of the boats churning through the mouth slow and easy. One by one they made it through, throttling out and scooting across the bay heading for the reefs and deep water. There was another full-on day ahead, but he thought he might be able to take time later to go for a dive, or go night fishing, bring in a couple of congers for the New Year hangi.

Then he remembered that he'd woken earlier and heard a boat out there at some funny hour after midnight—which was all wrong. Too early, too dark and not a good tide to be going out, though you never knew what some mad holidaymakers would do. Whoever it was wouldn't have got through the inlet at that time without their propellers ending up in sand and their motors breaking down.

After a while he had realised it wasn't a boat going out that he was hearing, but one returning, motor on slow, passing by the inlet because the tide was too far down. Even with the tide right they wouldn't have been able to see well enough to get through in the dark.

But maybe they hadn't wanted to come in at the inlet anyway in case they were copped. Doing what?

The boat had gone into the distance, on to the next bay he reckoned, where it would take at least four men, two entering the water from the beach, to get it in. Then what? Then there'd be a four-wheel-drive vehicle with a winch waiting and they'd be on the road within an hour.

Off somewhere in the dark with a load of crays? Who?

Couldn't be Brad and Horomona who hadn't been seen since Atawhai sent them back to Oz.

'I know they've been selling. I know they've found a market somewhere,' Atawhai had said. 'I should've got the police but ahh, didn't want to upset my sister. Anyway I told them to sell up and get back to Oz quick if they didn't want the cops or the brothers on them. Next thing I hear they're packing up. They skedaddled pretty fast.'

So who, when it was only themselves who knew about the cray rocks? Or maybe just some crazy tourists joy-riding with lights? He'd got out of bed and gone down to the beach from where he could hear the boat somewhere out by the point. There were no lights.

'Picking plums for Those Two,' Kid said when he asked where she was going with her plastic bags.

'Your Aunties.'

'Those Two,' she said.

'Well, you want to?' he asked, 'Pick plums for them, for Those Two?'

'Me, Georgie, Hinewai. Those Two making jam for their stall.'

'Want to or not?' He knew she could hear something disapproving in the question, knew he was putting her on the spot.

'It's OK,' she said.

And of course it was OK. If someone didn't find time to pick the plums in the next day or two they'd fall and rot on the ground. It was a good job for kids, one of the jobs he'd always enjoyed and it wouldn't take long at all. Kid having fun with her cousins, doing what other kids did, was what he'd always wanted.

Those Two had been grinning all over themselves lately, greeting him as though there was nothing wrong between them, everything to do with Kid on hold for the moment. Crazy Mamas.

But after all this business was over he was going to get Wai and Arch to bring everyone together to talk, because he didn't believe they needed family court sessions. If they all got together the older ones could talk Amiria and Babs round, no problem, no mucking around. One good hui, put the squeeze on, and Those Two would give up once they found they had no backers and once they realised their case wasn't strong enough to take to court—which was what Heke Norman believed.

Anyway that was for later. They'd all been flat out since the campers arrived—rubbish collecting, cleaning showers and loos, loading and unloading. Now today there was wood to collect and cut for the hangi, a trailer load of stones to get, a hole to dig and benches to set up. It was a long time since he'd been able to do that sort of work and he was looking forward to it.

'Spent half the day looking after their beers,' Para was saying when he went into the tent just on nightfall. 'In and out the fridge truck. Holy shit I was getting a thirst up.'

'It's a fact. Bloody hot day.'

'So how come this woman here conned us into going dry, new year and all, new millennium and all?'

'Ah, suckers,' Wai said, coming in with choppers and knives.

'True, suckers all right.'

'It's a fact, suckers.'

'Never mind,' Wai said. 'Once we see the last one off in a week or so, we'll have us a big hua of a party.'

'There's talking.'

'Party-up large.'

'Archie been doing up our knives,' Wai said. 'You coulda rid to town bareback on these.'

'Ah, knives.'

'Chopping and cutting 'til millennium, us.'

'Well maybe we have us just a mini celebration while we work,' Wai said. 'Get us a few cans, a chateau cardboard, just enough to see the New Year in. How's that?'

'Ah that's the one.'

'That's the story.'

'Now you're talking, Sis.'

He could see that there was a big enough crew getting the meat ready, peeling spuds, hacking up pumpkin, diving into breadcrumbs, so he thought he would have time to get over to the cove. 'You want a few congers to put in the baskets?' he asked.

'Ah, we do.'

'Mmm, Son,' Arch said. 'Take a hunk off my piggy here to bait your hooks, my little Yumyum.'

'That's me too,' said Jase. 'I get me some shorts.'

'And us, us,' Kid said from outside the tent in the dark, where she was hanging around with Georgie and Hinewai. Younger children were already asleep in the wharenui but the three of them were staying up all night with the older kids, according to them.

'You should stay,' he said. 'Bonfires, crackers, all that.'

'We come back through the hole after, when it all starts,' Georgie said.

Well they could, the hole would be empty by then, the tide was on its way down already.

'A torch, then we're off,' he said.

Even in the dark he could see the buoys. They were like gaps, opposites of themselves, holes in the water rather than solid things on top of it. There were two close in but he knew there would be more. Dumping the gear on the ground he sat to remove his limb and his shirt. Jase was already heading down to climb round the barricade of rocks and up onto the banks with the torch.

'What?' Kid said, 'What you wild about?'

'Stay here,' he said to Kid, Georgie and Hinewai. 'Stay here and light us a fire.'

It was a hot night. The heat of the day had collected in the basin, and without a breeze to shift it had remained there. It was topped by damp air filtering from a low sky.

The water sprayed up in phosphorescent drops about him as he struck out in the dark for the first buoy, and on reaching there he dived down, feeling about at the end of the buoy rope, hearing crays clicking away as he went. He clutched the struts of the first pot and tried hoisting it, surfaced, then went down to try the second one. Already too heavy. Jase, on the track above him with the torch, was too far away to make good light.

'Low tide we could drag them out,' he called, 'or cut them. Could be more.'

Jase tried to keep up with him along the track with the light as he began swimming in the direction of the deep rocks. There he found a cluster of buoys, which meant there'd have to be a big boat coming to collect. Maybe two boats, or one boat making more than one trip in the dark.

'We need help, need gear,' he called but Jase was already making it back along the track as fast as he could.

'Ropes and cutters. And take the kids home,' he called as he started out for shore.

He returned to the first cray pot and began shifting it little by little without making much progress, so he decided to wait for help, for gear, the low tide. When he got back to shore he found that

Georgie and Hinewai had gone but Kid was still there putting the sticks in the fire. 'You shoulda gone home,' he said.

'What you wild for?'

There was a weightless rain falling, a steamy heat and the fire the kids had made was becoming smoky and scented. Water was pulling back from the hole. He began drying himself down with his shirt wondering why the cove was always so thundery, so exploding, so full of everything—like Te Aro Park, like the city streets, all of life always going on.

'Cray pots out there,' he said. 'Someone robbing crays. It's people's crays, our aunties' and uncles' crays, your crays getting stolen. Set pots there, catch heaps all at once, then the crays are gone. Gone, that's it. Nothing.'

'Who done it?'

'Our relations maybe.'

'What for?'

'Want to get rich maybe.'

The first rockets were going off when he heard voices and saw the torches as Jase and the others began returning through the blow-hole. The fireworks burst out into white stars and coloured balls, fuzzy-edged against a watery sky. Water was still going out through the hole and he knew the ones coming would be making their way in against the walls, feeling for each foothold as they came through in the dark. He boosted the fire. Eight he counted, coming out in fragments of torchlight. Bones, Eva, Reggae and Dion with torches, Moana and Jase with ropes, Jackson with an axe, Joeboy with a gun and a belt full of ammo. But what they really needed was cutters. Without cutters they'd have to get the crays out of the pots one by one.

Anyway with two ropes they could get two teams working. He swam with the ropes to the nearest buoys and made his dives, securing the ropes through the struts of the pots. Eva, Jackson and

Dion were in the water behind him while the others had gone to the near banks to begin hauling in from there.

They pulled the first pot towards the banks, hoisting it over and around rocks, through the crevasses, moving aside the heavy weed and steadying it through the channels of rushing water. Once they'd got it near enough to the water's edge they lifted it out and returned for the second one.

The axe was useful after all because once they'd taken some of the crays out of the pot they were able to tip the rest to one side and chop enough of a gap to free the remaining ones which went flicking back into the lagoon.

Out at the far rocks where the water was still deep, he and Jackson dived down together making many attempts to get the rope tied to the struts, but in the end had to be satisfied with tying it to the buoy line. The pots then had to be tipped up and dragged from the centre. There was nowhere to anchor themselves so the others got into the water to help, the fire on shore giving them a line. It was going to take hours and he was thinking about Bones and Jase. Not the kind of job either of them should do for too long.

With two more pots to go they lay in the grass resting, listening to the shouting, laughter and music coming from over at the beach. Beside him Bones was creaking. 'Go back,' he said to Bones. 'Take Kid back.'

'Nah, it's OK.' A glow from the bonfires outlined the ridges, an occasional burst of stars littered against the sky. Dion was talking, on on on. But now there was something else he could hear, something knocking in his head, knocking, slow and even.

'Hear it,' he said.

Jackson stood and began scooping handfuls of sand on to the fire. 'Ha, ha, let's go,' he said, picking up the axe and the torch and making for the banks with Joeboy behind him doing up his ammo belt, slinging the gun over his shoulder.

'You gotta come with me, stick with me,' he said to Kid.

'Better get your leg on,' she said and when he'd done that they followed the others down the slope round the edges of the water, which had pulled right back now giving them space to pass round the shore side of the rocks, then round the hill slope, all the time listening.

Boat sounds fluctuated, now and again becoming lost as the vessel made its way past the outer reefs, round the bearded island and towards them. Voices, whispers travelled across water, a small light went on and the motor was cut to its lowest.

They could see a man lying along the prow of the boat, looking down into the water, sweeping the light from side to side as it came trundling in over low humpy waves.

In the neck of the cove they saw the light turn to pick up the outline of the two buoys, then settle ahead again as the boat made its way through. A second man in the boat switched the motor off, tilting it up out of the way of the rock and weed of the now shallow lagoon. They watched as the boat drifted towards the two buoys and the man with the light reached out, hooking the near one with a gaff.

Jackson, from where they all were on the ledge, switched on the torch and shone it down. 'Happy New Year, Cousins.'

In torchlight they saw one man roll off the prow into the water while the other scrambled towards the front of the boat.

'Swim,' Jackson called, and as the man still in the boat, reached for the ignition switch the gun went off, the shot shattering the water's surface like chased herrings, and the second man went overboard, the two clinging to the far side of the boat with their heads hidden from view.

'Swim,' Joeboy called sending another shot echoing round the cove, dislodging rubble from the bank opposite.

There was splashing, and the big sound of Jackson laughing as the two men scrambled for shore. 'Stop when you get to Sydney,' Jackson called.

'Seedney, ha ha,' Joeboy called.

They watched the men, two shadows, leave the water, untangling themselves from weed, pulling themselves out over the rocks, up the side to the hole and disappearing into the water that was now spilling out through the gap.

Gone.

Running by now over rocks, along sand by dying bonfires and a few last explosions.

Joeboy was up again, aiming.

'Ahh, ahh Cuz,' Dion was saying, 'it's a pretty good boat. Won't be so good full of holes.' Joeboy lowered the gun.

'Serve themselfs right,' Kid said.

'Come on Cuz,' he said helping Jase up. 'Going up the old house,' he said to Jackson, 'taking Kid and Jase.'

'We do it then, me and Joe,' Jackson said. 'Take the boat, empty the last two and take her up the inlet.'

'Wait round 'til daylight then take her in,' he said. 'Give them the gear to take home. And take Bones.'

'Uncle Arch'll come and pick you up,' Moana said. 'We'll tell him.' She was on the home track with Eva, Dion and Reggae. 'Get yourselves back in time to do the hangi fire, ha, put the hangi down,' she called. 'Happy New Year.'

It was as though several days had passed since he'd left the hangi tent to go get them a couple of congers. He took Kid's hand leading her through the trees, along the narrow track to the house. Jase, close behind, was beginning to stagger, needing rest and food. There was music still coming from over the hill, people waiting for the rise of big-dollar, dining-room sun, but it was too cloudy for a sunrise.

The old place smelled of dried insects and mice, old boards that had been damp during winter and were now scorched and heated, and there was a whiff of old fruit and wood stacks, soot and ashes.

It was as though the old house was full, like a pod ready to bust open scattering old brooms and cooking pots, books, rags and blankets, breaking mattress, old blood, old bones, dried juices.

He lit a candle and found a towel for Kid to dry herself with and an old shirt of his for her to wear, then went out to where Jase was sitting with his back against a tree making noises like, Ah, ah, mmm. It ah, ha ha.

'Talking crap Cuz,' he said as he went about gathering dry wood, starting the fire and putting water on to boil. 'Load a shit. Worse than Pop Henry, you.' Jase's black eyes had gone creepy and his black face was the colour of an eel underbelly, '*Lucy Lula, you love that silver belly tuna*, an old Archie song, ay Cuz?' He put teabags in the pot as the water came to the boil and went inside for tinned milk. 'Going to town on the uke, ay Cuz, Uncle Archie?' he said as he returned. '*Lucy Lula, make a hula*, no sleeping, no sleeping.' He scooped a cup of tea from the pot, let the milk drip into it and put it into Jase's hands. '. . . *And in the morning, you will be my lady*. Come on, come on . . .' He watched as his cousin drank the tea then took the cup from him and refilled it. '*Hiki dula, he the fella*. Come on, come on Man. *Lucy Lula* . . .'

'*You love that silver belly tuna*,' Jase sang.

'That's it, Cuz, that's it. You got it . . . Well you know, you know, that was a go ay? Horomona and Brad?'

'Boom,' Jase said.

'New Year with a bang, Bro.'

He went back to the house, where Kid had gone to sleep on the busting mattress, the busted bed, and returned with dry shorts and tees for Jase and himself, pleased to see his cousin on his feet, then pleased to remove the limb, the gritty stump sock, the steamy clothes.

By the time he went back inside Jase was already in there asleep, stretched out in front of the fireplace. He shook old mason bee nests and spider legs from two old bed covers, spread one over Jase, then lay down beside Kid pulling the second cover up over them.

THIRTY-ONE

IT WAS something for the rafters, truly, even though it was some time before the rafters picked up on all of it.

There was what took place before dawn on the first day of the new year, the new decade, the new century, the new millennium, and then what took place soon afterwards—soon after the sun didn't rise to the big photo opportunity, instead hiding itself giggly and wobbly and beside itself, behind its cloud screen as the earth turned.

It was some months before it all sorted and settled up there in the beams, after arriving only in instalments at different times, in differing versions, all out of sync and chronology. Not that it mattered how it came, or when, or in what condition. Every scrap and tatter contributed and became part of a mass that sprouted whole in the end. (But what does 'end' mean where there is forever the potential to add or embellish and when rafters are such inclusionists?)

It was past midnight when Wai and the team completed the cutting up of meat and the preparation of vegetables for the hangi. They cleaned up, stored the meat in the fridge truck and finished off the drink ration which had lasted longer than it should have because in the end there were fewer of them than expected. They'd lost half their work force and therefore half their drinkers.

'Disappeared outside,' Arch said. 'Jase come talking secret to his cousins. Nex'thing they disappear outside—for a smoke or what? Nex'thing, huh, gone.'

'Off and said nothing. Half our workers.'

'Buggers, they better be on deck in the morning.'

'Blast their earholes in the morning,' Wai said.

It was as they were finishing off the last of the drinks that they heard the shots, which they later thought they shouldn't have mistaken for the sound of fire crackers, but it had been a long eve.

They left the preparation tent to go home for a few hours sleep before it was time to light the hangi fire, stopping first at the beach to round up children who were still out playing in the dark. There was a crowd still on the beach, the music was blaring out and the bonfires were diminishing now that even the children were retiring from the work of keeping them going. Some families were returning to their camps to have a few hours' sleep before getting up to see the dawn, and they hoped, the first sunrise. Others were intent on seeing the whole night through.

'Two men come running out the sea,' the kids said as they were called out of the dark to go home.

'Hard out, them. Running hard out.'

'Wetsuits, them.'

'Down the beach.'

'Running, running, hard out.'

'Down the beach, down the road.'

The adults didn't take much interest in what the kids were trying to tell them, about what? About campers playing silly buggers in the dark? Or what? The work and the last bit of wine had slugged them.

Babs and Amiria had not been present at the hangi preparations in the tent. They had their own work to do for the next day, as they had had during the previous nights as well. Their Hot Bread

Shop had been a great success—cleared out by lunchtime every day, which sent them home with great smiles on their faces to make more loaves of bread, more and more sponge cakes which they decorated and sold whole, banana and carrot cakes which they sold by the slice, afghans, shortbread, peanut brownies, coconut clusters, yoyos, and chocolate slice which went six to a tray. And now they were doing jars of plum jam as well.

But not only were the loaves and goods a success, The Two themselves were a success as well. Among the campers were regular customers, some of whom made straight for the tent when it opened each morning in order to be first to make their morning tea selections. Some would buy what they wanted and go. Others would stay on, chatting to The Two, whom they found to be charming and interesting and who could tell them a bit of the history of the place, and who were willing to show them round.

Amiria and Babs were happy to do this, more than happy, and had time to do it because once the goods were set up on the table, displayed to their liking on the polystyrene trays covered with gladwrap, prices showing on coloured stickers, they could leave the selling in the hands of Moana and Reggae.

The sisters were photographed many times linking arms in front of the wharenui or other scenic places, with people from all over the country, all over the world. Among these new friends were two in particular, Americans Francis and Molly from Maryland who loved the home cooking and loved The Two. They were intent on photographing every single thing, getting the very best shots of every single thing to take home with them.

For New Year's Day Amiria and Babs were preparing something special to go alongside the usual array of cakes and loaves. It was to be two triple-decker chocolate cakes which they would decorate with chocolate icing, cream, and chocolate-dipped strawberries. So the cooking on the afternoon of New Year's Eve had taken them through to almost midnight. At that point they decided to leave the finishing touches to be done the next morning so they could join their new friends down on the beach to welcome in the new millennium.

They arrived down on the beach where the radios had been turned up high for the countdown, the bonfires had been boosted and the rockets were lined up ready to be fired. There was a dampness in the air that wasn't quite rain and was not enough to affect the fires or the fireworks or the spirits of the people. As midnight broke out of its egg Babs and Amiria, cold sober, but quickly able to get into the spirit of it all, walked down into shouting and tears, hugs and wishes, and especially into the arms of Francis and Molly who wanted to hug every New Zealander in the world.

'We made it, we made it, waddaya know?' Francis said, taking Amiria and Babs into his arms and breaking into tears.

When, not long afterwards, two men popped out of the tide and sprinted through the crowd, past the fires, spraying drops of water and kicking up sand, it was like all part of the happening.

'What is it? What is it?'

'Hey, hey, you guys.'

'Hey Happy New Year.'

'What? First Iron Man of the millennium or what?'

'Ha, ha, where's y' bikes?' Some of the children followed for a short distance, running after the two men in the dark.

In a glimpse by firelight Babs and Amiria thought there was something familiar about the two runners but were enjoying themselves too much to put thought to it. They didn't get to recalling their view of this, this scrap for the rafters, until many months later.

Apart from the music, the beach became quieter as some families returned to their camps to have a couple of hours' sleep before getting up to see the first dawn and, they were still hoping, the first sunrise.

The fireworks were done and the fires were going out, but it was while they were sitting by the last of the fires, with the last of the drinks, that Francis had the idea of going up on the hills to photograph the new millennium sun as it popped up out of the sea. It'd be such a great shot, and it'd be seconds ahead of any taken down on the beach, he thought. He was enthusiastic about it, so he stood, brushed himself down and asked Babs and Amiria to point the way. Molly stood reluctantly beside him.

'Why bother?' someone asked. 'You might lose yourselves.'

'And won't be any sun showing its face this morning, it's raining for God's sake.'

'If the sun don't happen the dawn'll sure happen,' Francis said.

'There's a track up,' Babs said, who didn't like the way these drunk Kiwis were discouraging their overseas visitors.

'We'll take you,' Amiria said, 'You need good torches and good shoes.'

Well, there were still a few hours to wait and some of the people were starting to feel a little slumped, wishing they hadn't promised the kids they could stay up all night. Kids were racing about being a pain and throwing sand up all over the place. A hill climb would fill in time, might be just what they all needed.

'OK, why don't we join you?' someone said.

'How long, how far?'

'Half an hour,' Babs and Amiria said. Both knew it would take longer, especially in the dark, but didn't want anyone to be put off. They were dead keen on living up to this super-hostess image they'd acquired recently.

All these details were beamed up eventually.

The last thing Babs and Amiria wanted to happen in front of these national and international visitors on their way along the tracks on this night time guided tour, was to meet with a bunch of young relatives, wet and barefoot, rowdy in the trees, coming into torchlight bearing weapons. There was no chance, out on the track, which was lit up like a street by all these flash torches the campers had, and with kids barging in and out around trees with their glow-sticks, that Amiria and Babs could pass by unrecognised. Nor could they pretend not to know the four coming toward them, all hyped up, calling, 'Happy New Year Aunty Babs, Happy New Year Aunty Miria,' hugging wet all over them. Bloody kids, hugging and kissing everyone else as well.

'These two lovely ladies are taking up us to view the sunrise,' Francis informed them. 'And what have you all been up to? How did you all see in the New Year?'

'Ancient water ceremony,' Dion said.

'We should move on,' Amiria said. 'Otherwise . . .'

'Sorry we missed it,' Francis said. 'Maybe . . .' he was unclipping his camera. But they were gone and the group was moving forward, 'Maybe we could hear more about this special ceremony sometime. Maybe our ladies here . . .'

'Looked like a pretty dangerous ceremony to me, weapons and whatnot,' someone said.

'Ah, they're pulling your leg.'

'Here's where we start our climb,' Amiria was thankful to be able to interrupt. Those nieces and nephews of theirs had themselves a plantation she wouldn't mind betting. In cahoots with that Jackson and that Joeboy growing dope, that's what. Now if they walked into something like that . . . plants . . . well . . . how would they explain that to their friends? 'It's not too far,' she said, 'and just gets a little steep near the top.'

Being up high made them laugh, though this is no mountain we're talking about. It was a rise that sloped quietly upward to one side of Rua's breaking-down house. It was the way Rua would take if he was to go round and out to the ledges of the cove rather than down onto the grassy shore banks. It was the way to the plank, the way Ani Wainoa had gone with her bundle. It was a hump in the foreground of the much greater heights that stood in layers beyond it.

The rain had begun to fall more heavily since they left the beach but they hadn't noticed while they were under the shelter of trees. Now it made them feel foolish, made them laugh. They could've been down on the beach larking, back under canvas snoring, home making coffee in their campervans. Instead they were perched on a slippery slope in the rain and in the dark, a more dark dark than they had ever seen, with their torches and cameras and two lovely ladies, waiting for a good old Y2K sunrise that wasn't going to happen. However it was a warm night and after a while the rain stopped. Eventually the birds piped up and the sky lightened in its sneaky way.

And it was so great, you know. The whole world was so . . .

A little later, though the sun didn't actually show its face they were able to tell where it was, see the tinge that it made on the clouds for some seconds, way out there over the water. You could cry.

'And you can say,' parents said to their kids, 'you'll be able to tell your grandchildren that you saw the dawn of the year 2000, and that you were one of the first in the whole world to see it.'

'Is that it?' kids said.

'Big deal.'

'Spare it.'

Though Tamsin was really pleased.

In full daylight and with the sky clearing they made their way down the slope through the trees to where the house was, to the beginning of the track leading out.

'What have we?' someone asked.

'One of the old places,' Amiria said.

'It's done for,' Babs said. The Sisters were wanting to hurry everyone along now, thinking of the work they still had to do when they got home. They needed sleep, needed a shower, clean clothes, make-up and hair fixing. God knows what they looked like in all this daylight.

Some were of the same mind about getting back as quickly as possible to showers and sleep. Others needed to straggle and to go poking about and looking in windows. Tamsin followed her Mum and Dad and put her nose over the windowsill of the old house and looked in. What she saw was two bumps under an old sheet, two heads, mainly hair—straight and black, spread in strands at the top end of a split mattress.

She came away from there, running and yelling after Max, Leanna and her brother, 'Lovers, lovers,' she squealed at them down the path.

The three older children did their best to ignore her, pretending they didn't know what she was on about.

'Run for it,' she yelled, cracking into her brother who gave her an unfriendly shove. 'Lovers,' she tried again, then she shut her mouth. Her father had her by the arm and he was shushing her. There was something here she wasn't getting quite right.

Amiria and Babs saw the remaining people on to the home track then returned to the house to find out what it was that Tamsin's father was shutting her up about. What they saw was Kid asleep, Rua asleep, the door open, all the windows half falling out and that silly Jase stretched out there on the floor. They hurried after their friends and thought no more about it, not until weeks later when they realised how it could seem, what they could make of it all.

When Rua and Kid woke the sun was shining. They went out to sit by the creek in the steaming grass while they waited for Jase to get up. The rain had not been enough to get the creek moving and the banks were high and dry. After a while they decided to wake Jase so they could all go home. There was work to do, there was plenty to talk about and he was eager to have a good look at the boat they'd acquired.

Rua lifted the sheet off Jase. He'd seen this before, knew his cousin wasn't dead but knew he wouldn't be able to wake him, knew that he could die. He sent Kiri for help to carry Jase home.

It took some weeks, but Jase did get to float his version of these events beamwards.

THIRTY-TWO

BECAUSE OF all else that happened, the hangi that had been planned to come up just after midday wasn't ready until evening. This didn't matter and turned out for the better since campers were only beginning to get themselves up for their first cups of coffee by midday.

Early in the morning, at fire lighting time, there were only the older men and a couple of teenagers at the site arranging the wood and the stones in a pile above the hangi pit. The men were just about to light the fire when Bones, Eva, Moana and Dion came out of the bush all hyped up and with a story to tell.

So the men postponed the lighting of the fire while the young ones went with Archie to lift his boat off its trailer, hitch the trailer to the station wagon and take it up river to the ramp to wait for Jackson, Joeboy and this new boat.

When they arrived back they could see that they needn't be in a hurry to get the hangi down, so they went to shower and change and have breakfast. They had returned to the site and were again about to light the fire when Kiri came telling them something they were all too busy to listen to at first. 'Rua wants you. You got to come and carry Uncle Jase.'

'What's that, Baby, you want to mind away.'

'Someone got to help Rua.'

'We all busy, Girl.'

'Rua, my Dad.'

'Where's he?'

'Up the bush?'

'What doing?'

'Bringing Uncle Jase.'

'All right Girl, you better mind away.'

'Dead.' She thought it might be true, knew it would catch an ear.

'What you say?'

'Dead, Uncle Jase.'

'Who said dead?'

'Nobody.'

Everything came to a halt again. The boys went running along and up into the trees while Arch went to ring Atawhai and to let people know what might've happened. People left what they were doing and hurried along to the bottom of the track to wait.

This could be it, the end of all this camping business.

Over.

Jase.

Soon afterwards Atawhai arrived, hurrying up the track to meet the men coming down.

'Out to it,' Rua said to Atawhai. 'Can't bring him round.' Atawhai took a look at Jase then came back out of the trees to where there was enough signal for him to be able to phone for the helicopter.

The fire was eventually lit in the afternoon. This was after Tini and Cass, who had accompanied Jase to hospital, had rung back to say he had recovered consciousness and was going to be all right.

Campers were all up and about by then—swimming, fishing, off sightseeing—or just hanging about taking photos of the sweaty men, the fire, the white-hot stones, their dinner in food baskets going down on top of the stones, the covers going on and the whole lot being damped down, dirt being piled over everything to keep the steam in. Well I'll be darned.

Though there was no first-hand camper input, everyone's version of everything got to the rafters eventually.

THIRTY-THREE

IT WAS a long two weeks. There was all that was going on in the planned game as well as the drama going on round the sidelines. Host energies were stretched, especially as after the first week their numbers dwindled, some people returning to their other homes and their other work. Jackson and Joeboy left on business but said they'd return for the clean-up and the party. Atawhai had made sure that nephews Brad and Horomona had really gone back to Australia this time. Information that he'd given to the Ministry of Fisheries was likely to lead to the bust of a significant cray smuggling racket and he'd managed to do that without having the good boat taken away or any of his relatives implicated. So far.

There was Jase in hospital, making a recovery then coming home.

They saw the last of the visitors off, thankful that that part of the business was over. Now they'd have a break before talking about how they were going to get Dining Room Two Thousand up and running.

Amiria and Babs were the only ones with tears in their eyes as they said their goodbyes to visitors. They had notebooks full of names, addresses and phone numbers from all over the country, all over the world. America.

They had invitations to call, to visit, to come and stay, and they were going to do it too they promised their friends and promised themselves. They were going to save their money, go on holiday, make their way north, go south maybe. Go to America. After everyone had gone they began to fill the hole left in their days and their lives by writing letters and sending off cards.

The clean-up and the party were hardly over before Amiria and Babs began lobbying among members of the whanau to have the campers back the following year, but there was little enthusiasm for the idea. From some quarters there was downright opposition.

'No way,' Wai said. 'It was a oncer. We got our money, that's it.'

The Two couldn't understand Wai. This was an opportunity to put their little settlement, their end of the beach and, most importantly, their side of the inlet, on the map. This place of theirs was full of history that people all over the world were interested in. Why not share it?

They had ideas, too, for additional activities that they knew would interest visitors, such as guided tours, bush treks and boating activities. There could be social evenings with disco, karaoke or live bands. Although there'd been a few nick-nack stalls this time, these could be extended to stalls for more traditional crafts—along with demonstrations of carving and weaving. Another idea was to get some of the young girls to dress in piupiu, bodice and tipare and be available to have photographs taken with tourists. These tourists would then have something of the *genuine culture* to take home with them. There could be tee shirts with a picture of the meeting house on them, and calendars depicting the bay at sunrise.

Well, it seemed some people just weren't interested in progress, Babs and Amiria sniffed, but they didn't give up. They took the trouble to speak to some of the business people round town, and found that the local garage and bottle store were keen on it all happening again. Other proprietors were not quite so enthusiastic since they felt they'd had potential custom taken away by food stalls and all that underpricing. Amiria and Babs were selective as to what information they used to support their case.

Most of the letters that they sent out to new friends went unanswered, though they did receive a handful of notes and cards sending thanks and good wishes. Once or twice a photograph of themselves slipped from an envelope, sometimes accompanied by a request for bookings for next summer. They felt abandoned on the whole, but anyway they armed themselves with these requests and took them to wave under Wai's nose in an effort to persuade her.

'Forget it,' Wai said. 'We got a building to put up.'

'Look here,' they argued, 'we got these new loos and showers, good camp sites. What use are they?'

'For our own families coming back for holidays,' Wai said. 'Then they won't have to camp on our front lawns, won't have to squeeze into our houses and we won't have to look after them because they'll look after themselves. We won't have to collect their rubbish, clean their loos and showers, feed them. Holidays can be for holidays.'

Wai was hopeless.

In among all of this Babs and Amiria hadn't lost sight of other important matters which they were waiting to hear from their lawyer about. When Cath Wyman eventually called them to meet with her, they found that it was with the intention of persuading them not to take their custody application to court. Cath thought it unlikely that they would win considering there seemed no doubt that Rua was the child's father, and that he had an agreement from the mother regarding him having custody. And though a full report from Martin Henderson, who was acting for Kiri, showed that either party was capable of caring for her, it did show that Kiri was happier with her father and strongly preferred to be with him. It was also the case that Rua had full support of other family members including elders.

'So,' Cath Wyman said, 'unless there's anything further that you think might strengthen your case, I wouldn't advise that you continue. You'd be much better off with an out-of-court agreement. That way something can be drawn up between yourselves and the father that could give you some access, depending on what you can all work out.'

This treacherous lawyer in whom they had put trust, with whom they were on first-name terms, and to whom they had brought peanut brownies on more than one occasion, had given up on them, just like that.

Abandoned.

Again.

But The Two wouldn't give up that easily of course, being far too hard-boiled for that.

'What do you mean by "anything further"?' Amiria asked.

'It would have to be evidence of neglect on the part of the father, or something serious to do with the father's behaviour, doubt about his suitability, skeletons in closets,' Cath said.

Well, if it was neglect that she wanted to know about, bad behaviour she was interested in, or suitability, skeletons in closets, The Two knew they could come up with plenty. Plenty, if they put their minds to it.

It was enough to cause twitches even among old, hard-bitten beams once the rafters got wind of it.

THIRTY-FOUR

HE WAS about to go to bed after a day of laying concrete for the new building when Heke Norman rang. It was work that he could do now that his hands and arms were free—a day working with others, hard work with men that he'd enjoyed.

Taku and Shania and half a limb.

It had taken him long enough to be ready for the half limb, long enough to need the missing piece, long enough to be able to do without the ghost bit, the fish-shaped gap with its shadowy flap and knobs and its moving shadow parts, but now he was glad.

'Thought I'd better give you a ring,' Heke Norman said.

There are same-age cousins who are too close to you ever to be brothers and sisters. Older brothers and sisters have grown more than what you have, younger ones have grown less, neither have ever grown the same—which means you can never be equal.

But your same-age cousins are joined by the shoulders to you, and have same-age thoughts and understandings. There are strings that loop from head to head of you, heart to heart, and you realise that it would be possible to fall into their skins and be them.

Between your same-age cousins and you, you have languages.

There is one that grows word by word in all of you at once—ah and ga, ma and ta, ha and haa, wha and far, kaa and car. The other is a secret language, which is secret only because others don't know of it. It has no words, or it has ghosts of words, mists of ideas that creep into all of you at one time. There are same-age eyes seeing from a same level and time, and memories storing on same-age shelves. The same tides run through all.

Born together doesn't mean you die together.

It had taken time for him to be willing to interrupt ghosts, to allow himself to detach himself from the space about his shoulders, the space below the knee, the gone people and the chopped-off piece. He'd spent all those months expecting someone to do something about Kid when he now realised he should've been the one to do it, but he'd had an attachment to a space which had allowed some part of him to keep on being a child himself, or at least had stopped him from being a father.

The cove, a physical life, minder of people's fish? He'd thought living alone was the right thing then, that surviving on his own freed him and was proof that he stood on his own . . . what? Ha . . . Bullshit. Hiding himself from himself.

Kid.

He thought of her stalking him, her spider eyes watching him and the boiled arm forcing him.

Also he thought of Maina, the fire times, and the night of the party when there'd been no need of fires, when Archie had been hunched over his uke, racing it, one twist of sweaty hair loose and swinging on his forehead, knees jumping and feet going toe to heel. Songs creaking out of Arch, out of his satchmo, with Amiria and Atawhai on guitars, starting in on the golden oldies as Maina came in with her family.

There'd been a move forward to bring the family in, a stir and a whoop as the singing continued and they came in shifting their hips, their arms, their hands and their eyes: *Kei te awhi to tinana, Aue*

Aue, E te tau tahuri mai, all of them with rocks of teeth. Hani had led the family in their round of greetings, *While you sleep, The spirit goes walkabout, And the heart, Goes on pumping.*

After they'd been round people had made room on the long forms for them while the guitars were moved on to Jase and Joeboy. He'd gone across to sit with them and held little bits of conversation with her in among songs, not fire and candle conversations but talking mainly about Kid who at that time was out playing on the marae in the dark with her cousins. She had come in not long afterwards to sit with him.

In a while Eva and Moana had come in carrying flowers and packages, one of which looked like a giraffe wrapped in red paper.

'We got some formalities,' Wai had announced. 'Before you all get off your faces we got some thank-yous.' In among all the woos and hoos she'd given a brief account of progress of plans for Wharekai Two Thousand and then had presented the lampstand, the flowers and the CDs to Maina for her and her family. Everyone had got up to support Wai's song, those who'd gone to sit outside coming back in to sing, joining in the actions—something else he could do now that he hadn't been able to do for some years.

Hani, taking his turn to speak, didn't look like someone who'd been sick, with his big head and shoulders, his even-coloured skin, his eyes lit and black. At the end of the speech they'd had to wait for his song while he retuned the guitar, wired it the way he liked it, loose and tinny, on the edge of off-key, on the edge of out, pick and pick, jangle, then singing big and scratchy.

Maina's turn. She'd spoken briefly, given her thanks then taken the guitar and passed it to her son, waiting while he tightened it up again. Wide face, like her father's, hard hair pulled back in a big clip—hair hard, that twisted hard and trapped your fingers, her eyes a dark weed colour with a flick of fish. Chunks of earrings and a sleeveless dress that could've been blue or black, breasts flattened by the cloth of it and pulling against the front buttons. Big arms as she leaned, the armholes of the dress cutting in against her underarms, the dress draping loose from the top, down over the fatty rest of her. The voice, starting from a deep place, came loose and caught him, had him pulling his breath in, pumping his chest to make room for his heart. They'd kept her there a long time, and finally let her go, bowing, laughing, big spread arms coming down.

Later she'd told him and others around them that she had a trip coming up, in a week, to Taiwan, then would be home in time to do bookings for another group who were going to Japan.

A-hula a-hula a-hula to the ten guitars, Englebert was a cuzzie bro if only he knew it.

'Lucky you, lucky you.'

A-haka a-haka a-haka to the ten guitars. A-boog it a-boog it a-boog it to the ten guitars, until it was time for her to go, time to get the old man and his pacemaker home.

'You could stay,' he'd said. 'I could take you home, tomorrow, whenever,' making room for his heart.

So she'd gone to tell her family she was staying, and Hani had gone off with the others laughing and calling out, 'Look after my daughter, all youse. Have another one of these shindigs when the roof goes on.'

They'd gone home leaving Kid asleep in the wharenui with Tini, Moana and her cousins.

He'd been looking forward to the work again the next day when they'd be taking away boxing, maybe starting on frames, but now here was Heke Norman on the phone saying he needed to see him urgently.

'Something's come up. Bring a couple of the aunties or uncles,' he said.

'Can't be that bad.'

'Bring them,' he said.

'What I've got here,' Heke Norman said, 'is notes from Amiria and Toi's lawyer regarding what The Two are saying, that is, what they intend going to court with. We need to go through it. They're now putting less emphasis on who has the right to be Kiri's main caregiver and are concentrating on suitability. In other words they want to bring a case that will show what they believe is Rua's unsuitability to be a father.'

'There's the report from Martin . . .'

'They want to dig dirt, go in for a bit of character assassination . . . Here, I've summarised. We'll go through . . . The first here is to do with ah, drugs, the second to do with what they're calling theft or intended theft.'

'They're porangi.'

'We'll take those two first. They're alleging firstly that Rua here is a user and an addict, that secondly he and his cousins have a marijuana plantation up the back somewhere and are part of a drug ring. They don't seem to have any evidence apart from the fact that they say they've seen nieces and nephews, not Rua, coming down from the hills where Rua's house is, with implements. I mean, all I need to know is they're not going to come up with a list of convictions or a bunch of evidence . . .'

'It's a load of rubbish,' Wai said.

'Not true then, no convictions?'

'None,' he said. 'But I got a plant or two.'

'A bit for yourself?'

'Cousins and me . . .'

'If it was going on big we'd know,' Wai said. 'We got nephews into dealing but they keep it away from home. Nothing to do with him.'

'So they can't come at us with anything in court. People coming out of bushes with implements. What would you say . . .?'

'Out busting cray poachers on New Year morning is what they're talking about. They know. Everyone knows . . .'

'Good, OK . . . Anything else . . . other drugs?'

'Nah.'

'You drink?'

'Yep. Same as them.'

'OK, it's just we don't want any surprises. Ah let's see . . . well, this land business. They wouldn't expand on it at all, and if they're not going to talk about it I don't see how they can expect it to have relevance, and anyway it doesn't have bearing on a person's ability or suitability to be a parent. Depends what comes out I suppose . . .'

'So, what . . . what they saying?'

'Saying your only interest in having Kiri is so you can steal land. That's as far as they'd go. No evidence, nothing to support . . . They'd have to show somehow that you didn't really want the girl and are only interested in what she's got. They wouldn't even say whether Kiri was a landowner or not, or an asset holder.'

'Mad in the head, them.'

'Rua here's got his own land,' Wai said. 'Clear title to some, shares in other places. He don't need land.'

'And the girl got nothing yet,' Tini said. 'Except what she got coming later, like anyone else.'

'Have you had any land dealings?' Heke Norman asked.

'None. Like they say, I got my own.'

'Buy, or swap, or talk to anyone? Not that that would affect your ability to be a father as far as I can see.'

'None of that.'

'All right look, I reckon we can deal with all that. They certainly don't seem to have much support for any of those things they're saying. But . . . E Kui, Whaea, e Rua, there's more . . .'

'What is it then, Heke Norman?'

'To do with . . . well to do with what they're calling the abduction, and they're giving their own version for the reasons for this so called abduction.'

'And?'

'Well let's come to that. E Kui, Whaea, what they're alleging is to do with Rua's relationships, first with the mother of Kiri, then with Kiri herself. Putting it clearly they're alleging Rua here had an incestuous relationship with the girl's mother, the mother of Kiri being his sister . . .'

'They got no right . . .'

'And ah, if I just finish off here, tell it all. They're saying, and intend to take to court, that there was this relationship with the mother, and now this same relationship with the daughter. An incestuous relationship with the mother and now he's sleeping with the daughter. Only telling you what they're saying.'

'Porangi, them.'

'Evil.'

Dead meat was what he felt like. He knew it wasn't up to him to speak for himself now and waited for Wai and Tini to get themselves together. Wai was up pacing.

'It's all in their heads then?' Heke Norman asked. 'They made it all up?'

'Rua here, and the mother of Kiri have the same mother,' Wai said. 'So, that's true, they're brother and sister . . . but there's no way . . . no way those two are going to put that round any court. It's family business. No right telling that lawyer of theirs our family business, or telling you, Heke Norman. It don't go past here, Heke Norman. No business having all that written down on your papers.'

'E Kui, Whaea, Rua . . . I think we can deal with it,' Heke said. 'What we'll do, what we'll do . . . I can talk it over with Cath, probably cancel that part of it out of the equation as not being relevant to Rua's suitability to be a father. We're talking about suitability *now*, in the absence of the mother, whoever she might be. What's more important may be . . .'

'Those Two, Those Two . . .'

'What they doing . . .?'

'Look ah, maybe . . .' Heke Norman said.

'They want trouble, we give them trouble . . .'

'More important may be the rest of it . . .' he said.

'What rest of it?'

'They say they saw . . .'

'Lies.'

'Rubbish, they saw nothing.'

'New Year's morning, they're saying, and saying others saw.'

He had to think back to the night and day of so many happenings. Fireworks, bonfires, cray pots, gunshot, Brad and Horomona, Jase in a coma, carrying him out and the chopper arriving.

Before that he and Kid asleep. 'Nutters,' he said. 'What they're talking about is me asleep on my bed up at the old place. Kid asleep on the same bed too. Nuts.'

'Poison.'

'And Wellington. You took her, they're saying . . .'

'Went there, stayed with his cousin while he got his limb fitted . . . They know . . .'

'It's what we're up against if this all goes . . .'

'Not going anywhere . . .'

'It's the damage allegation can do,' Heke said. 'The doubt that can be put into people's minds.'

'Not going anywhere, not after we get our hands on them. They want trouble, we give them trouble.'

But Heke wouldn't let go. 'Help me,' he said. 'Kui Tini, Whaea Wai, e hoa e Rua, it's the doubt that can be put in people's minds. You have certainty, other people haven't—that is if the worst happens and Amiria and Babs can't be persuaded.'

'They gotta be told.'

'Awhina mai,' Heke said, and they waited while he considered his words. 'Would you agree, for example, to your mokopuna being talked to ah . . . by a professional?'

'No way,' he said.

'E Kui, Whaea, Rua would you consider a doctor's report?'

'Examination?' Tini asked.

'None a that, no bloody way,' he said.

'If you think how . . .'

'Look here Heke Norman . . .'

'How it could seem if you refuse . . . I'm only trying to explain the position.'

'There's no position,' Wai said. 'Look, it's not your fault Heke Norman. We understand, and you're right. If we were fighting this in court we'd need back-up. But it won't happen. The sooner we get home, take a piece out of those two the better. Knowing their big mouths they could be spouting this all round the place already. It could've all crossed the inlet by now.'

THIRTY-FIVE

WAI WAS right to be concerned. Tongues were going for it over the bridge at the Post Shop. In this now slowed-down time, Babs found space between dealing with customers and paperwork to write cards and letters to new friends, as well as to keep up a flow of information to old friends and other-side relatives.

When customers or casual callers first noticed the absence of Kiri and asked after her, they received abrupt replies from Babs who said she had gone to hospital with a burn on her arm and that her uncle had taken her to Wellington without their permission while he was off getting himself a new leg.

'Ah that one, Tamarua's son who was in the accident,' they said.

It was one of these customers who first suggested Babs should've called the police—him going off with somebody's kid like that, not even saying. And he was only a kid himself wasn't he, Tamarua's son? They knew him.

Inside the shop doorway, to catch the eye of holidaymakers, overnighters and other casuals, were shelves of magazines, newspapers, sweets and drinks. There were fishing lines, hooks and sinkers for those who might wish to drop their lines alongside others who fished regularly from the bridge. Packets of cards and a shelf of printed shirts gave greetings from Aotearoa, New Zealand.

The shop had been built during an era of windowlessness. Going into it was like entering a cave, though there was an attempt at lighting via a fluorescent tube which served to brighten the front counters and cast candlepower over the front ends of the shelves which became darker and darker towards laundry goods, coils of rope, light bulbs, work socks, pop-out clotheslines and jandals.

Much of what had once been front window was now taken up by the rows of red post boxes. Of the remaining window space the bottom third had been painted over with white paint. Maybe there was a reason. The top portion had posters and notices advertising past events Sellotaped to it.

It must be said that Babs was selective regarding who she gave hard core information to. There were people and people. Old ones, new ones. The true informees were people she'd known all her life because they were related to her and she went to school with them or with their families, even if they were other-siders. It was mainly through Babs, and to a less extent her sister, that news travelled from Dogside to Godside and vice versa. Sometimes Dogside talk spread more quickly through Godside than it did through its own home territory. Likewise God goss through Dog.

It wasn't that Babs was above yarning with strangers or newer residents but she was able to give information a different slant when talking with them. Kiri had had an accident, spilt hot water. They'd sent her off on holiday with her uncle while she recovered. From the Post Shop, the informees could go along the street and call in on a less-giving Amiria at Bay Fish.

After the holiday period was over there was plenty to keep tongues busy until well into February, by which time the school term was well underway and there was still no sign of Kiri. It was a dead time with summer visitors gone, no one with money, a few old ones out getting their milk and bread, collecting bills and junk mail and going along for their Lotto tickets.

'So what . . .? What's with this girl?' Godsiders wondered.

'So, now he's saying he's the father, Rua,' Babs said. 'Thinks he's keeping her.'

'Ah, ah, well ah . . .' and it would be likely to be some days later that the caller would return to check on her own recollections. 'Ah, the girl's mother, Ani Wainoa, right?'

'Right.'

'Daughter of Ramari. Right?'

'Right.'

'Him, that Rua, saying he's the father of the girl, is son of the same Ramari. Right?'

'Right.'

'Ah.'

In her position as Post Shop attendant, Babs was first to see the postcards and letters coming to her and her sister from all over the country, all over the world. Or would've been first to see them had they come.

Once in a while there would be something to make her heart leap, some lonely card with a disappointing message scrawled across it. It would enliven her enough to ring Amiria along at Bay Fish and the two would make what they could out of it. Also it was something to show to friends, relatives, acquaintances and even talkative strangers who came in. It sustained them for a time.

Even expectation can be sustenance for a time.

But generally, opening the bag with hope in her heart each day, flicking the bits and pieces of mail into boxes and then looking into their own empty box at the end of it was a souring experience. You were like *that* with these people, then they took off and you never heard from them again. That included Dawn Anne and her folder bunged with notes. Thin air and not even a kiss-my-foot.

'He wants her land.'

'Her land, ah. She got land?'

A visit to Babs was usually followed by a call into Bay Fish to see Amiria who might be in the process of cleaning down stainless steel, mixing batter, heating fat in the vats, flipping onion slices and beef on the hot plate. Amiria already damp.

Amiria, though nowhere near as free regarding solid information as her sister, was useful in that a person could go to her with a sentence beginning, 'I hear,' and receive a statement of what they could take to be confirmation, such as, 'And he'll get what's coming, the little rat.' Or, 'Out for what he can get, little rat. Bugger-all by the time we finished with him.'

And if over the counter at the Post Shop there was a snippet of conversation such as: 'Who knows what he's up to?'

'Ah?'

'And her.'

'Him, and her?'

'Sleeping. Broad daylight. The whole world . . .' Along at Bay Fish they could get from Amiria: 'Get what's coming to him, little brat, when the shit hits the fan.'

What it did hit was rafters, Godside rafters, from where it eased down in drifts and spread itself. This was weeks before it ever touched base in its equivalent place on Dogside.

The rafters on Godside, taking first the main beam—the tahuhu, backbone of the ancestor from which the ribs descend—is a beam densely carved in ancestral figures whose heads sit squarely on only slightly rounded shoulders. These ones are open-mouthed in a rather innocent looking way, a round-mouthed rather than a gaping, fiery-mouthed way. They're round-eyed too. Surprised looking. Their tongues are not greatly elongated, protruding only as far as their chins. The stance that each takes is not particularly wide-legged and they're all somewhat uniform, differing mainly in what is held in the hand, or the patterns used in decoration of face and bodies.

Austere, they are. The workmanship is impressive and Godsiders would claim their main beam to be superior to any they'd seen. In the first place there was the very size and weight of the slab that enabled the fullness of the figures and the depth of the chisel work to be brought out. Also the work had taken time. It was serious and proper.

Dogsiders, however, might describe the work as lifeless, the figures as half asleep or half dead, gutless maybe, or boring—just like the praying hypocrites that gathered underneath it, that lot—the canoe-breaking fatheads.

The figures on the main beam in the Dogside house had been brought out from much lighter slabs and their heads were on sideways, alternately to left and right. Tongues flopped down to bellybuttons or slid out over shoulders, chests, arms. They squinted, ogled, peered, challenged and cheeked. Decoration was minimal.

Dogsiders were proud of the liveliness of the figures and their stuff-you attitudes, while Godsiders thought the work to be rough, careless, hurried and undisciplined, and believed the figures wayward, typical of fly-by-night, canoe-snatching runaways.

Now the heke—these painted ancestral ribs in each house—also invite comparison. In the Godside house, the central unbroken line which is where the heartbeat is, zig-zagged down the centre of each plank. The scrollwork following this heartline tucked itself into each angle, curling in on itself while at the same time maintaining an unbroken flow from the top edge to the bottom. The designs in black and red on a white background, that they'd replicated from the old house, were part of tradition that Godsiders were proud to follow.

It made Dogsiders yawn.

The heartlines on the Dogside heke were more sinuous and the coiled shapes in the indentations were unattached, open in shape as though they could be flying or swimming, or they were like dancers facing each other and seemed likely to break out as if they could evolve to some other form. A bit of yellow, a bit of blue had crept in there.

Godsiders said the reason that everything was so skimped and gaudy in the Dogside house was because their other-side relations had run out of the right paint and probably owned only two paint brushes, in other words they'd been short of materials at the time. This happened to be true but Dogsiders believed the results were all the better for it.

What does all this amount to when it comes to information retention, rafter ears, rafter story? Nothing much. Capacity is limitless no matter what the workmanship or adornments. Maybe there were fewer prayers hoisted up in the Dogside house but there were equally as many words, stories—equally as much gossip, slander, secret and history. The rafters handled it all, not a problem.

That's enough about beams.

Enough about Godside.

So, what was revealed to Wai, Tini and Rua when they went to their meeting with Heke Norman many weeks into the New Year was already hot on Godside. It had all crossed water via the bridge, via the footpaths and stores, via Post Shop and Bay Fish.

The three left the lawyer's office chopping out of the room and along the insecty boards in single file like a row of axes. Heke Norman, holding the door for them as they went out, caught up to Tini who was leading the three and hurried along beside her. 'What I'm saying, what I'm saying is, if it does, does get to court, don't leave me with nothing, no back-up.'

Chopping along.

After calling into Tini's place for an overnight bag the three drove mostly in silence through to the main street—where the countdown clock was well into ticking off its next three hundred and sixty-five days—over the new traffic humps and flagstones, round the roundabout, past the town clock in its new millennium paint, past the flags and decorations and the fatigued kerbside palms.

'What got into them?' Tini said, 'What they on about?'

Looking towards the beach, the temporary seating where the big celebrations had taken place was gone. There was a man jabbing papers onto a stick, putting them in a rubbish bag, and past the roadside veggie trucks and the whale graveyard the big beach was empty.

'Well, they can't. Not going to . . .'

The tide was a long way out, the spread of flat rocks making dark animal shapes all over the vast shore.

'You know, deep down . . .'

'Deep down rotten,' Rua said.

'Well . . . I don't know. Bad-mouth yes, but . . .'

'Rotten in the middle.'

'Deep inside . . .'

'Fly blow . . . shit gone to the brain.'

'You know, it was Lady,' Tini said. 'If there was anyone bad it was her . . .'

They came to the hills and began to wind upwards. They'd lost sight of the sea again but there was the big sky dipping beyond the hills.

'Mean,' Wai said. 'And they got their own disappointments. They want the campers back but no support for that. Like we took something else off them.'

'Well all their lives, all their lives same story. But in their hearts . . .'

As they were about to turn into their home road Wai remembered she needed milk, so they crossed the bridge and Wai went into Bay Dairy where she met Pani from Other Side who was pleased to ask, 'What's with that boy of Tamarua, that one-legged, that haua? They should lock him up.'

'Lock your tongue up,' Wai said. 'Or you find it coming out the back of your head.'

Pani went out the door feeling good and being sure to show it, but she had enough sense to make sure to be out of earshot before making her next utterance which was equivalent to: A dog will do what a dog will do. Sister, mother, grandmother, mother-in-law, it makes no difference to a dog.

'What's this, the whanau police?' Babs asked as Tini, Wai, Arch and Atawhai walked in with Rua. 'What's this, the vigilantes or the village aunties?'

It wasn't a good start. The Big Four were put off guard by this entirely unwelcoming attitude, this unexpected attack on elders. Nevertheless they disregarded rudeness for the time being while they really searched for this deep-down good place somewhere in hearts of The Two, for this little bit of shine that they really believed was there.

But The Two, from the vantage point of Babs' initial attack (which had made Amiria, who at other times would've thought her sister too big in the mouth, giggle behind her hand), had their theme song ready. This was—'If you don't want all this coming out in court, tell *him*,' their two heads swinging in unison to nod, downmouthed, in Rua's direction.

After a time when the talk became more animated and persuasive, The Two's response became abbreviated to, 'Tell *him*.'

So when they were challenged regarding truth, when they were told over and over they had no right telling family business they kept it up, 'Tell *him*.' When they were called out as liars and troublemakers and when one of the four lost her head and began to swear and threaten and tell the two to get that up-you look off their faces, Babs and Amiria opened their mouths only enough to say, 'Tell *him*.'

It was no good. They got nowhere. But it wasn't the end of it. Tini decided she was going to stay a while. She knew The Two better than anybody and intended keeping at them until they cracked. They would. They had to.

THIRTY-SIX

KID.

Daylight was sliding away from ceiling and walls and taking itself out wide-open windows. He moved about the house notching them in.

Kid asleep.

He could pick her up and go, but it was only a thought.

'You have to get in there and fight,' Heke Norman had told him. 'Give me every bad thing you know, the lot, then let me sort it.'

He'd done that as best he could, remembering the way the Aunties had treated Kid, the things they called her, and how she'd never been able to do what other kids did. There was the dead cat, the home-alone, the lock out, the burn—told it all even though he didn't want to. It was all wrong, all this court business and now there was a case building up to be ten times worse than when they started if what Tini and the others were worried about was old bones being let out to dance on prime time television and talkback.

It was two weeks after they'd all gone to talk to Amiria and Babs that The Big Four had walked in on him and asked him to change his mind about going to court. Tini had been unable to persuade

Amiria and Babs and now they had come to ask him to give up his daughter—just in the meantime—and they'd see to it she was treated all right. In a few more years she'd make up her own mind and come to him of her own accord, they believed. There was no way that they could have Those Two going to court spreading their evil and their lies, digging up the past, having their family business all over the newspapers, on the telly news and all over talkback radio.

'No way,' he'd told them. 'I'm not leaving her, not giving her up.'

'All that and you could lose in court anyway.'

'Lose, then there's all that family business all up and down the country, all for nothing.'

'Don't see how I lose,' he'd said. 'Only if you say you don't back me, only if you reckon I . . .'

'No.'

'No, but we think it's better . . . better you back out. What people say . . .'

'Let them . . .'

'Whanau dragged through the mud.'

'All for nothing, could be.'

'But,' Atawhai had said, 'if you want to go through with it, go to court . . . maybe . . . just for court . . . maybe you want me to have a look at her.'

'Nope. No way.'

Heke Norman believed the four were overreacting about their case making it into the news. 'The court's not here to crucify people,' he'd said. 'Though it might look like it. No, our case won't rate. You're not criminals after all.'

'But . . . a brother and a sister . . . have people flapping their ears.'

'Well . . . Irrelevant to suitability now etc. As I said we'll keep it out . . . unless they want to be sneaky and try to attach it to . . .'

and that's when Heke Norman had brought up again the possibility of a psychologist's report, an examination for Kid. That's what made him feel like picking her up now, and going.

'We have to do everything we can to rule out interference, and having done that it wouldn't leave them much to hang their case on. Who knows they might give up, if you'd reconsider.'

How could he? How could he explain something like that to Kid? What reasons could he give her? Why should he have to when Babs and Amiria *knew*.

But now he thought he might have to. Those Two were never going to give up the idea of going to court and from what he could tell they seemed to be looking forward to it.

Bad time. They had it in for him and he didn't know why. Worst time of his life.

Heke had asked him to name witnesses, anyone at all who could back up any of the statements he'd made, anyone at all who would give a character reference. 'One or two from outside the family would be good,' he'd said. 'Give me contact numbers.'

So he'd given Heke Maina's number, but so far, even though Heke had left messages for her more than a week ago, she hadn't called in to see him. Nothing from her.

And it seemed that no matter what information he gave, and even if he agreed to the examination, Heke was unable to tell how the case would go.

'You just can't predict outcomes with these custody cases,' Heke had said. 'And you can't stop attitudes coming into it. Outcomes should be based on suitability, where Kiri's lawyer's report would play a significant part, along with other firm evidence. The report from her lawyer is in your favour, I think. But there's also evidence that she's grown well and healthy in her situation so far, and is seemingly well adjusted—although there's the burn incident. We'll make as much as we can of that for evidence of emotional disturbance, as well as evidence of neglect. But we don't know . . .

You can mud-sling all you like, but most of it can usually be countered in some way—unless there's something really serious, and provable.

'Otherwise, if there's nothing too drastic, too obvious, then you're up against attitude, depending on the judge—towards your sex, your age—the idea that a man can't manage kids especially a daughter, that a girl must have a mother, or that mature parents are preferable. Who knows?

'And for us . . . what I have to make sure I get across is that Kiri is part of a whanau, that she has you as biological father and that she has plenty of mothers as well, also plenty of older people who are also her parents and grandparents. Cultural stuff. You can say that sort of thing a hundred times and mostly it doesn't sink in. There's a tunnel-visioned attitude that believes that a person has only two parents at most . . . in this case only one.

'But then again, it doesn't help any of our cases if there's something amiss, something gone wrong in the whanau.'

'A brother and a sister . . .'

'Let's put that one aside. Let's say whanau into drug dealing . . .'

'All the same whanau. Their whanau too . . .'

'Or whatever, but you see what I mean.'

'And it could all blow up in my face if I go too hard at it. Like, if there are all these so-called parents then why haven't things been better? They could think it's six of one, half a dozen of the other and finish up with some joint arrangement since you live practically next door to each other. Not what you want.'

None of it was what he wanted.

The door opened. Jase came in switching the light on. 'Bad,' he said, 'what they been blabbing, Those Two.' Bones came in behind Jase carrying the baby who was asleep, followed by Remelda.

'I should pick her up, get out, take off for Oz,' he said, knowing he never would. It wasn't what he wanted for Kid, or for himself— hiding, being on the run. What he wanted was a life here, a life for her growing up with cousins and doing what other kids did.

'Anyhow they can't take her. You're her father, that's it,' Bones said.

His cousins and Remelda moved in and settled themselves, Jase taking up the guitar and picking at it. The door opened again and Eva came in. 'Need putting out of their misery Those Two,' she said. 'And as for these so called kaumatua, Nan, Uncle Arch and Nan Tini, what're they on about? Dodgy, them. You don't know which way they're facing. Say they support you, same time as they want you to give up your daughter.'

'Give up on me you think?'

'Seems like.'

'Them, and Maina too,' he said.

And just then Maina came in. 'Ha ha all having a tangi here,' Eva said. 'Join the party.'

'What's going on?' she said, moving round to make her greetings then sitting at the far side of the table facing them. 'What's all this shit flying round all over the place . . . Look, Eva, go and get Nan, Arch, Tini if she's around. I got something to say.'

'My father went back into hospital two weeks ago,' Maina said. 'Back into intensive care. Pulled through all right, again . . . well, so far. It's not what I've come to talk about, but I was hardly home over the last two weeks and that's the reason I didn't get to answering Heke Norman's message until today. Anyway I got to see him this afternoon.' She was looking down on her hands which were spread in front of her on the table, then she looked up, at Wai, and from one to the other, 'What's going on? What sort of a whanau is this? Is this supposed to be a family, or what?'

No answer from Tini or Arch or Wai.

'Heke Norman went through the lot,' she said. 'I couldn't believe . . . Well, never mind all that now. You know all that. What I've come to say is . . . I've come to get him.'

Nothing from Tini, Arch or Wai.

'Because how can I leave him here if you don't support him, if you're telling him to give up his daughter as if he's done wrong, if you're letting all this rubbish fly around all over the place and doing nothing about it. So, I'm taking him with me, taking his daughter with me, if they'll come.'

Nothing.

But there was a shift from Arch as he lifted his head and looked around the room. Wai and Tini lifted their eyes too, glancing Maina's way as she paused, keeping her eyes on her hands.

'And if they'll come then at least no one'll be able to keep on saying what they're saying about him and his daughter. Will they . . . ? I mean . . . I know here is where he wants to be, know he's got plans for here, for his daughter growing up here. We've talked. We know we've . . . well . . . got different pathways. But . . . I can't . . . I can't leave them here . . . someone I love, if his own family don't . . . if it's how he's going to be treated.'

Nothing to say Wai, Arch, Tini.

'For as long as he needs, or as long as he wants, if he'll come.'

Arch shifted his feet, leaned forward while Tini and Wai sat back, doing the circuit with their eyes but not speaking. Rua felt himself moving, standing, a weight lifted. 'I'll pack our things,' he said.

'He goes, I go,' Bones said. 'Back to Reld's old place, ay Reld?'

'That's me,' Jase said. 'Not stopping here, no way.'

'Not me either,' Eva said. 'Not sticking around. I'm off.'

'Not going anywhere, Granddaughter,' Wai said.

'I'm off Nan . . . going with Cousin and Reld. Anyway it's nearer the Polytech.'

'Dining room?' Jase said, following the others out. 'Youse can do it yourselves.'

THIRTY-SEVEN

ALL THROUGHOUT the fundraising project and the events that occurred during that time, Wai, Arch and Tini had forgotten to remember their deaths. Life had been too interesting to think of leaving it.

Not that any of the three were in the habit of dwelling on the time when they would achieve their ultimate chieftainship, but having reached a certain age or state of health, it was natural that dying came into their consideration from time to time.

Wai, for example, had looked death hard in the face on more than one occasion, but a triple bypass had put her on her feet again. At those times she'd found the face looking back at her to be undramatic, disappointing, kind of goofy she reckoned.

Arch would regret leaving Cass behind when his time came, though he knew she'd manage all right without him, that there'd always be someone to clear debris from the creek and buy the Lotto tickets. 'Only wanted a cook and look what I got,' he'd say and she'd give him that snooty look of hers that took him right along with it, put the two of them in some secret place as if she was a waitress who was really a queen giving him food. But how could he want to leave her? She was like a sunny room, made him feel like bending double and groaning. Bloody hell, little fish swimming in his furry veins. She killed him every day.

However, he knew he couldn't expect too much more time and work from his smoked lungs and pickled liver, which had become a kind of party piece duo that he liked to pay tribute to in song from time to time.

Tini, at eighty-three, older than Wai and Arch by twenty years, was dwindling in every way but faculty. What she was now, was a few sticks tied together with a nosy bird perched in among them. She understood, as she became smaller and smaller, that she would one day come down to nothing. Didn't care really.

But now Maina had walked in and caused a walkout.

All three were jolted by it. All three lay awake, that night and on many nights afterwards, considering their deaths. Everything that happened or didn't happen in the week that followed, served to throw their deaths up in their faces.

Tini, Wai and Arch were upset at first that blame had been dumped on them—on what was seen as *their* lack of action, *their* lack of support. If there was fault on their part, if there was blame due to them, it was for what had happened ten years earlier. What they were trying their best to do now was some kind of damage control, wanting to protect people from the venom of tongues, protect the family. Maybe they could've done more about the present situation if there'd been more time, but with court coming up they knew there was no time and believed they'd done the best they could under the circumstances. What more could be expected of them?

Experience had shown them that matters righted themselves given time and if you didn't jiggle them too much. Could they just wait and see? In time Kid would leave her aunties and go to Rua of her own accord. In time the young ones who had left would come home.

But they all knew there was no time if they were going to see all this with their living eyes. Also they were afraid there'd be too much fall-out from playing the waiting game and none of them wanted to leave a mess behind.

Another alternative was to just forget it, let it all go to heck. They could sit and watch television, go lala like Pop Henry, match their footsteps into his even though they knew the old man was well ahead of them on that particular path. If they chose to forget, the tide would still come in, go out, twice a day.

These were tired thoughts however, and in the end they had to admit there was something not right that had to be put right, and that it was up to them to do it. They couldn't allow themselves to sleep, die or go gaga until they'd given it their best shot.

Besides there were other consequences as well if it wasn't sorted. For example there was a dining room to build. All the materials had arrived but now there was no work force, or only a small and disabled work force to build it—blocks and timber, bags of cement, stones in piles, and silence. There was only so much that those with frailty and crook internals could do, though they might carry blocks and mix cement up to a point. There was only a certain amount that mothers with babies could do, and though there were others, young and more able-bodied, who had said they could spend weekends working, once they found out what had happened they had become disinclined. These ones wanted everything sorted first.

The big question that everyone was asking was, what was the use of having a kitchen and dining facility if the houses were all emptying out leaving no one behind the pots, no one catching fish, collecting watercress, no one to help put the hangi down?

For that matter what was the use of the wharenui itself if there was to be no family, if there were to be no speakers, no one to call the people home, no one to look after the visitors or to retell the stories, no one under the beams to create the up-draughts and down-draughts. Where would be breathing?

OK. Tini, Arch and Wai had to pick themselves up out of tired thoughts and find a way. In order to do that they had to seek inside themselves and remember who they were.

What they remembered was that if you came down to bone there was always the matter of survival, which had all been done before—of oceans, of war, of illness, of theft and starvation. Compared to all that this was nothing, only a bit of yack yack that had been stopping them from seeing. After all they were not court, they were bone, and they'd allowed themselves to be bullied.

There had to be a hui.

Pop Henry was in his armchair by the door where he slept through the meeting, waking every so often to mumble into the spaces about him before dropping off to sleep again.

Arch who had the floor was pulling old stuff down, telling about the death of Rua's mother, his father's remarriage and how he and his sister Wai had undertaken to look after him. He told what happened between Rua and his sister Ani Wainoa, of the night when Kiri was brought home, leading up to recently when Rua had decided to acknowledge his daughter and take charge of her.

All of this was already known to those present, but perhaps it was known in a fragmented way. Arch wanted to make sure they got it right, but also Arch was wanting to settle people. They were here to bear witness. He kept his eyes going round the circle, watched as people relaxed, watched Amiria and Babs.

The Two were there under sufferance, sitting side by side, straight-backed, flicking their eyes about from time to time sizing up the height and weight of what they were facing. Rua was there, home for the first time since he'd left with Maina.

Arch moved on to speak about the matter of custody that Amiria and Babs had taken to court and the background to that. A point that he kept returning to was that he didn't understand why his nieces, Amiria and Babs, were so determined to take the matter to court and why they would want to take family business there, why they would want to insinuate abuse when they had no reason for believing it had ever taken place. 'We got to find that out,' Arch said.

From there he came to the main point that he wanted to make, explaining to Amiria and Babs and everyone, that court or no court he, Wai, Tini, Atawhai and others he'd spoken to were supporting Rua. They wanted Kiri to be with him since he was her father, and they knew Kiri preferred to be with him. But aside from those reasons they all knew if they didn't support Rua now they were allowing him to be taken away, and allowing all the young ones to take themselves away too. 'All gone, house empty,' was how he put it.

What Maina had done when she came to collect Rua was nothing new. It was all part of custom to remove a loved one from a situation where it was considered they were not being well treated. Tini could remember when her brother Henry had worked for Maori Affairs that her aunts and uncles had gone there to inform them that they were removing their nephew because of insult by the Department to Henry and his people. On another, more recent occasion, they'd all gone as a group to collect a niece who was being ill-treated by her husband's family.

What Maina did was only unusual in that it was not family removing a family member from a situation, but rather someone coming from outside the family to take someone away from it.

Tini, Arch, Wai knew they had no room for objection. The whole incident had shamed them.

'We don't want this thing going to court,' Arch said. 'But what we come here to say this morning is . . . if it go to court let it, because it's on'y court. If our nieces win in court, they win, but on'y court. If they want to say all round the shops what they been saying, then they say it, on'y yack yack. Want to send it all across the river, then they send it, on'y yack yack. But in that case . . . in that case . . .maybe they want to follow their tongues.'

This last statement caused a stir in the house, a wiggle in among the heke and tahuhu, caused a shift of eyes to see how The Sisters were taking it. It had been years since a dog-poisoning forebear had been told his actions were more suitable to life across the water and had been told to go and live on the other side. He had moved away for a time, though not to Godside, and had returned some years later by which time talk of what he'd done had mostly been confined to rafters.

But it was not so long ago that people had known without being told that they needed to leave for other places. There was Ani Wainoa for example, though she would have gone sooner or later anyway. Very recently it had been Brad and Horomona who'd received the message.

For The Sisters to be told they should go and live on the other side was hard stuff, especially coming from Arch. It drove their chins up, narrowed their eyes.

'We been done over before,' Arch said. 'And somehow we get through. But, our kids leave and they don't come back, well, we don't get through at all. Kids go, that's it. Had it. Finish. Who to clean the cobwebs down? Who to paint the pou? Who to get the house ready for the dead? Who to call the dead home and who to bury the dead? Who to light the fire, keep the fire burning? Who to cook the kai and put the hangi down? Right now, who to build the wharekai? Who to get the fish? Who to see the mokopuna eat their fish?'

When Arch finished Wai stood to push the message home that the girl would stay with her father, no matter what. 'If Rua wins in court, and we give every bit of support to see that he does, then OK, the girl stops with him. If he don't win, same thing, the girl stops with him. We see to it, court or no court, no difference. You want her,' she said to The Sisters, 'you have to knock down every door to get her. Behind every door you find me, triple bypass and all. You knock me down, you find someone else. I tell you, if anyone has to leave here it won't be the young ones.'

Again Sisters getting the squeeze, the message that if they didn't like what they were being told they could go, but by now their chins were almost pointing ceilingward. They sat like concrete, eyes wide and unmoving.

'You forget how close I know you,' said Tini, standing as Wai sat down. 'You forget it was me who was a mother to you, whenever I could. And . . . I know what I saw when I was a girl.' There was a shift from those listening, who didn't know where Tini had decided to take them, or why.

'What I saw was your mother, who was my same-age cousin, with ribbons in her hair, dresses with long sleeves so that the sun would not touch her arms, white socks to her knees so the sun wouldn't touch her legs, pretty hats to keep the sun from her face. The only child with shoes.

'What I saw was a pretty girl with pretty white skin who had black sisters to do her washing, who fetched things for her, cooked for her. Black sisters who got a hiding from their father if ever Little Lady cried. I saw brothers who carried her on their backs to school, saw them coming out of the trees with her, carrying her so that no speck of dust would get on her shoes or her clothes. They were brothers who would get a hiding if she complained, and who carried her on their backs everywhere until she was ten years old. After that they led her on her own horse that no one else was allowed to ride. They fed the horse, watered it, groomed it, took it to the school paddock for her.

'We her cousins, didn't think it strange.

'She was a round girl with a round face, round body, round arms and legs that were like cream, like butter. For lunch at school we had a piece of eel, a piece of crayfish or a piece of bread wrapped in newspaper. She had condensed milk sandwiches, fried bread with golden syrup, cake with plum jam, carried by her sisters in a billy with a lid.'

Tini spoke into a mainly still house, but maybe there was a shift made by The Sisters, a slight lowering of chins, a wariness entering the unshifting eyes.

'In winter she had warm scarves, tunics, wool coats and socks, but I think the very coldest days would be the only times we wished to be her. At thirteen she was kept at home, fed on pigeon and fish, cakes and cream. She had her hair brushed for her, chairs taken outside for her so she could sit under a shady tree.

'Later her brothers escaped to the war. Two of them never came home. Her sisters escaped to nowhere. All The Lady did was grow from a little soft girl to a soft big girl who sat and watched her sisters rub and scrub, and who she began to blame for all that was unhappy about her life.'

And now there was definitely a shift, a turning of two heads. 'Shut up you,' Babs shouted, 'about our mother.'

'But what was her life? Nothing was her life.'

'Shut up you, about our mother.'

But this was not going to be tolerated. People were beginning to object, and Atawhai and Cass moved to sit one each side of The Sisters to see if they could bring about some control.

'We her cousins, got married. Some of us moved away. Her sisters married too but still they looked after her, cooked for her, sewed her clothes, took her with them to card games and socials. At thirty years of age she surprised them all by getting married. Her marriage lasted for three years and after that she returned to the family home with you, her two daughters.

'Her sisters gave the house to her, built homes of their own from tin and boards. I was the one who helped her with you, her children. My own kids were grown by then. I bathed you, fed you, carried you home with me when your mother took to her bed complaining.'

Cass on one side and Atawhai on the other were talking The Sisters down, telling them to wait, wait, their turn would come. Even though they blocked their ears it didn't prevent them hearing what Tini was saying.

'As soon as you could walk you fetched and carried for her. As soon as you were old enough you cooked and cleaned for her. You were good girls, pretty girls, slave girls, clever girls that hardly went to school. One of you stayed home with her every day.

'You were ragged girls who wore what was left of my children's clothes, who carried bags of shopping home from the time you were seven, shopping which you paid for with money from all the shares in land that your grandfather had left to your mother. She lived on the very best of land that was left only to her, with its beautiful freshwater springs, its wood pigeons, its tui and korimako, its ti-kouka, its nikau and ponga—in a house cleaned and shined for her by two daughters she didn't at all love, who she sent away into the bush when visitors of importance came by.

'She treated you all the time unkindly. Like dogs, except that dogs are better treated. You ate leftovers, slept on broken beds. You were beaten. And all you wanted was for her to love you. I understood that because of the look of hope you always had, the quick way you moved in your wish to please her, your half smiles, your half afraid movements, the way you tiptoed.'

'Aii aii . . .'

'Aii, aii . . . Stop her. Make her stop.'

'Our mother . . .'

'Aii, aii, aii, our mother gave us everything.'

'Your mother hurt you, ordered you, beat you, slaved you. You went here and there doing everything for her, feeding her, feeding her, until her precious skin began to split and her teeth rotted away and the only time she moved from her chair was when there was a meeting to do with land.'

'Thief. He's a thief. He wants to take everything.'

'And when she held her bandaged arms out that evening in the house we watched, not believing what was happening. There was our grandson, wet and shaking. There was this new baby wrapped in a rag. There were the terrible arms reaching out . . .'

'Land-grabber.'

It was a shocking word which caused a long silence. It was a word the rafters hadn't heard since government acts had placed land belonging to everyone into the hands of a few, causing great disruption and loss. Just what it was that Those Two were nutting off about, was what everyone was trying to fathom.

'But we could let it happen because of these two girls,' Tini said, 'who were women now of course, women in their thirties with no lives of their own, who waited hand and foot on their mother who had no love for them.

'They looked after this mother of no love, and now they cared for a baby as well. But now. But now, here was The Lady's child to love, the child she chose to love, just as her father had chosen to love her. But was it love? Or was it another way of showing her unlove of her lovable daughters. I tell you I was the one who was your mother then. Was it just another way of punishing daughters for their father who had turned her out? Little Kiri had the best of everything for the first two years of her life while my cousin was alive. She saw in this baby what her father had seen in her.

'But the night that she took the baby home was her last night out of the house, out of her chair. There was poison growing from the inside of her, breaking through bathed and shaded skin. Her daughters fed her, fed her, changed her weeping bandages. The poison grew. It came breaking out of her. It touched others . . . '

'He's a thief, a snatcher.'

'Land-grabber, thief.'

'He takes her from us, he takes everything.'

'Wants everything.'

'Our mother . . . '

'Our mother gave us everything.'

And surely Tini was going too far, stirring the pot when it didn't need stirring. People watched as Babs reached into a bag, took out an envelope and flung pages into the middle of the room. 'Look there, and tell us he's not a thief.' Dion collected up the pages, put them in order and handed them to Atawhai who began to read through.

'Somewhere, wrong has to stop,' Tini said. 'To make it stop we got to know what it is. It's why I had to tell it all, so poison don't go on infecting. But who? Who can stop it?'

'Look there,' Babs called. 'Look there and you'll know all about Rua, just waiting, just waiting, his own house falling down. It's only now he decides he's her father.'

What's all this? No one knows. It's awful.

'*She* told him,' Amiria shouted. 'That kid did it. We know, we know she told him. We know she snooped through our drawers, read our papers when we weren't home. She's in it too, with him.'

'It's a legal document,' Atawhai said. 'Signed and witnessed. It's Lady's will. The papers show that our aunt . . . has left land, house, shares, in fact everything to her whangai daughter Kiri. Her first daughters, I'll say her true daughters, have been given guardian status. That is, they have been allowed custody of house, land, shares, everything, only for as long as they have Kiri in their care.'

'Aii, aii, she gave us everything, gave us everything.'

'Now you turn us out.'

'Take our land our home . . . ' They were on their feet shouting and no one could really blame them.

'He knew, he knows, that Te Rua . . . ' Amiria wailed.

Atawhai sat down and Tini rose to her feet again. 'He knew, he knows nothing,' Tini said. 'Just like the rest of us. He's not the thief. It's your mother who is the thief. She stole from you. She stole your young lives, she hurt you, slaved you, blamed you, and after she died, we now see she stole from you again.' Here Tini had to wait while Atawhai tried to calm the sisters down. 'But we won't let her steal from you any longer. I tell you take your papers, burn them. It's rubbish. All it is is legal, that's all. Nothing. Before all the new laws were made land was for everyone and people decided where they would build their houses. Think of that. We here today know where your land is, where your house is. You don't need a piece of paper to show us.'

Tini looked round for agreement for what she was saying, knew she was getting it. 'Now your mother's unlove has been written but you can't have, we won't let you have, a piece of paper that steals from you and which is only something a law has made, which has only the eyes of two witnesses to say it's true. We are your witnesses, and we know your land, your land with not one broken tree. Free yourselves from her. She wasn't your mother. We were your mothers. We were the ones who loved you, and we are the ones now.

'Ngarua and Maraenohonoho held jealousy in their hearts and in some ways the quarrel between them has never ended. In another way it has become unimportant because one night Ngarua took matters into her hands. After that it became a rivalry cloaked in story, part of who we all are because Ngarua freed us.

'Free yourselves. Don't carry the bruises, or pass on bruises. Your mother's poison has to stop right now. Free yourselves. Begin with a burning.'

THIRTY-EIGHT

HE FELT sorry for Arch who'd been father and grandfather to him for a long time now, so close to him he hadn't noticed him get old. Old on his feet, telling it, telling it in the house, making a way home for Kid and him—cutting away crap, cutting it away to get to what was important. Wanted to get up and tell them all it didn't matter anymore.

'I think I got to bring my dog,' he'd said to Maina once they'd packed the car and bundled Kid into the back seat with covers and pillows.

'Policeman coming?' Kid had asked as she stirred and woke.

'No. Tell you tomorrow,' he'd said, at the same time wondering what had made her ask the question, what had been said to her that was worrying her in sleep.

'Yes, bring him.' Maina had put her arms round him briefly. 'See you at home,' and she'd driven off.

After watching her go he'd stood with Eva, Jase, Bones and Remelda for a while, arranging to help them shift the next day. 'But you don't have to,' he'd said.

'Not stopping. No way.'

'Nah, going,' Bones had said. 'Bring us a trailer from Uncle Harry's.'

As he drove away he'd been thinking about what he would say to Kid the next day, wondering how she would feel about being taken away from her home, her family, her school, and beginning to think he should've put more thought to what he was doing. Could this shifting about be used against him in court? Also he didn't really think the fact that he was going to live with Maina would make any difference to accusations Babs and Amiria were making against him, or was she his minder now?

And no difference to the question of whether he allowed Kid to be examined or not, whether he should call Atawhai or not. That was the thing, the rock in his stomach.

But he'd wanted to leave with Maina, had to. Apart from wanting to be with her he'd felt stuck, not knowing what to do and knowing nothing was changing. For something different to happen you had to do something different—had to try to alter the tide, or struggle against it until it turned so you could see what was there once it went out again.

As he turned down the no-exit street he'd seen her waiting out by the gate for him, seen her cigarette glowing in the dark.

'I rang hospital. Dad's asleep,' she'd said, going ahead of him to open the door as he carried Kid through to a bedroom. 'So, won't go back up tonight unless they ring me.'

'It's what to tell her, what to do,' he'd said as they unpacked the car. 'All this . . . just putting her in the middle of shit.'

'Eating stones, you,' she'd said. 'I'm throwing a couple of tonics into you,' and he'd laughed, felt himself relax.

'A couple of rock crackers you reckon?'

'You, me both.'

'Time to party you say?'

'A bit of crying, laughing, dancing, something like that. Think about the rest tomorrow.'

The next day he'd gone round to Harry's place for the trailer and to tell their uncle that Jase wanted to come back and stay, then he'd spent the afternoon helping to move Bones, Remelda and Eva's things to the cottage behind Remelda's Aunt's place.

He and Kid had spent the rest of the week looking after the house, doing shopping and cooking while Maina went to work and to the hospital. On some afternoons they'd gone into town to see Heke Norman and the following week he had enrolled Kid at the local school and begun looking for work.

He still hadn't spoken to Kid about why they'd moved and she hadn't asked. He'd been thinking more and more that he would have to allow Kid to be tested by a psychologist and examined by a doctor—not even by Atawhai—who now said it would be better done by one of his colleagues as being someone outside the family.

'Wait right 'til the last, is all I can think of,' Maina had said. 'Or get the psych report and put off the examination to the last minute. Something might happen.'

What did happen was that once he decided to talk to Kid it all became easy. 'People say I stole you,' he'd said. 'They say I don't treat you good.'

'Policeman coming?'

'No. People—Aunty Wai, your Aunties, know where we are, but . . .'

'Sick of all them.'

'Your Aunties . . . they going to court to try and get you back.'

'Who cares?'

'Well it means . . . See . . .'

'Who cares, Rua?'

'Judge might say, might say, give you back.'

'Don't make a difference.'

'And then the policeman . . . '

'But I won't.'

'Policeman . . .'

'Won't go, Dummy.'

'Take you back to them.'

'No way. Can't you listen? Get out the window, hide in the trees, hide in Aunty Wai's place, hide in Uncle Arch's, Pop Henry's, Georgie's house . . . Or, if we live here with Maina and Pop Silver, I run away to here . . .'

'Might come for me . . .'

'Not you, Dummy, running away. Not you stealing me . . .'

And she was right. She'd brought it all down to nothing. The Two could win in court, but what could court do? Nothing to him, nothing to her. So easy it made him laugh.

Now here was Arch telling it, giving it heaps, saying the same thing—it's on'y court, on'y yack yack, we been done over before, on'y court.

After Arch, Wai dished it out too, supporting him, making it clear, driving the nails home. The girl stays with her father, knock down every door, girl stops with him. Across from him The Two sat like rocks. They'd break, he thought, or go.

Break? OK.

Go? Good riddance.

'You forget how close I know you,' Tini was saying to The Two. 'I know what I saw when I was a girl.' Tini was reaching back, a long way back and he didn't know why. To him it was all done. Kid had done it, Arch and Wai had done it, said it all and it didn't matter any more. After the court hearing, no matter what happened now, he was coming home with his daughter and was just awaiting an opportunity to stand and say it.

He'd found three days' work doing shelves for a downtown café and another five making frames for a vineyard, but hadn't liked going to work because it meant Kid having to wait at a neighbour's place after school until he returned, and though she'd waited patiently enough he'd seen she wasn't happy. Also he could tell she wasn't happy at the school he'd enrolled her in.

But without work he'd felt cornered, useless, as though all he was doing was waiting for night and for Maina to come home, which wasn't how he wanted things to be.

Two days after the court hearing, Maina would be gone for six weeks to Taiwan. After that there'd be other groups that she would be asked to manage, though it hadn't been an easy decision for her to stay with her new job—a job that would frequently take her away from home—knowing Hani Silver could check out any time. But her father had made her hold on to the work, threatening to put himself into care if she didn't stay with it. 'If you don't stick with it, Daughter,' he'd said, 'I'll know you're waiting for me to die so you can get on with your life.'

At first she'd been wild with him for saying that, then she'd laughed. 'It's true,' she'd admitted. 'True, I actually thought of it. Thought, give it up for now, there'll be time for me later.'

'Ha, snapped,' Hani had said. 'Snapped. But think of me alive another twenty years and don't worry. Don't put yourself on hold, otherwise I take myself off to one of those places. Anyway, I want my granddaughter and baby to come and live with me. They need a house, ne?'

After the dining room was up he was going to build a house, a good home for his daughter and himself, and big enough for her cousins to come and stay. He'd get the electricity on, widen the track and make it suitable for bikes.

Tini was telling sad stories, everywhere quiet. Ngarua looked out from one wrecked eye, a wink, a blink, but what did she know?

He thought of the cove on a day with cloud covering it, backing up for a storm, water packing down grey and weed shadowy in it.

Up on the bank the two of them had cleaned fish, scales flying, birds waiting to snatch up guts and hearts and bleeding pieces—birds dangling there, dropping and snatching. They'd bucketed water into the tub of cleaned fish and gone out into the water to wash themselves.

Hard, salted hair, black weed floating.

Making his way towards shallow water at the base of the ledge, he'd cupped his hands over one, then the next of the round stones lodged there, pulling himself along and she'd followed, out from him in the deeper water, pushing a log in front of her, resting on it every now and again. Gradually the stones with their spongy growths had given away to the sharp dark rocks that in several places leaned out into the water.

There he'd divided the heavy weed that trailed in the slow movement of the water and which covered the dark openings between the rocks. He'd dived under, gone in feeling blindly for kina, touching up and down the ridges of rock until his fingers found them, easing the shellfish away from where they clung, then coming up to breathe, to lift the kina onto dry rock before he parted the weed again, thrusting in and reaching.

She'd taken her shirt off, collected the shellfish into it, lifted the shirt-bag onto the log to push through water, and they'd taken the long, long way to bring them to shore. They'd cracked through the red centres and the flattening spines. The red juices and brown seed had spilled as they loosened the wide orange tongues in the cups of shell.

What did Ngarua know?

Maybe she knew where Tini was going with her talk, and why. There was movement from The Two and their barracuda mouths were opening, telling Tini to shut up, shut up about their mother. Cass and Atawhai had gone to sit with them, talk them down while Tini kept on, rubbing it in, rubbing it in about their mother, he didn't know why. Because not even he, who now didn't care much for the feelings of Amiria and Babs, wanted old stuff thrown up. What use was that?

'Aii. Aii. Make her stop.'

Tini was telling about him wet, out of the sea, an undrowned baby with anemone eyes, arms and legs like bones of birds, hands like shells that opened out as fingers. He'd never been scared before. Reaching out were the awful arms and he had put his child there.

'Land grabber.'

It was a bad word but he didn't care. Tini was making everything worse, so much so that people were now objecting to it. They were beginning to comment, and Jase was whacking down on guitar strings to cause an interruption.

Enough, enough, enough.

But Tini, on her feet, wouldn't sit, kept it up while The Two nutted off completely about something Kid was supposed to have done, something he and Kid were supposed to have cooked up between them.

Take it, take it, take everything.

Porangi as. Biffing papers. But even so Tini hadn't given up calling out Lady Sadie. Noise all around. Everyone fed up. He felt like walking out, taking Kid, going.

But then he began to see it all come round.

Trees fall, the mud banks up behind, and there you are guts up in mud pulling away rubbish and silt, until first there's a trickle, then a flow. You've done as much as you can do but it's a day or two before water runs clear.

Maybe not in the trees. Maybe not right for a girl living in trees. It would be better to build his house out on the front part of the land closer to cousins, closer to mothers and fathers. Yes, and leave the old place to its strange memories.

There was silence now, while they all waited, waited, waited, for a right time.

Watching The Two.

Waiting.

Watching them drying their red eyes, blowing their red noses, dabbing, dabbing with all their tissues, blowing and dabbing, sniffing, fingering back their hair.

And maybe one day they'd go off and see the world too, he and his daughter. Yes. Grandfather, aunty and uncle in Oz. A mother who wanted to be an aunt on the other side of the world.

Waiting.

People spoke to each other in whispers while Jase plunked a little, and they all waited.

Waited.

Amiria stood, holding a hand out for the papers, taking them from Atawhai, crossing the room and handing them to Jackson. 'Burn them,' she said.

THIRTY-NINE

IT'S TIME for the song.

But who will begin it? What will it be?

Jase with the guitar is gearing up, picking at strings, bouncing a few chords. His sickness is taking his eyesight away but he doesn't need good sight for that. He waits for a note and a beat.

Jackson has taken the papers outside, flicked his cigarette lighter under them, put a hand behind the flame letting it grow, then putting the burning papers into the empty two-kg-sliced-peaches tin that smokers use for an ashtray. He holds the tin up by his face for a moment, lighting his cigarette as the flames rise.

Other smokers come out to join him and when they've all finished Jackson returns to the doorway, rattling the tin to show those inside it has been done, there's been a burning. Good job too, or words similar to that, is what people call out to him.

He leaves the tin and its butts and ash out on the veranda and goes back in.

It's time for the song. Which song and who will begin it?

It won't be Arch or Wai or Tini to begin. They're still recovering from their deliveries, from the hard words said, from the revelations made. They're relieved it's done and are free now to remember their deaths. They need time.

It's not up to Amiria and Babs who are still in their tissues, needing days, weeks, months, and help, to lift themselves. The Two could not do it.

It won't be Te Rua who also needs recovery time, which will be time in water. He's waiting, and while he waits he thinks of the house he'll build on the front of the land and of the journeys he and his daughter could take one day.

He'd like to be gone from there, like to be in water over at the cove where today there's light from a struggling sun; where there are crosswinds brushing cold water up into small jagged waves; where the blowhole is emptying, uncovering the nubbled boulders as the heavy weed shifts in the remaining water. Wherever he is there'll be a pattern in his mind of stones in shallow waters, an image of the places where the sand shifts, of rocks and dark spaces, of sliding and shunting weed, and of channels where the fish will swarm away from him as he swims to deeper and deeper places. Wherever he goes there'll be a voice in his heart.

He'd like to be gone but the time hasn't arrived yet when he can get up and leave, go and find his daughter. He has to see it through to a first song, then to a coming down through more talk, more songs, until it's time.

So who will begin this particular ending?

It won't be any of the younger ones because they know they haven't lived long enough to take such responsibility. They can only wait.

It won't be Cass, or any other newcomer because they know it's family business. This must take its own time in its own place.

It'll have to be Atawhai, who is old enough to understand the extent of bruising, experienced enough to read the faces and know the right moment and the right song.

What will it be?

The first could be a love song to warm the spirit, followed by songs that will rouse it. After a time it won't matter who begins the songs as one picks up from the one before. The singing is likely to continue until the tide has turned and high water rises full above the sharp rocks, dark spaces, shifting weed, and spills out through the opening.

It will continue until there has been enough time, and when that time has come, people will leave at intervals and in twos and threes so that exit is not too sudden, so that the house is not left too suddenly alone.

The patterns on the heke-of-many-colours, of which visitors from Northside have whispered that they thought they'd come to Disneyland, swirl and spin.

The carved figures of the tahuhu with head-this-side, head-that-side, as bold or as shy as the moon, chuckle and dance and flash their eyes, while the leatherclad Ngarua on the far end wall dips her paddle, sings final words, watching from a ruined eye as she is made whole once again by the closing of a door.